# Project Dream

...in the desert where they learned to
dream...

A novel by

# CJ Zahner

Author of
*Dream Wide Awake*
*The Suicide Gene*

PROJECT DREAM
COPYRIGHT © 2019 CJ Zahner

For more information contact Cyndie Zahner
www.cyndiezahner.com

Cover art by Diane Huber

Published 2019
Printed in the United States of America
Print ISBN: 978-1-7332391-0-3
First Printing, 2019
www.cjzahner.com

# Dedication

In memory of my grandmother, Margaret Gifford,
who died when I was three years old.
I like to think I would have called her Gee.

And in memory of my mother, Donna Mae Gifford
Filutze,
who so lovingly cared for her during the six years
after her surgery while she lay bedridden.

I inherited my love of reading from my mother
and my compassion from my grandmother.
My mother would lay me in the bed next to my
grandmother
to help pass her long days.
These were the women of faith and strength
who inspired my strong, passionate female characters.
I think they would have liked Gee, Rachel, and Izzy.

# Foreword

**The Children "Dreamers"**
Izzy
Lenny
Rachel

**The Jimenez Family**
Bela & Belo
Mama & Papa
Isabelle "Izzy"
Enrique "Ricky"

**The Emling Family**
Mary Alice
Lenny

**The Callahan Family**
PopPops & Gee
Momma & Daddy
Rachel "Sissy"
Lisa "LeeLee"

**Project Dream Officiators**
Commander Randall Scott
Jerry McDaniel
Ken Swarthy
Joanne Merryman
Annie Sherman

# Chapter 1 Izzy

Red glints danced through the dark chapel. Izzy loved how the candles' scarlet flickers throbbed against the brown brick walls. She liked everything about the little sanctuary: the red-touched statues staring toward heaven, the sturdy mahogany pews, the marble communion table flaunting hand-polished candelabras that sent a soft glow into the room.

*Stay away, white people.*

That light from the wicks' flames rose, ebbed, and fell foggily over the tabernacle. The mist expanded and hovered around the altar before lazily rising toward the ceiling mural.

She stared at the haze despite what Mama had warned. The smoke swelled and brightened until it reached the Blessed Mother and Baby Jesus painting on the ceiling. Slowly, the white vapor transformed into the figure of a woman, her long, wavy hair flowing gently.

*Oh, no.*

Izzy glanced at her mother.

If Mama caught her talking to angels again, she'd make her spend next Saturday afternoon in church praying. She dropped her gaze to the ground.

The little sanctuary, nestled in the back corner of an old building behind St. Paul's big church, was open seven days a week, twenty-four hours a day. Volunteers manned the perpetual prayer space even in the middle of the night because St. Paul's pastor insisted the room remain accessible to anyone who needed to pray, anytime, and Izzy's mother needed to pray often. For Izzy's papa and her brother, Enrique.

Maybe a smidge for Izzy.

She remained chin to chest but dared to glance upward again. The mist had traveled toward the back wall.

She lifted her chin. Stared straight ahead at the windows embedded in the wall across from her. She purposefully ignored the mist, which lingered beside and behind her now. She concentrated on the windows. Their tinted glass sent vibrant hues in every direction.

Izzy sat in her pew and counted the colors, breathed in the sweet candle scents. She sang songs in her head, swung her legs, and focused on the various shapes formed by the little black frames that separated the pretty stained glass, preoccupying herself with anything to keep her mind from the mist.

Her mother, kneeling beside her, reached a hand back to stop her jittery legs, and Izzy wiggled into a straight position. She glanced around the dark room to see if anyone had noticed her mother's silent chastising.

Four other people knelt in prayer. Two she recognized, Fred and Jean. They volunteered on Sunday evenings when Izzy's mother typically frequented the tiny side chapel.

The woman, Jean, raised her eyebrows, smiled, and winked at Izzy. Her lips never stopped moving, and her fingers continued to work the rosary beads in her hands. Izzy liked the lady named Jean, who never talked but often smiled and made funny faces when Mama wasn't looking. The woman's husband, Fred, knelt somberly beside her, his head bobbing every few seconds as he tried not to doze off.

Izzy smiled back and then dared to glance toward the others in the room. She kept her vision low, away from the air above them where the mist often hung. One tall gentleman knelt with his hands clasped, head down, and another woman, someone Izzy hadn't seen before, clutched rosary beads in the back row.

Curiously, Izzy squinted toward the lady. She wore a black mantilla that fell to her shoulders. Her face was somber. Her cheeks, tear-stained. She looked almost as sad as Mama had been when Bela Jimenez died.

Suddenly, the white mist swooped downward, swirled around the woman, and drifted over her like a window sheer blowing in a gentle wind. The woman's sorrowful mien beelined across the room and stung Izzy.

Izzy nudged her chin against her chest again.

*Don't look at the angel. She'll ask you to do something.*

She busied her mind with upcoming events. Concentrated on her brother's basketball game, her swim meet, and Christmas. Christmas was the only time of year Mama bought toys or clothes other than school uniforms, and it was less than four months away now. What did she want?

Mama was "broke." But Papa sent an envelope from Mexico last week, and Mama's face lit up like the statue of St. Theresa when she had her vision of the Blessed Mother, so Izzy hoped to get her bicycle this year.

She opened one eye. The filmy white mist had grown taller. Quickly she snapped her eye shut, but her shoulders sagged in defeat.

Mama had been scolding Izzy all her life not to stare at the cloudy haze. But Izzy's mind could never erase the white people—that's what she called them because Mama simply wouldn't tolerate her calling them angels or ghosts. Mama said never to talk about them. Look away when they appeared. But Izzy found it impossible to ignore the white people, who desperately longed to give her messages.

Reluctantly and defeatedly, she lowered her chin, turned her head sideways, and opened her eyes.

*What?*

The white lady looked directly at her.

*What do you want? Quick.*

Izzy waited.

Ghosts were funny. They appeared and then you had to figure out what they tried to tell you. She didn't understand why they couldn't whip up a voice and talk. If they spoke to her, communicated clearly—that's what Mama said Papa didn't do before he went away—the messages would be so much easier to understand.

The white lady floated forward and gradually transformed into the clear form of a thin, older woman with short hair. She held a cigarette in one hand and made the motion of coughing violently. Izzy's chest tightened.

*Okay, I got that. You were sick. So what do you want?*

The woman swirled her hands and drew three letters in the air. NYC. She slashed the letters with a harsh swipe, violently crossing them out several times

Izzy closed her eyes. Concentrated. What was the woman saying?

Suddenly, the room swayed. Had an earthquake struck? She placed her palms flat on the pew. What was happening? In her mind, she no longer sat in the chapel. She stood in a building, an office. Big gray floor boulders buckled beneath her. The building was collapsing.

Her eyes shot open, and she shook her head free of the frightening vision. She glanced toward the mist.

The white lady's form whirled and danced. She spread her hands wide apart, and roses fell from her arms. She nodded toward Izzy, her eyes pleading.

Izzy sighed.

*Okay, I'll tell her.*

She sprung onto the kneeler, stretching her lips toward Mama's ear.

"Mama, does NYC mean New York City?"

"Sh, yes, sit back and say your prayers."

Izzy slid back onto the pew, wondering how she would approach the sad woman.

Revealing the messages the white people relayed always perplexed her. How did she tell someone a ghost followed them around? And more importantly, how did she do that without alarming Mama? She wished her Belo Jimenez had given his gift—curse—of seeing angels to Enrique, not her.

"The gift skipped a generation and fell to you, Izzy," he once said.

"But Belo, I don't want your darn-blasted gift."

Her grandfather had set one long finger against her lips to quiet her. "Listen to the angels, but be careful who you tell. They'll come for you."

"Who will come for me?"

Belo had scared the daylights out of her.

"Who?" she asked over and over, but Belo would never respond, which made her worry until hives forced their way out of her skin. Every time she asked, he set a finger against his lips, closed his eyes, and shook his head. So Izzy was darn careful who she told.

She gazed toward the sad woman wearing the simple clothes. The lady had no jewelry and wore no makeup. She looked harmless. Was it safe to tell her?

The woman made the sign of the cross, kissed her rosary beads, and slid back onto the pew to gather her things. The spirit above her clasped her hands and begged.

Izzy sprung onto the kneeler again.

"Mama, may I get a drink of water?"

Her mother leaned toward her, whispering, "Yes, but quickly."

Izzy darted toward the door; the woman was coming. She stepped into the hall and rushed to the drinking fountain. She sipped water, listening for footsteps.

When the woman neared, Izzy turned. "Hello."

"Hello." The woman nodded and walked by.

Izzy closed her eyes and scratched her forehead. If only she had been born with a flowing tongue like Belo said of Enrique.

"Ma'am." She couldn't open her eyes when she heard the lady turn. "Did your mother die?"

Oh, that sounded horrible. Why had she asked such a thing? She wasn't even sure the white spirit was her mother.

"Of lung cancer?" Izzy opened her eyes. "She smoked, right?"

The lady stared but didn't say a word.

"She says you shouldn't go to New York City."

The lady's face wrinkled. "What?" She sounded cross.

"I'm sorry. It's—well." Izzy scratched her nose. She might be breaking into hives. "I saw this lady by you and she kept slashing the letters NYC like you shouldn't go there and she wouldn't stop, so I thought I better tell you. She kept doing it over and over and, well, I know she doesn't want you to go to New York City."

The woman took a step toward Izzy. The wrinkles melted from her face. "I do have a trip scheduled to New York. Next week. For a conference."

Goosebumps crawled over Izzy's skin. Whenever people, real human beings, confirmed what the white people told her, chills spread through her.

The lady stood still, waiting for Izzy to say more.

Izzy scratched and the lady stared.

"What was her name?"

"What?"

"My mother. What was my mother's name?"

The woman appeared hopeful. She held her breath, waiting. But Izzy didn't know the woman's name. She had difficulty hearing the white people. Usually, they simply gave signs.

Yes, signs.

"Oh." Izzy held a finger up. She remembered the sign. "Rose? Is your mother's name Rose?"

The chapel door opened behind Izzy, and she heard her mother's voice. "Izzy, what are you doing?"

"Nothing, Mama." Izzy sidled down the hall toward her mother.

"I hope she wasn't bothering you."

The woman said nothing. She stared at the two of them, a perplexed expression tainting her face. After a time, she left the building without saying more.

"Izzy," Mama barked. "What were you talking to that woman about?"

"I only said hello to her, Mama."

Her mother gazed at her skeptically. "Remember what Belo said. Don't talk to anyone."

"I didn't, Mama. I promise."

"Go collect your things. Your brother called. It's time to pick him up."

Izzy hurried back into the chapel and grabbed her coat, missal, and satchel. She smiled and waved goodbye to Jean as she exited.

Eight days later, the World Trade Centers collapsed. Izzy prayed the woman from the chapel had not been inside. She watched for her in church on Sunday and at the chapel during the week when she and Mama went to pray for the people who had died, but Izzy didn't see the woman.

Three weeks after September 11th, Izzy and her mother visited the chapel on a Sunday evening once again. The lady was sitting in the pew next to the woman named Jean. When Izzy walked in, she heard the lady say, "That's her. That's the girl."

"That's Isabelle Jimenez," Jean said.

The woman stood and rushed toward Izzy. Jean followed.

"Mrs. Jimenez?" The lady glanced at Izzy's mother.

"Yes?"

"Mrs. Jimenez, your daughter saved my life."

Izzy's mother made her spend the next two Saturday afternoons praying in church. But it was too late. Saving that woman's life would prove Belo right.

They would come for her.

## Chapter 2  Lenny

Lenny had no friends. At his sixth birthday party, his mother invited all the boys in his kindergarten class, and not one of them showed. That single incident represented the most traumatic day in his mother's life. Even worse than the day Lenny's father was struck and killed by the drunk driver.

So when Lenny begged his mother to have another party for his eleventh birthday, Mary Alice made an appointment to see a counselor. Not for Lenny, for herself.

"I'm afraid no one will come. I can't bear it."

"You must have some family in town who will come."

"No, we have no one." Her heart wrenched.

"Friends? Coworkers that might have children his age?"

Well, there was Sherry at work, Mary Alice thought. She had a son about the same age. And Karen, an older lady she walked with, had two granddaughters in fifth grade. Maybe they could come. She sighed. This fear of no one showing had uprooted her psoriasis. She itched an elbow. Then a shin.

"Maybe one child. Possibly two. But Lenny won't know them."

"How about talking to the teacher? Surely, there has to be someone who will come. A child in a similar situation. Sometimes you don't realize other children are going through the same cruel ordeal until you speak up. Talk to the teacher."

Mary Alice did. She contacted Lenny's teacher, Mrs. Hill, and discussed the dilemma at length with her. Mrs. Hill said since Lenny had grown taller this year, some of the boys were picking him for dodge ball. A few of those boys might come.

So Mary Alice gave her invitations enough for the entire class, and Mrs. Hill sent her own personal note home with the students.

Mary Alice also gave invites to neighbors. In total, she handed out twenty-eight invitations. Then she walked two streets over to the little plaza on the busy street with the mailbox on its corner, and she held her breath, staring at the twenty-ninth one. The envelope was addressed to the Callahan home. The Callahan girls lived around the corner, but she didn't dare deliver theirs herself. She closed her eyes and slipped that last invitation into the mailbox, praying they accepted.

She was elated when an Adam's mother called to say Adam would come and three other mothers called to say their sons, who went to school with Lenny, would also attend. Karen's granddaughters were coming. Sherry promised to bring her son, and finally, the call she was waiting for came. The Callahan girls, Lisa and Rachel, would be there.

She prayed no one reneged.

On the day of the party, Mary Alice generously set out fourteen places. Lenny counted them and smiled from ear to ear.

"Are that m-m-many k-kids coming, Mom?"

"I'm not sure Lenny. But we have to have a few extra plates, you know."

"Ok-k-kay, Mom."

"Remember Lenny. Try to look your friends in the eye. When you look down it's disrespectful."

"I will, M-mom."

The party started at 2 p.m. and at 2:01 Mary Alice's eyes welled with tears, but she forced herself to remain calm. She watched Lenny hitting balloons in the air all by himself. Then, mercifully, the doorbell rang. There at the door was her friend Karen and her twin granddaughters, Mila and Mallory. The twins ran in. Karen set a hand gingerly on Mary Alice's arm.

"Did anyone else come?"

"No, not so far." Mary Alice could barely get the words out. Karen leaned in and hugged her.

Then the miracle happened. The doorbell rang a second time.

Mary Alice hurried to the front door. When she opened it, the Callahan sisters stood staring at her. Behind them were three little boys. The sisters had brought three neighborhood boys along with them.

Seven children.

The doorbell rang three more times after that. Mary Alice broke down and cried. The children didn't notice. Karen ushered them in.

"Go on," Karen waved Mary Alice away. "Compose yourself. I'll line them up for some games."

Mary Alice ambled to the kitchen and leaned over the sink. She could not contain herself. Tears of relief streamed down her cheeks, blurring her vision. She grabbed a clean dishtowel from a drawer, wiping her eyes. When she tossed the towel onto the counter and dropped her arms to her side, five wee fingers slipped their way into the palm of her hand.

She hadn't noticed the child had entered the room.

Mary Alice glanced down and stared smack into the eyes of LeeLee Callahan. The Caribbean blue of them pierced her.

"It's okay, Ms. Emling," the child said. "Lenny is going to be fine. You'll see."

Mary Alice Emling would think back on this moment of her life for many years to come.

# Chapter 3  Washington D.C.

Jerry McDaniel hated his bosses. He spent day and night imagining ways to frame both his supervisor, Bart Conrad, and his director, Randall Scott.

Scott was a narcissist too high up to touch. He insisted people refer to him as the commander. Probably because his name conjured so many skeletons in the closet their bones clanged if the door blew open. Scott spent most of his military career nailing that door shut. When his superiors promoted him to Washington, that closet entrance magically disappeared into the woodwork. Funny how a transfer to Washington could turn man into magician.

Conrad was no angel, either. Give that guy a dime, and he'd slit Scott's throat.

What a pair.

And now the CIA was cutting them loose. White House personnel had decided to create a stand-alone department for the secret program Scott and Conrad headed. Without question, Scott would abuse his new-found autonomy. Sovereignty could corrupt an honest man. Give a deceitful man supremacy? Disastrous.

Then, as if those two devious idiots didn't yank Jerry's chain enough, there was this slippery kid coming up the ranks. The nephew of some bigwig. Someone Swarthy. Between Scott, Conrad, and this Swarthy kid, Jerry was juggling fruit— not balls, because in his opinion none of them had the balls to oversee this program. And despite seeming a fruitless, lost cause in the past, Jerry believed in this project.

They just needed to find the right kids.

While scads of White House officials scoffed at the idea—training children to remote view? Preposterous!—Jerry had done ample research. He studied the Stargate files. Researched clairvoyants. Talked to scientists, not quacks but hard-core, fact-driven experts, who believed this specific proposed training technique would work.

Today, sitting in front of the CIA director's right-hand man, Jerry perspired underneath his suit coat. So much sweat accumulated in his pits, he could have wrung his shirt out and filled a swimming pool.

Outwardly, he remained calm.

He shifted slightly in his seat. Waited. In the past few months, the head of the CIA had been preoccupied with a search for weapons of mass destruction. The top men didn't give a damn about anything else; hence, officials welcomed Scott's request to disassociate the CIA from the remote-viewing program.

But while the men at the top kept their noses buried in Iraq maps, Scott began pilfering dollars from other defense budgets to the tune of fifteen million dollars. That greed set off a slew of cabinet-member complaints. Scott was sequestered to a meeting in Washington.

Scott brought along Bart Conrad and Jerry for that D.C. day of reckoning.

"Every indication from the 1995 closeout of the project said flop. What makes you so sure this will work, Randall?" Steve Larson, the right-hand man assigned to investigate, tossed a report onto the table.

"The University of Arizon—"

"No more bullshit about Arizona and that afterlife experiment. Talk to me about remote viewing."

Conrad spoke up. "Past programs were inconclusive. However, last year a college professor worked with an Indian reservation school, and the kids identified objects in a building across the road."

Larson looked from Scott to Conrad and back to Scott.

"This is what you developed an entire department for? Because some half-assed teacher said his kids could see through walls?"

"Steve, Bart has been researching remote viewing for ten years."

"You did the study?" Larson cut Scott off and turned toward Bart Conrad.

"No, sir." Conrad wiggled inside his collar. "Central Intelligence did the study. With impressive results."

"Central Intelligence?"

"Yes, sir. Under my authority, they brought in—" Conrad's Adam's apple rose and fell. His determined demeanor slumped. He looked like a grade-school kid in a principal's office. "Five people to investigate psychics, sir."

Larson glanced back at Scott. "This has got to be a joke."

Jerry watched Scott squirm and, in his head, Jerry howled. He'd been waiting six months for this moment. He began counting down.

*Five.*

"Absolutely not," Scott replied indignantly. "We recruited the best researchers in the country. Explain, Bart."

Bart fumbled with the papers in front of him. Jerry had never seen him so nervous.

"The men who participated—" Conrad hesitated. "And one woman."

*Four.*

Scott looked like a leopard ready to pounce. Conrad's hands shook. The report he fingered had wet spots from his sweat.

"Sir, these men are—men and woman—are esteemed. Five highly-respected military officials."

Silence reigned. The tension in the room was worse than a stretched rubber band. Clearly, Bart Conrad was screwing it up for Scott. Steve Larson slammed a fist on the table.

"I don't care if John McCain is on that list. All you've done is test the same theories everyone else has tested in the CIA for the last thirty years. You simply shuffled the results."

*Three.*

"We gave you eight million dollars, but you weren't happy. You took an extra seven million from other budgets for the implementation of a defunct project."

"But, sir—"

"Not one ounce of evidence exists that remote viewing works. We never intended fifteen million dollars to be transferred to this program. Unless you give me some hard-core proof that this project will succeed, we're pulling it."

*Two.*

Scott and Conrad tried interjecting, but Larson overrode them.

"I've had all I can take of your bullshit, Randall. Tell me. Who the hell of these five superstars can stand up in front of the head of the CIA and Congress and say they've proven remote viewing can be taught to kids still wetting their pants?"

*One.*

"Major Bern Selig and—Annie Sherman," Jerry blurted out.

*Lift off.*

Here's the thing. The idea of training hadn't been Scott's or Bart Conrad's. It had been Jerry's. And he'd done his homework.

He knew cabinet members would complain when Scott skimmed money off the top of their budgets, and top CIA officials wouldn't have time for budgetary trivialities with their heads so far up Middle Eastern asses they couldn't see light. So they'd send their hatchet man, Steve Larson. Larson had lopped off the heads of so many CIA officials that the hair from their scalps could cover every bald head in D.C.

Jerry had no intention of stepping up to the guillotine.

Steve Larson respected the American hero Major Bern Selig. As eighteen-year-olds, the two had spent time cleaning bathroom floors with toothbrushes in a military academy. West Point to be exact. Later, they dodged bullets in Middle Eastern trenches together before Selig transferred out of Larson's division and single-handedly saved the lives of fifty-six men. Larson often bragged about his war-hero friend.

Jerry had acclaimed friends, too. One golfed in Selig's foursome. Jerry needed to pull only a few strings and rack up a few favors to secure a spot in a tourney with the American legend. Jerry studied Selig's golf swing on the first round, let him win a few holes on the second round, and clobbered him on the third—the guy didn't know what hit him.

Next, Jerry taught Selig how to straighten his shot and pick his clubs. He gave him three private golf lessons. With that, Selig lowered his handicap and sent a case of Kentucky's best bourbon to Jerry's home.

They began playing together occasionally. To garner Steve Larson's approval, all Jerry needed to do was convince Selig, Larson's idol, that they could train kids in remote viewing. Three professors from the University of Arizona and one from Cornell did that.

Why had Jerry selected tenured profs from those two universities? Because Selig was a University of Arizona graduate, and his only daughter, his princess, had received an acceptance letter and committed to attend Cornell next fall.

Selig loved the professor's report and with his stamp of approval, Jerry simply sealed the deal by introducing one last piece of the puzzle to Steve Larson. A very nice-looking piece.

"Sherman?" Larson's voice suddenly strained.

"Yes, sir. Sherman and Selig oversaw the project. Sherman actually requested to work at the facility once up and running."

For the first time during the meeting, Steve Larson looked Jerry McDaniel in the eye. The stare felt penetrating, electrifying, wonderful.

"What's your name, son?"

Larson was older than Jerry. A decade older. Some might consider him at that perfect age. Old enough to have amassed a fortune and made a respected name for himself, but still young enough to be considered a looker.

"Jerry McDaniel, sir."

Jerry could feel Scott's and Conrad's eyes on him, the lousy good-for-nothings. They had treated him like some backseat lay, a roll in the hay. Ordered him around as if he was an intern. Never had they asked for his opinion. So while they wasted time cajoling government officials at fancy dinners and private meetings, Jerry had researched hatchet-man Steve Larson.

"Who signed off on the research?" Larson picked his glasses off the conference table and placed them on his nose, shuffling through the reports.

"Both of them, sir. Peruse the Anomalous Cognition report." Jerry waited for Larson to find the report he himself had slipped in the file on the way to the meeting—carry the files, Commander? Sure, I'll carry your files.

When Larson found it, Jerry said, "Page 387, sir."

Steve Larson didn't move a muscle. His eyes, however, snapped upward, and he peeked over his glasses at Jerry, his stare so hot Jerry thought the hairs on his face might singe.

He did everything in his power not to smile.

Larson shuffled to page 387. His lips moved silently as he read the findings of Major Bern Selig and Ms. Annie Sherman. A minute or two lapsed. He tossed the report down, removed his glasses, and tucked them in his shirt pocket. He leaned his elbows on the table and stared directly into Jerry's eyes. Jerry stared joyously back.

"And what do Mr. Selig and Ms. Sherman want to see happen?"

"Well, sir, they weren't entirely sure but they estimated a six-to-nine-month study would do it. An entire year would be grand."

Jerry struggled not to break into a laugh during the long, silent seconds that passed. He forced himself not to glance toward Scott and Conrad though he desperately wanted to witness their dumbfounded expressions.

Finally, Steve Larson spoke.

"You—they—want one year?"

"That would be more than enough to complete this—" Here, Jerry hesitated briefly and continued, "secret…project."

Silence befell the room again. Jerry was one hundred percent confident no one understood what was going on except himself and Steve Larson.

Larson stood. Picked up his briefcase. One by one he transferred the reports from the table to the bag.

"One year."

"Thank you, sir." Jerry stood.

"Yes, thank you, sir." Bart Conrad tried interjecting. He held out a hand, but Steve Larson reached for Jerry's instead. Shaking Larson's outstretched hand was the single best moment in his career up until that point.

"You have a name for this project, son?"

And before Bart could tell him his cockamamie Operation Crux name, Jerry blurted out, "Project Dream, sir."

Steve Larson turned toward Randall Scott and said, "Let's go sign the papers, Scott."

When the door shut and they were gone, Bart Conrad inched into Jerry's space.

"What was that all about?"

Jerry took a step into Bart's space, paused there a minute, and exited the room laughing. He drove seventeen miles away to his mistress's house, stopping only once to pick up a bottle of Champagne imported from France.

Six days later, Project Dream was born. Jerry McDaniel was named the director, and the compromising pictures of Steve Larson and Annie Sherman remained locked away in Jerry's safety deposit box.

## Chapter 4  Izzy

Izzy stood sideways, tilting her head and gazing into the mirror. She had no idea what those kids were talking about. Okay, she had a wee bit of extra meat on her, but her stomach wasn't big. Not that big anyway.

She turned and faced herself, staring into her brown eyes.

"You are such a dork." She frowned at herself. How could this be? Her gorgeous big brother, the toast of the town, every inch of him so popular, and her?

"Chopped liver."

Now that her brother had decided to return to Mexico with her father, there was no hope of her ever sitting with the popular girls in the cafeteria. Everyone at St. Mary's Grade School, students and teachers, remembered the much-loved Enrique from three years ago when he played ball there—baseball, basketball, football. His name would be etched in the auditorium for years to come. Not only for his accomplishments in these three sports but for soccer, track and field, and swimming as well.

As if those accolades hadn't been enough, his nomination to walk Melissa Delavern down the aisle in his eighth-grade year sealed his fame. Melissa had won the coveted part of Mary the Blessed Virgin in St. Mary's May crowning ceremony. Enrique had walked down that aisle beside her, playing the part of Joseph. What a laugh her Mexican relatives had gotten from that.

Her attention returned to the reflection in the mirror.

"Well, you might not be popular but you're smart. At least you don't have to worry about grades." She tucked in her white shirt that had snuck out over the top of her uniform skirt. "You're just uncoordinated."

The door flung open. Enrique took two steps into her room and jumped onto her bed.

"Hey, muchacha, you aren't uncoordinated."

She straightened her spine and turned sideways. "I'm not worried about being uncoordinated. I'm worried about being fat."

"Fat, my Lord, you have no ass."

She turned and look behind her. "Something about your brother saying you have no ass is just wrong."

Enrique laughed. He sat up and crossed his feet at the ankles, leaning back on his arms. My God, he was nice looking; no wonder the girls in the neighborhood were nice to her.

"And maybe you're right that I have no ass, but the boys call me jelly Isabelly." She put one hand above her stomach and one below. "Tell me the truth. Do I have a big stomach?"

Enrique squinted his eyes and rubbed his chin. "Well, let's put it this way. Is it flat?"

She picked up her sweater, twirled it around, and snapped him with it, laughing. "Your gut is bigger than mine, and your head is fatter." She loved Enrique, even when he teased.

He sprang from the bed and jumped toward the door.

"Ah, the truth comes out how you feel about your big brother. Well, we swimmers have to have some body fat." He leaned toward her and winked. "For buoyancy."

She snapped the sweater at him again, but he blocked the snap with her bedroom door. The wool against wood made a cracking sound.

From the bottom of the stairs, her mother yelled, "Ricky leave your sister be. Get down here. Your father's on his way."

Izzy screwed up her lips and meandered back to the mirror. How alone she was going to feel. First Daddy left for Mexico and now Ricky. She and her mother had no other relatives in America. Her father was one of eleven children, and the only one to gain citizenship—through marriage. Her mother was born and raised in the good old USA. The only child of two only children. Both in graves for over ten years. Her mother was solo en el mundo—alone in the world.

Izzy looked in the mirror. Despite about a million ghosts hanging around all the time, she felt alone, too. She grabbed her bookbag, jerking it forcefully, and as she did, her art class's long tube of red acrylic paint flung out of the bag and into the air.

*Oh, no.*

She held her breath. Concentrated on catching it. Mama would kill her if she stained her bedroom rug again. She watched the tube fall toward her fingers.

*My God, I'm going to catch it.*

The tube slipped into her hand. Elation swept through her.

*I'm not uncoordinated!*

Her lips widened. She tightened her grip on the tube.

The scene switched to fast motion. The top of the tube popped off, and a spray of red splatted over her starched white shirt.

She raised her head, catching the reflection of her white, blue—and now, red—uniform. She looked like a smeared flag. The tube in her right hand, a paint brush. She dropped her arms to her sides. The tube squirted more red. This time onto her skirt.

She clenched her teeth together and forced words out of the spaces in between them.

"Mary, Mother of—"

She was tempted to let loose a barrage of swearing but refrained. She would remain the completely obedient Catholic girl that she was. Well, her mind danced on, except for the shoplifting, of course. But it wasn't her fault they had no money for bras. She had to wear a training bra. Girls were making fun of her.

Now, this. A ruined uniform.

How she would ever get out from under this gray cloud, she didn't know. How could a ten-year-old be burdened by such black luck?

"Santa Marie, pray for me," she said, signing a cross under her chin. "Mama is going to kill me."

Twenty minutes later, after her mother gave a grand lecture on the cost of Catholic school uniforms, somehow, the red had at least been removed from her skirt. Her mother hurriedly ironed a new white shirt and left it on her bed. Izzy slipped into her uniform, snapped her cross tie, and dug through the closet for her shoes.

She descended the stairs and scrambled to the kitchen in time to witness her mother hugging Ricky goodbye, tears streaming down her face.

She had only seen her mother cry once before, when her grandmother died. Even when Papa left, she'd hid her emotions. Always a pillar of strength, her mama worked two jobs, distributed communion to the sick for their church, volunteered at Izzy's school, and never demanded support payments from Izzy's father. Izzy thought she still loved him.

But who didn't? He was like Enrique.

From the doorway, she choked back her tears and listened.

"Mama, I'll be back." Ricky tilted his head and talked out the side of his mouth.

"Of course, you will." Mama snapped a tissue from a box on the counter and wiped her eyes. "I don't know what's wrong with me."

"Papa said it's a six-month job, that's all."

"But you'll enroll in school there, right?"

"I promise."

"And stay away from that girl."

"Maria Luisa? Ma—" He stood back, flashed that irresistible smile that Izzy was sure the entire universe loved. "I have no time for that girl."

"Oh, I heard how you had no time for her last summer."

Izzy smiled as she listened, glad her mother never sulked long.

"What? You don't want el nieto?"

"Ah!" Her mother shoved Ricky's shoulder. "Don't say such things."

Her mother covered her ears and walked away. Enrique turned. His eyes met Izzy's. He winked. "You complain about our small family, and yet you don't want a grandchild?"

"You are sixteen years old. Don't say that." She made the sign of the cross.

"I'll be seventeen in two weeks," he said.

Instantly, his mother froze. Izzy glared at her brother, and he lifted his shoulders at her, shrugging.

"What?" he pantomimed.

Izzy shook her head. Reminding Mama she would miss his next birthday tortured her. They shared silence for a moment. Then Izzy's mother turned and threw her arms around Enrique, squeezing mightily. Enrique buried his face in her neck.

"Ma—"

"Goodbye." Mama wept softly. "I love you, Enrique."

She released him, grabbed her purse, and went out the kitchen door without looking back.

Izzy and Enrique stood motionless in the quiet. The TV blared from the living room. News anchors spewed words about a shooting, a death, and some secret government program that politicians refused to talk about. But there in the Jimenez family kitchen, the crumbs of breakfast and the dripless faucet, which Enrique had fixed last night, sat silent.

Finally, he turned his palms outward and lifted his shoulders. "I didn't remind her of my birthday on purpose."

She couldn't take it. She ran to him, tears spilling down her face. "Please don't go, Ricky. Please don't leave Mama and me."

He stretched his arms around her and set his chin onto the top of her head. She hugged him tightly, squeezed so hard the beating of his heart throbbed against her cheek. He placed a hand under her chin, tipped her head upward, and set his forehead against hers. "Don't cry, Izzy. Please. You know it's the one thing in the world I cannot stand."

She couldn't stop crying. She held on to her brother, savoring how every inch of him felt, so she could remember the embrace—in case—in case he never returned.

The horn of the school bus blasted outside, but Izzy didn't let go. And Ricky didn't tell her she had to.

Instead, he placed his hands on her forearms, pushed her away, and glanced into her eyes. "How about I walk you to school one last time."

"It will take twenty minutes, and Papa will be here soon."

"He can wait," Enrique said, and he gave her the sign. The secret code that meant they would always be there for each other.

He touched the tip of one finger to one ear lobe, his lips, head, and heart. Something he did when they were in trouble with their parents and couldn't talk in front of them. A gesture he used in the neighborhood playground after Izzy told him the kids teased her because her big brother always called out, "Isabelly, I love you."

Only this time, when he finished the secret sign they would take to their graves, he said the words out loud. "I won't say the words, but I think them and feel them in my heart. I'll always love and protect you, Isabelly. Always."

Izzy threw her face against his chest and sobbed.

# Chapter 5  Lenny

"Mrs. Emling, the—"

"Ms. It's Ms. Emling."

"I'm sorry, Ms. Emling, our records show Lenny is the fastest and strongest boy at the Thomas Detention Center. We could use his abilities in our program."

Mary Alice looked the man up and down. What did he think? She was stupid?

"Mr. Grant, tell me the truth. You have spent the last hour and a half dancing around the subject and the past three weeks testing my son. Calling me. I'm tired. I want to know what this is about."

"An opportunity, ma'am, for your son to turn his life around."

Mary Alice raised her eyebrows. "Turn himself around?"

"Yes, ma'am."

"Officer, my son does not need turning around. Your legal justice department needs turning around."

"I know how you feel, ma'am."

"No, you don't, officer. Let's get that straight. My son came across three boys, one of whom was raping a twelve-year-old girl. The other two were waiting their turn, and so he ripped them to shreds. All three of them. You and the Pennsylvania State Police sent him to the Thomas Center for rehabilitation.

"He all but killed one of them, ma'am."

She hesitated, knowing the silence implied his words affected her. But they didn't. She let him wallow in his self-win for a moment. Then she let loose.

"I believe—I'm not completely sure because no one revealed the three boys' names, but I believe—one of those boys was—"

She hesitated again.

"Your boss's son." She snapped her chin to the side and squinted one eye. "Some Barnett boy. And correct me if I'm wrong but this boy—this somebody Barnett—never spent one second in a detention center."

The officer folded his hands on the conference table and cleared his throat.

"No, but the boy who—the boy accused of raping the girl is in a reformatory—"

"Well, isn't that nice." She set one long finger against the side of her mouth. "How fortunate, wouldn't you say? That this Barnett boy was lucky enough to be second in line?"

She dropped her hand from her face and straightened. "What about intent or abetting of a crime? Do I have to find myself an attorney, officer?"

"Ma'am…" He continued talking.

She jumped out of her chair and gathered her belongings.

"You're not taking my son anywhere," she interrupted. "He's a good—"

"Mary Alice." The man stood abruptly. She could see the angst building in him. "Your son is never going to get out of reformatory school, and my guess is Barnett will make his life a living hell when he turns eighteen, so you better sit back down and reconsider."

Mary Alice slapped her purse onto the table, heaved two flat palms on both sides of it, and leaned toward the officer. "Tell me the truth. What's this really about?"

"The truth is we have a new program for bigger, faster, physically-fit kids."

"Uh-huh." She kept staring. "That's it? You're going to send him to a private middle school and high school, give him free college, ensure him a job, and pay me a stipend because

Lenny grew nine inches the past year and runs like Usain Bolt. What do you want him to do? Run from Barnett?"

The officer sat down and rubbed the back of his neck with his fingers. "No, ma'am. He's not going to be running from anything or anyone. He'll be educated. Grow up with normal teenagers. Attend college and work for the U.S. government."

"Bullshit." Mary Alice didn't often swear, but she'd had enough. "Tell me the truth or I walk out this door. What do you want my boy for?"

He gazed into her eyes, studying her intently. She could see the truth dawning on him; she was going to make him tell her.

"They don't want him for his physical strength alone, do they?" She leaned closer.

"No, ma'am. He has an unusual way of—" The man slipped two fingers into the inside of his collar and wiggled his neck around. "Showing up at, how shall I say, some convenient times."

"Convenient times?"

"Yes, ma'am. More than once, he has averted—" He cleared his throat. "Incidents."

Yes, he had. Lenny defended those weaker than him. How he knew when boys would attack girls or break storefront windows to steal was beyond her. She pushed off the table with her hands and lifted the purse strap over her shoulder.

"So you want him for his mind, not his physical strength?"

Again, a coldness encased them. The clock on the wall ticked. The other officer, who stood by the door, shifted his weight, and the floor creaked beneath him. Outside the room, someone shuffled by on high heels, and muffled voices resonated from offices down the hall, but no one spoke in their little corner of the correction center. The silence lasted seconds but felt like minutes.

"No, ma'am." The officer's shoulders sagged. He appeared more relieved to tell her than defeated. "We want him for both."

*****

Two weeks later, Lenny Emling stood next to the black limousine in the parking lot of the Thomas Detention Center, his mother's arms around him. She squeezed as if she would never see him again.

"I'm sorry, Lenny," she mumbled. "The attorney said this was our only option. We'd never get you out of here unless you enrolled in the program."

"It's ok-k-kay, Ma." Lenny gave her an obligatory squeeze. "I don't c-care about leaving. It's n-not like I like my school."

"But you had such a great year in football. You were finding yourself. Had made some friends."

"They only liked me because I w-was big. M-made a good defensive tackle."

"I'm going to miss you. I know you shot up like a beanstalk this past year." She pushed him away, her eyes wet. "But you'll always be my little Lenny."

"Ma." He sighed. Acted annoyed. The one thing he couldn't bear in life was to see his mother cry. "I'm f-fine."

She licked her thumb and wiped something off the corner of his mouth.

"Ma," he said. "I'm twelve years old. You c-can't k-keep treating me like a b-baby."

"Oh, Lenny." She grabbed his forearms with her hands and began crying outright.

"Mrs. Emling," the driver said. "We have to leave now."

"It's Ms.," she whispered, throwing her arms around Lenny for one last mighty hug and kissing the side of his big head.

"Ma, s-stop."

"All right, sweetie. You go now. You get the best education, and you make something of yourself."

"Geez, Ma." He was surprised how easy it was to sound annoyed with her. He picked up his small bag and stepped away from her. "It's n-not like I'm n-never coming back or anything."

He jumped in the car, closed the door, and took a seat in the back, away from the driver. When he settled into a comfortable position, he noticed the partition. A plexiglass shield separated him from the driver. Thankful he wouldn't spend the two-hour trip to the Pittsburgh airport forcing conversation, he placed his bag on the seat next to him, refusing to gaze out the window at his mother.

While the driver rounded the car, got in, and started the engine, Lenny inspected the lunch his mother had packed him. He brought out the brown bag, dipped his hand inside, and pulled out a peanut butter sandwich. As he did, a small sheet of purple stationery fell onto the seat. He picked the note up and read it.

"No matter where you go or who you meet, remember, no one will ever love you like your mother. XXXOOO Mom."

Lenny held the note in his big hands for a minute, staring down at the words, thinking about how she was always saying no one would ever love him more than she did. Now he was alone. They were both alone.

For some reason, the stories his mother relayed about his grandmother popped into his head. His grandmother had lived for years with crippling arthritis. When the swelling and stiffness immobilized her, Lenny's mom packed up her things, quit her job, and moved away from Erie for a time to care for her mother.

His mother was the most giving person he had ever met. She visited the sick in her church. Provided them with lunches and hot dinners. In the winter, she shoveled their walkways from their doors to their mailboxes. She helped older neighbors plant flowers in the spring and weed their lawns in the summer. She drove the nuns from his school to their doctor appointments. Volunteered at the food pantry.

She was selfless. She did favors for people with a smile and never expected anything in return.

An only child herself, his mother had no other family, and Lenny had never met his father. Now she was alone, and she couldn't lift a full laundry basket or carry the trash container to the curb. Her knuckles were crooked. She bent at the waist most days as she walked.

Why hadn't he realized this sooner?

Lenny had to lift the cans off the higher shelves for her. Move the furniture so she could vacuum. Pack the food and clothes in the trunk for her to take to the homeless shelter.

Who would do that now?

Big wet drops fell from his eyes to the paper. The blue ink of his mother's words blurred into the purple sheet.

The car began moving.

"Ma," Lenny said, reaching for the door, realizing what she had kept from him.

The pain and soreness had set in. The stiffness in the morning. The swelling of her hands and feet. Why hadn't she said something? She had inherited her mother's debilitating rheumatoid arthritis, and now he was leaving her alone. With no one.

He jiggled the handle. The door was locked. The car began inching its way down the long driveway. Lenny slapped the hand with the note onto the window as he passed his mother. She was crying. Holding her face in her hands.

"Ma," he yelled, banging on the window and helplessly watching her as the limousine rolled away.

"Ma, I love you!"

He shouted I love you over and over until his mother faded from view. Then for the first time in his sad twelve years of life, Lenny Emling threw his big, awkward body down onto the back seat of that limousine and cried like a baby.

He vowed to come home and take care of her one day.

## Chapter 6  Izzy

"Isabelle, what were you thinking?"

"I was thinking I didn't want anyone calling me smelly-jelly Isabelly ever again."

"But to steal? Steal clothes like a juvenile delinquent?"

"I couldn't ask you for more money, Mama. I know about…I just needed some clothes."

"You know about what?"

"Nothing. Just…about the money."

"What money?"

Izzy hated when her mother hollered. She seldom yelled, but when she did, Izzy broke out into hives.

Blotches formed on her arms. She itched her elbow. "That you don't have much money."

She bent and scratched her knee. Lifted the cuff of her pants. Blotches mottled her leg.

"Izzy, I'm talking to you. What do you think you know?"

She slapped her pant leg down. "That Papa doesn't send you money anymore," she squealed. "There, I said it. I don't know why it has to be such a big secret. So what if he doesn't care about me. So what if he only loves Enrique."

She folded her arms and waited for her mother to scream. Instead of shouting, however, Mama slumped into a chair, punched her elbows on the kitchen table, and dropped her head into her hands. She cried so hard Izzy could barely understand her. "Is that what you think? Your father doesn't love you?"

Izzy stood stunned. Her mother hadn't cried in years—two years, to be exact, when Enrique left for Mexico.

So why now? The police were on their way.

She searched for something horrible to say. Something so hurtful Mama would stop blubbering and slap her. She had only slapped Izzy one time when Izzy said the F word. Other than that, not even a spanking.

But now Izzy wanted to be slapped. Punished. Screamed at. Anything but cried to.

"Well…well." There were things she could say to her. Like she worked too much. She never had time to take Izzy to the mall like other mothers took their daughters. She never allowed her to have a dog. Or even a cat. That she never sat in the stands and cheered at her swim meets. And that she let Enrique leave and now they could only talk to each other when he borrowed Papa's phone and he hadn't called in two months.

"Well, you—" She couldn't say such things. "Mama, please don't cry."

"Sit down, Izzy." Her mother rose and shuffled to the sink. She poured herself a glass of water and tottered back. "There is something I need to tell you."

She sat down and moved her chair in. Its legs made a chalkboard-scraping sound against the linoleum. Izzy flinched.

"I should have told you this months ago."

Izzy didn't like the sound of this. Wasn't it embarrassing enough she'd been caught stealing, again? There was more?

"What is it, Mama?" She responded out of reflex. She didn't really want to know.

If the officer wasn't on his way there, she would have run out of the house. Run right to Gina Rodríguez's and begged Gina's mother to let her spend the night. Instead, she sat down and folded her hands. Tried not to itch the fiery-red splotches prickling her skin.

"Your father hasn't sent money because he's sick."

She couldn't bear the itchiness longer. She scratched vigorously. Her fingernails made long red streaks on her arms.

"He is?"

"Yes, honey, he's very sick." Mama stretched an arm across the table and stopped Izzy from scratching. Held her hand. "He has cancer. Lung cancer. And it's bad."

"Bad?"

Her mother swallowed. Her face sagged. Izzy hadn't seen her so hopeless since—since Enrique left.

"But if he quits smoking, he will get better, right?" She yanked her hand from her mother's grasp.

The muscles of her mother's cheeks tightened. Her lips disappeared inside her mouth. She closed her eyes and shook her head.

"Well, the doctors can fix him, right? I mean I can get a babysitting job, and Enrique can take more building jobs to help pay the medical bills."

"Izzy, I'm sorry, honey. It's too late. The cancer is inoperable."

"Inoperable?" Izzy stood. "What does that mean?"

"It means there is nothing they can do." Her mother put her head in her hands and began crying again. "I'm so sorry, Izzy. I didn't know how to tell you."

The doorbell rang, but neither of them heard it.

"There's always something the doctors can do. Gina's uncle is a doctor. We can have Enrique bring him here."

"No, honey. He's in the hospital. He's too weak to travel."

"Well, can't they give him chemo?"

Her mother shook her head.

The doorbell rang again. Izzy began pacing back and forth, scratching so hard that now both arms were bleeding. She leaned down and scratched her shins, too. Streaks of red lines burrowed through her thin pants.

"I have to call Enrique. He can bring Papa home."

"No honey, he can't."

"He must!"

Her mother winced. "He has to stay with Lucia."

"Lucia? Why must he stay with her?"

"Izzy, honey, sit down."

"I don't want to sit down. What does this have to do with Lucia?"

"Ricky didn't want me to tell you."

"Tell me what?"

"Lucia had a baby."

"A baby? Lucia?" This was too much for her. First news of Papa. Now a baby? Enrique would never return to San Diego.

"When?"

Her mother sniffled. "Two months ago."

"Two months ago? Why didn't anyone tell me?" Her face grew hot. She paced and scratched. The doorbell rang. She fled to the back door, jimmying the lock. Her mother followed her, grabbed her shoulders.

"Izzy, I'm sorry."

"No," she screamed. She shirked her mother's grip and backed away.

"You should have told me. You never tell me anything. You think I'm a weak little girl. You don't know anything about me."

She ran toward the living room, the front door. She had to get away. Maybe to Gina's. Gina's uncle could help her father.

"Izzy!" Her mother screamed.

Izzy wrenched open the door just as the doorbell rang again. She barged outside and fell into the arms of a police officer.

"Whoa," he said, holding her back.

She swung at him and fought. He strengthened his arms around her. She screamed for him to let her go until her screams turned into sobs, and her legs went limp. She slid to the ground.

Her mother rushed out the front door and knelt beside her. Neighbors stopped raking yards and working on cars. Izzy could see everyone around her, but she couldn't process anything—the colors of the day swirled into a blurry mess.

Nothing, not her mother's arms or the policeman hollering through his shoulder mic or the sound of the ambulance's siren, could restore her mindfulness or soothe the ache inside her. She slipped into unconsciousness.

Twelve hours later, she awoke. A woman in a police officer's uniform sat in a chair beside her bed. The woman rested a slender hand against Izzy's cheek and talked into her shoulder mic. "She's awake."

"How are you feeling, little lady?" The woman inched to the edge of her chair. "You gave us a scare."

Izzy pushed up in the bed, and the nice officer adjusted the pillows behind her. Immediately, Izzy's mother dashed through the door and rushed toward her. A second police officer followed. Her mother fell onto the bed and buried her head in Izzy's neck, sobbing.

"They're taking you away from me," Mama cried.

"Shhh," the nice police lady said. "Everything will turn out fine."

"But." Izzy glanced at the lady and male officers. Behind them, a doctor holding a shot rushed toward her bed.

"Where are they taking me?"

"Arizona." Her mother wept. "To a program called Project Dream."

The doctor stuck the needle in her arm, and bit by bit, her awareness slipped away. Her gaze spanned the room, groggily halting on the wall mirror as her consciousness faded.

She noticed her image. Bulging red blotches covered her once smooth face. Some bled. She didn't look like herself. Was that her? Or someone else? A girl in a horror movie, maybe? Or a dream?

What had her mother said? A dream.

Yes, this must be a dream. The ugly, mottled girl in the mirror must be dreaming.

## Chapter 7  The Nevada Desert

The limousine rode past miles of barren road edged with rock and sand. Occasionally, Izzy spotted white trucks with black-tinted windows, and men, guns slung over their shoulders, riding three-wheelers that surged over mounds of beige earth.

Dust kicked up outside her window, swirling under a relentless blaze of sun. Not a single cloud broke the blue sky. After more than an hour of traveling through the desert, a blur of buildings emerged in the distance.

The scene made her stomach ache and her skin itch.

She tried not to scratch as they neared the so-called prodigy camp. A long, flat, one-story building sat embedded in the sand. Three smaller structures and a large hangar flanked its left side. A basketball court, tennis courts, and some type of obstacle course fringed the right. At least those amenities relayed a sliver of hope this place wasn't as scary as it appeared.

Behind the main campus, sand stretched a mile toward a mountain range. The first range hung low, flaunting hills, really. Halfway to those knolls, a domed-roof structure sat like an ostracized kid in a cafeteria. Izzy wondered why that analogy struck her. She prayed the thought wasn't a premonition of days to come. The man in the expensive suit at the airport said six girls and eighteen boys were already enrolled in Project Dream. Izzy was the last of the initial twenty-five to arrive.

Lucky her.

When the limousine pulled into the only outdoor shade Izzy could see in the entire complex, a carport attached to the main building, she gathered her belongings from the back seat.

The driver with the big head, the back of which Izzy had stared at for hours, carried her large suitcase inside. She followed him, carrying her duffel bag and purse, her stomach twisted into a knot.

A man—she was too nervous to recall his name—handed her a list of instructions to read. Places she was not permitted to go were noted on page six. Her class schedule was inserted as page fourteen. The cafeteria form for food allergies or aversions she would find on page twenty-seven and must be turned in at breakfast tomorrow. A list of personal goals and objectives on page thirty-seven must be completed by the end of three months. The pages in between, she should read at her leisure.

A woman, Ms. Sherman, led her to a plain dorm room with beige walls and a single bed made up in eggshell-colored bedding. Unpacking her meager belongings took all of fifteen minutes. As instructed, she placed her clothes in the single dresser, personal items in the bathroom, and her writing pad, pens, and other articles in the unadorned desk. When she finished, she sat down on the bed, bounced a bit to test its comfort, leaned toward the window, and pushed the curtains aside to peek outside.

Nothing but desert.

She glimpsed the wall clock. 5:27. She had to be at the cafeteria by 5:45. The instructor said tardiness was greatly frowned upon and punishment, justifiable.

She wondered what justifiable meant.

She tucked her suitcase beneath her bed and wandered to her closet. She flung the doors open to find a straight line of perfectly hung clothes.

She removed one hanger and assessed a uniform. The material and colors mirrored her old school's uniform—navy blue and white.

*Figures.*

She twisted the hanger back and forth, and as the white shirt whirled, she caught sight of a rectangular patch on the bottom edge of the inside hem. She lifted the blouse and read the words out loud, "Project Dream."

She screwed up her lips and shoved it back inside. As she did, she realized the clothes weren't all uniforms. She shifted a bunch to the left. A rod-scraping noise echoed through the quiet room. Her eyes widened.

"Oh my God."

She removed a mustard-colored silk blouse and matching jeans—designer jeans. She sidled to the mirror and held the clothes in front of her. Would the jeans fit? Was it a zero? She fumbled to see inside the top of them.

Yes, size zero.

She tossed the outfit on the bed and pulled out a second. Gray jeans and a black top. She eyed the outfit up and down. "Wow."

She flung it onto the other outfit and reached for the next. She fingered the smooth material of a sweater that hung over knee-length pants. "Must get cold at night."

She slid that outfit forward and inspected the next one, and the next. A few slides down, she found a pink and lemon-colored sundress. She practically bent the hanger ripping it from the closet. She bolted to the mirror. Hung the wide part of the hanger over her neck and tucked the sides of the dress around her.

She had never seen such gorgeous clothes. Wearing materials and colors like this would have made no-uniform, dress-up days at St. Mary's bearable. She turned sideways and pulled the dress close. Did the material hang loose a bit? Would her belly be covered?

Oh, what she wouldn't have given to walk into Sister Agnese's class wearing a dress like this rather than her crappy, dime-store stuff. Mary Ellen Wagner, the snobby rich girl, surely would have been envious. Instead of slewing a barrage of insults her way, she would have said, "Izzy, where did you find that lovely thing?" or "Can you come to my birthday party? It's at the San Diego Yacht club," or maybe ask the question every girl at St. Mary's wanted to be asked, "Want to sit at my lunch table today?"

Or—at least stop calling her smelly Isabelly.

She decided to try the dress on. She removed her clothes, slid the bottom over her head, and wiggled into the soft fabric. She stood for a minute smiling into the mirror. Then she hurried to peek at the next outfit, a thin velour tracksuit, and the next, camouflage twill pants with a long matching scarf and a white t-shirt. When she thrust that aside, a shoe rack on the floor called to her. She fell to her knees and sat back on her legs.

There were name-brand running shoes, flip flops in various colors, leather sandals, and plain high heels with open backs. My God, there were sixteen pairs.

She put her hands over her mouth, nearly crying. No one would ever make fun of her clothes again.

She squealed, slid off her knees, kicked her own ratty loafers off, and tried every single pair of the sixteen shoes on. Not until she slipped the last perfectly fitting shoe off her foot did she remember dinner.

Frantically, she glanced at the clock. 5:52. She was late.

She kicked the pile of shoes back in the closet, grabbed the yellow sandals that matched her sundress, and stood. She put one on each foot, hopping, and ran out of her room. She glanced left and right. Which way had Ms. Sherman said the cafeteria was?

She guessed and ran left down the long hallway, took another left, and a right. She was near the front lobby.

She ran back in the other direction, glancing down hallway after hallway until she heard the faint sound of clanging plates. With that, she charged down the hall toward two open doors, and the clanging escalated. She quickened her pace and barged through the doorway, noticing the disaster but unable to stop.

She dug her heels into the floor. One flip flop dislodged. The other hit a wet slippery patch. Izzy struggled to catch her balance as she slid further into the room. Kids glanced up from their tables. She was sure she made eye contact with every person in that room before tumbling to the ground. The hems of her lemon-colored dress wafted upward and exposed her underwear. She rolled onto her back and batted the edges of the sundress down.

Laughter exploded. A woman in a straight blue shift rushed toward her. Nasty comments slung off the walls. Izzy hustled to her feet.

"Miss Jimenez?"

"Yes, ma'am," she said, curtsying. More laughter rang.

"You'll go back to your room and change into your uniform."

"Yes, ma'am."

Again, a curtsy. Again laughter. Izzy squinted. Had she really curtsied? A second time?

"Children." The woman turned away from her. "We will wait for Ms. Jimenez to change her clothes before taking one bite of food."

A massive group groan followed. The woman turned and eyed Izzy again.

"You're excused to change, Ms. Jimenez."

"Yes, ma'am."

My God, she curtsied a third time.

She closed her eyes, turned, and walked as calmly as she could down the hall to the end. When she turned the corner, out of sight of the cafeteria doors, she raced toward her room.

"My God, my God," she uttered over and over while she changed.

She flew out of her room and toward the cafeteria, stopping reservedly to walk down that last, painfully long hall. When she entered, exactly six minutes after she had been excused, the woman, who Izzy would later find was Ms. Merryman, said, "Your food tray is at the window. Retrieve it and take a seat for grace."

She glanced around the room. To the right, a counter below a long window flaunted one idle tray. She walked slowly toward it, grabbed its edges so swiftly she nearly sent the plate and utensils on the floor. Recovering, she walked toward the first available seat she could find.

A boy slid over on the bench, so there was no room. She slowed. Glanced at the next table. A girl there shot a look so uninviting that Izzy moved speedily by. The third and fourth tables seemed suddenly filled. Kids spaced out with wide elbows.

She walked toward the last table at the back of the room, her head held low. She took a seat at a table where a big, cloddy boy with a scary face and a skinny, straggly kid with big feet sat. Neither glanced up when she sat down. They never looked at her once through the entire meal.

Two hours, a meditation class, and meeting later, Izzy returned to her room, changed into pajamas, and cried herself to sleep.

## Chapter 8  Rachel

Rachel stood in her grandmother's bedroom, waiting. She crossed her arms and tried to find her patience. She wanted to talk to Gee—that's what they called her, short for G'ma—about her little sister, Lisa.

Ever since the day Lisa lost her breath from a panic attack and fell down the attic stairs in their grandparents' home, Rachel had been picking up her pieces and fitting them back together. Gee said Lisa's panic attacks would eventually stop. Rachel wondered when.

Before they moved to the house where they lived now, they lived in a poor neighborhood with other penniless scumbags. Kids there showed their underwear, and dads drank beer on the porch in the morning. At least that's how Pops— they called their grandfather Pops or PopPops—described it. The only thing Rachel remembered about that old neighborhood was once someone opened a fire hydrant, and kids played in the flooded streets until police and firemen shooed them away.

"Get my granddaughters out of that rat-infested city playpen," Pops always yelled.

"I'm not living in any snooty, nose-in-the-air suburb," Daddy would reply.

Pops won that battle but only because of the lawsuit.

In between living in the hoodlum neighborhood and the snobby neighborhood where they lived now, Rachel's family had to live in Gee's and PopPops's attic for a year until the lawsuit over Gee's back surgery was settled. Gee never walked another step—as Pops put it—after that butcher carved into her spine.

Pops sued the doctor and bought a house for Rachel's mother with the award money. That new house, where Rachel lived now, was around the corner from Pops's and Gee's house. Living close to her grandparents was important because her mother had to help the nurses care for Gee.

Personally, Rachel liked her old neighborhood.

Lisa would have grown up tougher there where kids skipped school, lots of parents didn't have jobs, and gangsters—another of Pops's terms—walked the streets.

But they moved, Lisa saw the black devil, the panic attacks began, and Rachel promised never to leave her alone in that attic where they slept and where that devil had once appeared.

Then she did.

Lisa tried to climb the gate at the top of the stairway and came barreling down the stairs. She thudded on the wood floor at the bottom, and Pops rushed her to the emergency room.

On the morning of her fall, Rachel woke early and went downstairs with Momma because sometimes LeeLee—that was Lisa's baby name—could be a pest, and Rachel needed space. She wanted to eat cereal in front of the TV in peace and quiet. LeeLee chattered too much.

LeeLee woke, glanced at the empty space in the bed beside her, and screamed.

Rachel heard her, but she was exercising her vocal cords in a cartoon sing-along. The back door had slammed shut; Daddy left for work. Momma busied herself helping Gee, and PopPops hadn't put in his hearing aids yet. She ignored LeeLee's cries anyway.

By then angels were appearing to them often. So what was the problem? LeeLee could wait a minute. The day before, LeeLee said she wasn't as afraid. The devil had only come one time, and the angels had promised to protect her. Momma overheard that conversation as she walked by their room. She stopped and scolded them. Said neither of them should talk about the angels or devils again.

"Momma's right. If we stop talking about them, we'll stop seeing them," Rachel had told LeeLee.

"I don't want to stop seeing angels. They're pretty."

"Well, you can tell me when you see them, but not Momma. She gets nervous."

"I can tell Gee."

"Yeah, you can tell Gee anything."

"And PopPops."

"You can't tell Pops. He'll swing his fists at you like he does at Daddy."

"I can tell him. I can tell PopPops anything, too."

At the time Rachel was fairly certain she was Pops's favorite, and LeeLee was Gee's favorite. She didn't want LeeLee horning in on Pops, telling him secrets.

"No, you can't, you little weasel." She shoved Lisa.

LeeLee bounced against the bedroom wall, caught herself, crossed her arms, and stuck out her bottom lip. "You're bossy."

"Am not."

"Are so." LeeLee stuck her tongue out. "I told Gee you're bossy. She called you impulsive."

"What's that mean?"

She smiled whenever she remembered that conversation.

"Gee said impulsive is when your mind runs behind your mouth."

PopPops called Gee the word whisperer. She taught new words each day. Rachel and Pops didn't care much about Gee's words, but LeeLee did. LeeLee was smart and dreamy and kind like Gee. Rachel was loud and busy like Pops.

"I don't care what Gee says," Rachel said that day. "What did Pops say?"

"He called you gumption."

"Gumption?"

LeeLee nodded.

"What's gumption?"

"I don't know. Gee didn't teach that word yet. Maybe sticking your gum on the back of your ear?" Because that's what Rachel always did.

Now, whenever Momma said, "Rachel get rid of that gum," Rachel would stick it on the back of her ear and whisper "gumption" to LeeLee. They would giggle and laugh.

Rachel and LeeLee were like that, happy together one moment and fighting the next.

So the following morning when Lisa tried to climb the gate at the top of the stairway and came tumbling down the stairs, Rachel didn't care and she did. She didn't care that Lisa fell all the way down the stairs because Lisa deserved that for being such a fraidy cat. But she did care because Lisa thudded hard against the wood floor. Pops had to rush her to the emergency room. More importantly, Pops and Mommy and Daddy took Lisa for ice cream after the doctor had cast her arm.

People coddled—another of Gee's words—Lisa too much. And today Rachel was going to put an end to their babying by talking to Gee.

"LeeLee has to learn to take care of herself," she said.

Gee pushed the button on her bed, rolled slowly upward, and swung her feet over the side.

"Rachel, darling, give me a minute." Gee wiggled her feet, adjusted the pillows, and inched slowly back to the center of the covers.

Rachel didn't wait for her to settle in completely before she continued.

"The bigger kids pick on her. She's so quiet and door-mattish," she babbled, hurrying before Pops or Mom arrived with the wheelchair. She had to get her point across to Gee before they wheeled Gee away to the wide bathroom for her morning routine.

"Door-mattish isn't a word."

"Okay, quiet and wimpy. Too nice for her own good."

"Sissy, I understand how sweet and unassuming your sister is." Gee shifted in the bed.

Rachel sighed.

Did Gee always have to use new words? What did unassuming mean? She intentionally used words she and Lisa had to decipher. Decipher was yesterday's word.

"Decipher what the angels are trying to tell you," Gee had said.

Lisa got out the dictionary, sifted through the Ds, and read decipher's meaning out loud. Gee asked each of them to use the word in a sentence. Then she told them to close the door, and they talked about ghosts, while Rachel and Lisa put fresh pillowcases on Gee's pillows. She egged them into having a pillow fight, snickering and giggling while they knocked each other silly.

Gee yelled, "nothing" when Momma questioned what the noise was. That Gee could be both serious and fun was a rarity in Rachel's eyes. She taught and nurtured, but allowed them their mischief, too. And while Lisa loved Gee for her nurturing, Rachel loved Gee for her allowing.

Today, however, Rachel wanted to impress upon Gee's serious side.

"When I'm not around Lisa's going to have to know the ropes."

"The ropes, you say?" Gee chuckled, which made Rachel a bit mad. "Now that sounds like PopPops talk."

"Pops says you have to know the ropes. You don't want your sails to flap around."

"PopPops was a fine sailor." Gee glanced toward the ceiling.

Rachel loved the look on Gee's face when she talked about her grandfather's younger days. Rachel hoped someday she would fall in love with a man who had bulging biceps like Pops.

"He had the strength of two men. Not very tall, mind you, but he beat most men in fortitude, determination, and courage.

Lots of men wanted to fight him on the docks, and others were too afraid."

*Fortitude?*

Bam! Rachel's impatience resurfaced.

"I know, Gee, you already told me those stories." She glanced out the door and down the hall, hoping not to see her mother.

"Oh." Gee's gaze fell from the ceiling. "I'm sorry, darling. My old mind wanders."

Rachel's heart sagged into a sloppy lump in her chest. How could she grow cross with Gee? Lately, Rachel's mood turned hot and cold quicker than a faucet. Her temper flared. She had no patience. She said things that hurt people. Often found herself in trouble at school.

She jumped onto the bed beside Gee, and Gee swung a weak arm around her.

"I'm sorry, Gee. You can tell your stories about Pops if you want."

"Rachel, look into my eyes."

Rachel did as she was told

"Why do you apologize so often?"

"Because I say mean things."

"You are anything but mean."

"Okay, I'm impatient."

"Patience can be overrated. We need people like you. You're fast on your feet."

"And fast with my tongue. Pops says I talk before I think."

"He loves that about you. We all do. Never apologize for the vim and vigor you were born with."

"Huh?"

*Great. More words.*

Gee laughed and coughed and squeezed her as best she could with her weak arms.

"This one time, I won't make you look the words up." Gee smiled and Rachel moved closer. Gee wrapped her arms around her. Despite her weak hold, Gee's embrace felt as safe and warm as a cocoon might feel. "I'm going to tell you a secret. You must never tell anyone."

Oh, a secret! Her heart leaped. Usually, Gee only told secrets to LeeLee.

"A secret? For me?" Rachel wasn't good at keeping secrets. When her temper flared, she dumped them like a bowl of Cheerios.

"Yes, darling, a secret for my Rachel. Can you keep this one? Because you are the most like me, and heaven knows I couldn't keep a secret."

"You can't keep secrets, either?"

"I only ever kept one secret. All the rest I spilled. But sometimes secrets need to be spilled. There's no need to apologize for speaking your mind."

"No?"

"No. Never. You are so much like me."

"More than LeeLee?"

Gee squeezed again. She set the bottom of her chin on top of Rachel's head. "If only you and I could be sweet and kind like LeeLee. She needs protecting because she has so few bad thoughts."

"Well, she has bad thoughts about me all right."

Gee chuckled. "Sisters argue all the time, but the one thing about a sister is you can never get rid of her. She's always your sister. Friends come and go but a sister? Even if you don't speak to each for a long time, no one can break your bond."

Gee leaned and spoke softly into Rachel's ear. "Still, sometimes they can be annoying. Especially little sisters. They follow you around like a shadow."

Rachel spent a moment inside her head. Lisa was sort of like a shadow. Not as tall. Not clear. But always hitched to her heels.

Gee continued. "But shadows don't like the night, the pitch black. They disappear into its darkness. Lose their shape and melt away."

"They require light," Rachel said proudly.

"They do. They need light shining on someone to keep their form. The brighter the light, the more distinct the shadow. It grows."

Rachel realized they were no longer talking about shadows. Not really. Her impatience flared.

She sighed. "Tell me in words, Gee. What are you saying? You want me to take care of Lisa?"

Gee wrapped a second arm around her and squeezed, laughing as she did. "That is what I love and admire about you. You are no baloney. Yes, I want you to allow the light to shine on you, so Lisa can grow in your shadow. We both know she's more fragile than we are."

"You're talking about her dreams, aren't you?"

"I am."

Briefly, Rachel wished she had been born second. Wished she had panic attacks and everyone coddled her.

*I don't want to go to the desert.*

She didn't want to be the strong sister, but when you came right down to it, she didn't want to be a shadow in the background, either. Lisa shied away from attention. Rachel wallowed in it.

They were as opposite as an ice cream sandwich and a brownie-stuffed muffin. Rachel was cold and tough. Lisa, warm and mushy. LeeLee became frantic when their kitten ran away. She cried when the boys at school shoved the boy with the big ears into the snow at recess. She cowered in the corner, shaking when the dreams came.

Dreams and angels and bullies at school never scared Rachel. And despite all, she did love her sister.

"Okay, she can hide in my shadow."

"Not forever, mind you."

"Just until the day I die." Rachel's voice plummeted with annoyance. Caring for LeeLee was laborious.

"Not that long. Only for a while."

"How long?"

Rachel was so done with this conversation. She never saw the value in crying over spilled milk. Wipe the mess up and eat the cereal.

"Well, let's see." Gee grew pensive for a moment. Pensive was last week's word.

Rachel waited. A misty calm washed over Gee. "When the first girl comes."

She had no idea what Gee meant.

*The first girl. What first girl?*

"Well, she better come soon because Lisa's dreaming again, and I can't keep her from doing that."

Rachel jumped off the bed despite Gee's pleas for her to come back. She ran down the hall, through the house, and out the front door. She sprinted home, and when she passed Lisa in the front yard, she shoved her as hard as she could. Lisa fell into the mud that had formed from last night's rain.

"What was that for?" Lisa squealed from the ground.

"I'm not doing your dirty work."

"What work?"

"You know that man? That man you see in your head who is hurting girls? I'm not telling the police about him. You tell them."

She stuck her hands on her hips and stared down at her sister. When Lisa started to cry, she covered her ears, ran into the house, jumped in bed, and pulled the covers over her head. She swore she would never block the light from shining on Lisa again—ever!

But ten months later, Rachel would shadow her sister from the hot desert sun.

## Chapter 9  Lenny

By Lenny's seventh day there, all twenty-five places had been filled in the school. On his fifth day, some scrawny backwoods boy from Idaho, Todd somebody, quietly sat down at the opposite end of his table. On the sixth day, a fragile-looking girl, sort of a dark-haired LeeLee, took the seat smack-dab across from him.

Lenny didn't like or particularly want anyone else sitting at his table. He refused to look either of them in the eye.

Yesterday, on the perfect-klutz-of-a-girl's first day, she came skidding into the cafeteria on her butt dressed inappropriately. The entire room erupted in laughter. They were forced to sit and stare at their food until the girl returned, blotchy-faced and disheveled. By the morning of her second day, her blotches had heightened.

On the third day, it happened. She talked to him.

"Lenny, excuse me, Lenny? Can you hear me?"

She leaned across the table, her white shirt stained with jelly, her long black hair tangled, and a shadow of this morning's toothpaste still caked in the corner of her mouth. He shifted his gaze to the boy, Todd, who had moved closer to their end of the table now and sat in the seat next to the girl. Lenny was glad at least the elbow room on his side hadn't suffered.

"W-what?" he whispered back, but a few people from the next table glanced their way. Lenny's voice had changed last spring and summer. He found whispering difficult these days.

"I was wondering. Do you ever fall asleep during meditation?"

The boy named Todd snickered. Lenny shot him a scowl before returning his stare to his food.

"N-no."

"I'm having a hard time staying awake," she said rather loudly. Clearly, she hadn't read the Project Dream manual. "I keep losing my concentration."

"Sh." A girl at the next table set a finger against her lips. "Be quiet."

There were strict rules; no one talked during lunch. The afternoon schedule was cumbersome, and teachers didn't want kids wasting energy. Socialization was only permitted in the evening. But Lenny had yet to be invited into a conversation even then. That suited him fine.

He glanced at the girl, and in that split second when their eyes met, he read her like a book. He gazed down but kept her in his peripheral vision. Ignoring her didn't discourage her.

"I think I fell asleep." She glanced around and leaned across the table. "I woke myself up snoring."

Lenny slurped his stew without looking. In the few days the little girl had been there, she'd been the brunt of evening talk. In all of Area 51, where they were purported to be, there was only one set of stairs, in the observatory. Her first night there, she had climbed the stairs to see the night stars, and when she finished, she slipped on the top step and fell to the bottom. He heard she slit her hand on the metal steps, and the nurse had to stitch her up.

He changed the subject. "What happened to your hand?"

"Nothing." She stuffed her bandaged right wrist underneath the table and glanced at the other boy, Todd.

Todd laughed.

"W-what are you laughing at, f-farm boy?" Lenny glared at him.

"Yeah, what are you laughing at?" A tall, lean boy from the next table sauntered over to theirs. He glanced toward the doors to make sure Ms. Merryman hadn't reentered the room. Lenny watched Todd Kennedy's face turn red.

"Nothing, Ben," Todd said.

"He wasn't saying anyth—" The little girl named Izzy tried defending Todd.

*Another LeeLee.*

"Who asked you? Shut the hell up. You already got us in trouble once. Want to get us in trouble again? I was talking to Todd here."

"No, sorry, it's just, I don't mind he was laughing—"

"I'm not laughing," the boy named Todd managed to say. He didn't look frightened like Lenny expected he should. The Ben kid was twice Todd's size.

"I heard him laughing," the boy sitting directly behind the girl, Isabelle, said.

Lenny thought his name was John Michael but wasn't sure. There was a John and a Michael and a John Michael. All three were lean, fast, smart boys. In his short stay, Lenny couldn't tell them apart. Nor did he care to.

"How about you, big boy?" The boy, who might be John Michael, stood and joined Ben. He leaned his hands on Lenny's table. "You laughing?"

Lenny gazed deeply into his eyes, seeing everything about him, his strengths and weaknesses. He'd seen similar boys at his grade school in Erie. Boys too afraid to stand on their own, so they sought out a leader and joined a pack.

"N-no, I'm n-not laughing."

"N-n-n-no, I'm a b-b-b-b-big, d-d-d-dumb idiot," John Michael mimicked. The boys from his table whooped, egging him on. "You g-g-gonna wet your pants b-big Lenny."

"You're mean." The petite girl straightened in her seat.

"Oh, you got a crush on b-b-big Lenny, Isabelly?"

"Don't call me that. That's not nice." The blotches on her face reddened. "And, no, I don't have a crush on anyone. I just don't think it's nice to bully people."

"Yeah, well, I think the two of you are doing it."

The girl's mouth dropped open. "No! You're disgusting. Go sit back down and leave us alone."

"C'mon, Isabelly, tell the truth. You and b-big Lenny got a thing going?" The boy shoved her shoulder. Lenny grabbed his wrist.

"She s-s-said no." He stared straight into the eyes of John Michael.

"Stop it this instant. What are you boys doing out of your seats?" Ms. Merryman appeared out of nowhere. "Since you haven't used your time properly, you lose the remainder of your lunch period. Ben, John Michael, pick up your trays. You're done eating. In fact, everyone's done." She pounded her hand on the nearest table. "Stand up, everyone. There will be no talking, discussing, or arguing in the cafeteria. Until everyone abides by the rules, you all suffer."

Lenny lodged the last of his sandwich into his mouth and rose, tray in hand. Low moans reverberated across the room. Other kids shoveled stew in their mouths and grabbed sandwiches as they stood. One by one they headed toward the trash cans next to the kitchen, dumped food into the compost, and clanged bowls, trays, and silverware onto the counter.

As Lenny headed out of the room, he kept one eye on the kids still waiting in line to scrape their plates. Ben bumped his shoulder against little Izzy. She dropped her tray and the remainder of her food spilled everywhere. Her bowl shattered. People applauded. Ben and John Michael slapped backs and roared. Their faces reddened with jest.

Lenny slipped away from the line of kids parading out and waited by the cafeteria doors for the two of them. When they neared the doors, he stepped into their path.

"What are you looking at, freak?" Ben tucked his shoulder and walked toward Lenny.

Lenny spread his feet slightly apart and waited for the impact. Ben bumped him hard, but Lenny barely jiggled. He stood with his head down.

Like a pack of dogs, the others turned on Ben.

Mean kids were all alike. Lenny had learned that at a young age. Before he had grown so big, his classmates had taken turns picking on him, each of them vying for the title of most vicious. They picked on those littler than them until someone bigger stepped in and picked on them. The meanest, most backbiting kid won the leader's spot.

But no more.

Lenny watched the muscles in Ben's face tighten as insults flung: "He stopped you cold." "Not the big guy you thought you were, are you, Ben?' "Did you hurt your shoulder?"

Kids snickered. Lenny scanned their faces, gazing into their eyes. Only a few of these kids had kindness in them. Torn from juvenile detention centers, most held a savagery so deep, black stained their souls.

Life at Project Dream was going to be the survival of the fittest. But then, Lenny was a survivor.

He took a step sideways and allowed Ben and the throng to pass. Kids jeered both him and Ben. Lenny said nothing.

The remainder of the day and the next morning continued much the same as prior days. The following afternoon included mediation and the introduction on what exactly remote viewing truly entailed.

Ms. Sherman tested their abilities in what the kids called the room with the curtains. Desks in that classroom were separated by half walls on either side, so students saw only the person sitting in front of and behind them when they were seated. With the push of a button, heavy metallic curtains unfolded from the walls, further dividing the boxy room into cubicles. Ms. Sherman placed items in an alcove at the front of the room. Kids meditated. Concentrated. Each had a pencil and paper in front of them. Sherman instructed them to jot down what they saw in their mind's eye.

When the images materialized in his head, Lenny drew lines and sketches. After two hours, papers were collected, but no results were announced.

In the evening, they congregated for a rehash of the rules. Ms. Merryman said since they hadn't learned to conserve their energy during lunch, they must revisit the directives. The next morning, they attended academic classes, including English, mathematics, science, computer science, and a foreign language of their choice.

Lenny selected Spanish, as did his cafeteria chums, Izzy and Todd. When Spanish class finished, the three headed to the cafeteria. The little girl hurried up alongside him, practically running because her legs were so much shorter and his strides, so much longer.

"Do you think we'll be here an entire year?"

Todd Kennedy caught and joined them. "Of course, we'll be here a year. We can't even see our family for six months."

"What?" The little girl stopped abruptly.

"What do you mean six months?" She hustled to catch them. "So my mom won't be able to come?"

"Girl, what world do you live in? Weren't you paying attention at orientation?"

"Yes. Maybe no. I don't know. I was already homesick."

"We can't have visitors for six months. After that, they'll fly us to Phoenix as long as we don't tell them where we are."

"Six months?"

"Yeah."

"And we can't tell them where we are?"

"Right."

"Well, where are we?"

"In Nevada! My God, what goes on inside that head of yours?" Todd blew into one of her ears and lifted the hair on the other side of her head as if the breath had blown right through her. "Yep, all space. You must have lost everything inside on that spill down those steps. One set of stairs in the entire desert, and you come sledding down them like you're on a toboggan."

"I was tripped. That kid, Benjamin whoever, tripped me."

Todd snickered, quieting as they entered the cafeteria.

"I can't stay here for six months."

Todd shushed her.

She lowered her voice. "We'll miss Thanksgiving. And Christmas. They wouldn't keep us here for Christmas."

They queued up in the food line.

"Would they?"

A few heads turned, but the Izzy girl floundered frantically in her own world now. Not a care for the silence order. Lenny closed his eyes. This wasn't going to end well.

She resembled LeeLee in every way: kindness, innocence, sweetness—until she noticed some injustice.

Miss Merryman walked briskly by, carrying a food tray. She exited the cafeteria, her heels echoing down the hallway.

"I mean that would be cruel." Isabelle started up again. "I hoped I would be back at my school before the end of the year. Do you think they'll let us keep the clothes?"

"You're not going back to your school. Did you read the guidebook?"

"No."

"We are here for the duration."

"What duration? The entire school year?"

Kids both ahead and behind in line shushed them.

"Oh my God, my birthday. I can't stay here for my birthday."

"Shut up," Todd murmured. "You're going to get us in trouble."

"But they can't keep me here for my birthday." Now the little girl was blindly talking out loud to Todd as if she argued with him to let her go home. "My brother's coming to see me. I have to be home for my birthday."

She leaned over her tray of food, soiling her shirt.

"Excuse me, sir? You behind the counter, do you know anything about how long we will be here?" She rapped on the plexiglass panel, and four boys in front of Lenny left their trays in line, stepping toward her. Ben was one of them.

"Shut the hell up," he said. "You got us in trouble once. You won't do it again."

"But Todd said they plan on keeping us here six months. I can't stay six months."

"Quiet," Todd murmured.

"You did. You said they were going to keep us and not let us go home."

Kids in line began waving their hands at her. Last night they'd been warned speaking in the cafeteria wouldn't be tolerated. If students didn't obey that rule, the entire twenty-five would skip lunch.

"Shut up," another boy said, trying to keep his voice low.

"You, shut up." She thrust her chin his way.

Lenny sighed. This girl was going to learn everything the hard way. He kept his head down but watched her out of the corner of his eye. Kids turned on her like dogs realizing the measly mutt at the back of the pack hid a stash of raw meat.

Ben shoved her. "Shut the hell up or I'll knock the shit out of you."

"You shut the hell up." Her head bounced out and back in a quick, determined jerk.

Lenny couldn't lunge toward her fast enough to prevent what she did next.

She lifted her tiny hand, positioned her weight over the center of her feet, and shoved Ben with all her might. He flew forward.

What happened after she pushed him, witnesses would long remember. Ben swung at her. She ducked, and Lenny stopped his hand midair with a cafeteria tray. A fight between Ben and Lenny broke out, and although Ben was roughly as big, Lenny took him down speedily and easily. They struggled. Ben grazed Lenny's face with a punch. Lenny hammered him back.

"Get off me, you freak," Ben yelled.

Other boys jumped on Lenny, heaving him off Ben. Lenny didn't fight much. He stood watching the blood run down Ben's face.

Ben rose, dabbed his nose, saw the blood, and exploded into a punching frenzy. Fist after fist hit Lenny's face before he freed himself from the boys holding him. More boys stepped in, and they regained their grip on him.

"You flunky junky." John Michael took a turn wrenching his fists into Lenny's gut.

Lenny made a swirling motion with his arms, once again breaking free. He grabbed John Michael by his collar and hurled him across the room. John Michael landed on a table. Kids flew left and right out of his way.

In a blur of a moment, Lenny felt a bang against his head. His vision dimmed. Had the Todd kid hit him?

"Todd, what are you doing?" he heard the little girl say.

She jumped in front of Lenny right as his vision cleared. Ben's fist barreled toward him but hit her. Lenny watched her slight frame falling toward the ground, her arms and legs limp with a rubbery unconsciousness. Her head bounced once when it hit the floor.

Something inside Lenny clicked.

He remembered LeeLee. The schoolyard. Blood from her face mixing with snow. The big bully of a kid, Rob Robbie, laughing. Robbie had punched LeeLee when she stuck up for Lenny. Powerless to rescue her because of his puny size, Lenny never forgot the shameful feeling that unleashed inside him as he helplessly watched LeeLee bleed in the snow. She always stuck up for him despite his stuttering and despite the other kids hating him. Boys held him down easily back then.

No longer.

Lenny stepped over Izzy, tightening his muscles for what was about to come. Ben's fists plunged deep into his gut twice. Lenny balled a hand and flattened him with one simple punch.

Ben fell unconscious to the floor. Lenny straddled him and repeatedly hit his face. He only stopped when the boy named John Michael staggered toward him, yelling obscenities. Lenny grabbed him by the shirt and punched him until teeth flew out of his mouth.

When there was no more life left in Ben and John Michael, Lenny turned on Todd. By then three men from the kitchen were on his heels, but he never stopped hitting Todd until a fourth and fifth man appeared. It took five of them to hold Lenny down.

From the floor, he watched Ben, Todd, John Michael, and Izzy being carried off to the infirmary. A half hour later an ambulance arrived, and the boy named Ben was transported away. He never returned.

There were rumors Ben died, but no one confirmed that story. John Michael said Ben's parents lived in Long Beach, California, and kids attempted contacting them but couldn't locate an address.

Project Dream officials didn't allow Lenny to return to school for three days. He endured an accelerated anger management program that included a myriad of punishments. Some of those military techniques were considered torture and had long been banned, but he survived. His extremely high tolerance for pain helped him endure. Right before they allowed him to return to class, one official admitted he'd never seen a soldier, let alone a kid, with such a high pain threshold.

The button of a girl, Izzy, had returned the day before him. Her face was badly bruised. Lenny was glad he had stuck up for her. Defending her had somehow lessened the guilt he experienced for not having been able to help LeeLee.

After the incident, they attended classes and sat silently in the cafeteria. A month later, John Michael was moved to their table. Lenny wondered if they were testing him. Did they want to see if he had learned his lesson? Or did they want him to beat the life out of John Michael?

It mattered not to him.

He understood Project Dream now. His only goal was to survive. Somehow, he was going to get through this and go home to Erie to care for his mother.

And watch over LeeLee.

# Chapter 10  The Nevada Desert

"How are the parents handling the program?" Randall Scott fingered the report.

Jerry McDaniel refrained from answering. There was no use alarming the commander with minor details.

"Fine, sir," Bart Conrad responded. "We have a few noisemakers. A mother in Boston calls our Washington office. She wants her son removed from the program. A brother in Mexico is causing chaos about his little sister."

"And?"

Bart hesitated enough for Jerry to jump in.

"The brother is no problem. I put an order to stop him at the border. He won't be permitted to cross. His citizenship, shall we say, has disappeared. And regarding the Boston mother, we've added an incentive package. The boy's stepfather is cooperative. He's sure extra cash will calm his wife down."

"Are they worth it? The two kids?"

"Yes, sir," Jerry responded. "The Mexican girl has caught on quite quickly, and the boy from Boston has a genius's IQ."

"What about physicality? You can train a mind but not always a body. If they end up in the Marines, they have to have skills."

"The boy is thin and fast. You would never know it from his stature."

"And the girl?"

Jerry McDaniel couldn't help his lips from turning upwards.

"She's a slip of a girl but swims like a fish," he said. "I've never seen anyone like her. She's fast on her feet but in the water? She's faster than some of our best boys."

Scott paused for a moment and turned toward the three instructors.

"Are there any other children that pop out to you who you feel—" He hesitated as if he chose his words carefully. "Have qualities beyond the others?"

"Well, sir." Ms. Merryman adjusted her glasses. "I've studied them for months now, and I see three or four others that stand—"

"And they are?"

She hesitated. Jerry had warned her of the commander's impatience. Obviously, she hadn't listened.

Now she babbled hurriedly as if he would cut her off again any second. "One boy has the strength of Hercules but everyone fears him. He's a problem. Another boy resembles the girl. His remote-viewing skills are unmatched and his physicality above average, like the rest of them. One other boy has also caught on fast."

"That's three."

"Well, you know the other one, sir. Chase Finley."

The commander's eyes glazed over. "The pilot's son?"

"Correct. The aviator's kid."

"Is the son like the father?"

Ms. Merryman glanced toward Jerry as if she didn't want to commit an answer.

Jerry thought before responding. "Better."

For the first time during the meeting, the commander relaxed in his seat. "How does he do in the classroom with the remote viewing?"

"Top ten," Jerry replied.

"And in the field?"

Jerry hesitated, closed his eyes briefly, and nodded. "Like his dad."

"I'm not surprised." The commander shifted his elbows back to the table. "What do you hear from his father?"

"Nothing. Absolutely nothing."

"Never good." Scott sifted through his papers. "Keep an eye on both of them."

"Yes, sir."

"What about the herculean kid? The one who—" The commander chose his words carefully, and though he hated the man, Jerry respected him for his judiciousness. Caution could be virtuous. "Ended Benjamin Jones's time with us and sustained the…penalty. Is he as good as everyone says?"

The entire room quieted. Jerry rolled his neck around inside his tight collar. "Yes, sir. He is."

"Could he flare up, again?"

Everyone nodded concernedly toward Scott—except Annie Sherman.

"You there." The commander pointed the tip of one finger toward her.

Instantly, the expression on Ms. Merryman's face told Jerry there was animosity between the two women. Merryman appeared downright elated that Scott didn't recognize Annie Sherman. Jerry himself was surprised, but then Annie had certainly matured since her cadet years, and Jerry hadn't noted her on the attendance sheet.

"How do you feel about him?" The commander fixed his stare on her.

Annie seemed unaffected. Her eyes scanned the room, settling a moment on Ms. Merryman, who straightened in her seat.

Annie raised her chin. "I like him, sir."

"You do?"

"Yes, sir."

The commander gave Annie a once over, up and down. "You like him?"

"I do, sir."

He turned and addressed Merryman. "But you don't?"

She shook her head. "No, sir. He's trouble."

"Trouble?" The commander directed the question to the male instructor, Ken Swarthy.

"Yes, sir," Swarthy agreed.

"How much trouble?"

"Everyone is afraid of him," Merryman interjected. "Even some of the instructors."

The commander remained pensively still. After several quiet seconds, he leaned his forearms onto the conference table and folded his hands. He shifted his gaze back and forth between Merryman and Swarthy before settling on Annie Sherman.

Jerry glanced at Sherman, too. She sat musingly, her ponytail frozen and her large yellow-speckled eyes unblinking. Randall Scott had to recognize her.

"Do all the students fear that boy?" Scott spoke directly to her.

She remained perfectly still. Although Jerry didn't know her well, her reputation—along with her pictures—had preceded her. An army brat who followed in her father's footsteps, she would know the importance of the question. Someone her age with such military acumen was a rarity. A soldier with her looks? Deadly.

Women hated her. Men loved but secretly feared her. She was dangerously sexy.

She responded perfectly. "Not the girl who can swim, sir."

A silence vibrated through the room. Nothing felt calm about the quiet. Every eye turned to the commander. Finally, he spoke.

"Keep him." He stood and everyone in the room followed suit, saluting him as he exited.

When the door closed behind him, Jerry gazed into the lovely hazel eyes of the woman who had just saved Lenny Emling's life, and he smiled.

# Chapter 11  Izzy

In those first months, Izzy, like the other kids, slept with Bluetooth earbuds that played recordings of what their duties entailed. A soothing background melody softened the mood as a woman uttered the requirements of participating in Project Dream. Loyalty was essential. Secrecy, critical. Over and over throughout the night, the meek voice declared confidentiality imperative.

Essentially, they were hypnotized into silence.

After their first six months of brainwashing, desensitizing, coercing, threatening, and indoctrination, officials awarded the children monthly visits with their families in Arizona. They reminded them relentlessly that they worked for the government; everything they learned was classified. No one threatened death if they revealed information, but no one disclosed what the "severe consequences for both the student and their family members" would be.

During family visits, officials watched them closely. Kids slept in a dormitory-style building; families slept separately in plush suites. Both sleeping facilities were located in a campus-style setting where new buildings, recreational amenities, and pools were being constructed. A large concrete wall stretched for miles around the area. Between the hours of 8 a.m. and 10 p.m., kids could spend as much time as they desired with loved ones, anywhere on that campus—as long as they remained loyal to their Project Dream secrecy oath.

Izzy intended to prove her loyalty. She didn't want any mysterious consequences befalling her family.

Besides, after Enrique moved to Mexico, her San Diego homelife had been dull and boring. Her mother had no money.

Her school sucked. She had more fingers than she needed to count friends. Kids teased her because of her dime-store clothes. And the jelly-belly nickname had settled in as permanently as initials in cement.

Missing her mother and not seeing Enrique's baby were her biggest drawbacks. Not much else changed. Angels still visited. She was still uncoordinated. Unpopular. Even nice clothes couldn't make people like you. Much of her life had remained the same.

So when her brother Enrique snuck across the border and miraculously showed up in Phoenix for a visit, she had no intention of dillydallying about Project Dream despite his interrogations. But Enrique persisted. He had a stick up his butt about the program and kept pelting her with questions when all she wanted to hear about and see pictures of was Sammy.

"Stop," she finally told him. "I'm not talking about Project Dream. It's a military school. Boring as hell. Don't you have any more pictures of Sammy?"

Enrique tugged at her arm, slipped a hand around her shoulder, and led her down a less crowded walkway. He spoke softly, which was unusual for him. His head snapped left and right, and his eyes danced as if he expected a sniper.

"They don't know I'm here," he said.

She should have known. He never wore a ball cap. But there he was shifting his eyes back and forth beneath a brim. "They're not going to let me come back. I asked too many questions."

"To Phoenix? You can't come back to Phoenix?"

"To the country. They're not going to let me back into the United States."

She stopped walking.

"What do you mean? You can't visit Mama?"

"They'll stop me at the border."

"You never cross at the border."

"I may not be able to come across at all. They're watching me."

"Who?"

"The Federales."

"That's ridiculous. You haven't been in trouble for years."

He said nothing.

"Enrique! Are you in trouble again?"

"Maybe a little"

"No, not now. You can't get into trouble now."

He placed a finger against her lips.

She lowered her voice. "You promised you'd bring Sammy to Phoenix with you."

"I won't visit again."

"Enrique!"

"Sh." He glanced around. "It's okay. I asked Santiago to look into this program."

"Santiago? Are you crazy? His brother is in the cartel."

Now Izzy's eyes searched the area around them.

"Santiago is a good man. He owes me his life. He talked to some people. He said no one is getting out."

If Enrique had to go to Santiago to get information about Project Dream, then everything the instructors said about the program's secrecy and the possible punishments for participant's families must be true. She wiggled inside her tight clothes. Brushed a clump of hair off her hot face. Maybe she'd never get out of this godforsaken program.

"Well, I can at least enroll in San Diego for college."

"They aren't going to allow that."

"You don't know that."

"I do." He shifted uncomfortably. A glisten of perspiration shimmered above his top lip.

"Enrique? Should you be here? You always take chances."

He lifted a strand of her hair. "I had to come." His eyes told her what his words hid.

"What is it? Something's wrong."

He leaned rheumy, penetrating eyes toward her until they disappeared to one side of her face. He buried his lips in her hair and whispered, "I come today to tell you what you do not want to hear."

Oh, she didn't like this. His hands gripped her.

Cautiously, her gaze scanned the surrounding buildings and rooftops. She searched for cameras. Could they hear him?

"What do I not want to hear?"

He tugged her close. She leaned against him.

"Papa."

He need say no more. The whisper of one word told all. Her knees buckled, but he held her up.

She couldn't speak.

"They wouldn't allow you to go to Mexico for the funeral."

An agonizing moan escaped her. Enrique wrapped his arms around her.

"I had to tell you myself," he said, his voice so low she could barely hear him through her sobs. "I have a car waiting. Come with me."

A sudden sense of urgency struck her. She heard the angels in her head. She actually heard them.

*Don't go.*

She opened her eyes. Quickly, an angel sent impression after impression into her mind. Cameras. Men. She and Enrique running. Officers catching them. Mama crying.

"They're listening," she whispered. "I can't. They'll find us."

"No."

"Yes, they'll find me. They'll find you."

She went up on her tiptoes. Moved her mouth close to his ear. "Listen to me. They'll find Sammy."

She leaned away slowly, locking eyes with him. Then brusquely, she freed herself from his grip. She stepped to the side so anyone peering through a camera could see her.

All of her emotions built up in the back of her throat. She swallowed them down. Squelched her grief. She forced the memories of her father to the back of her mind. His sunburnt face, the twinkle of his eye, the way he danced on his board as wave after wave tested his balance. She would think of him later, but now, she must think of Mama and Enrique and Sammy. She thrust every image of her father into the depths of her memory.

"Enrique." She spoke loudly "Don't ruin this for me. I had nothing before Project Dream. No friends. No clothes. No place to go. I'm not like you. People don't like me."

"Muchacha, no—"

She cut him off. Shouted. "You couldn't call and tell me my father was dead?"

"Izzy," her mother appeared out of nowhere. She tried to step between them. Izzy nudged her aside and grabbed hold of Enrique.

"This is between me and him, Mama. Enrique, if you mess this up for me, I will never speak to you again. I will never meet your daughter, and you will never see me."

"But—"

"Stop. You hear me? What we once had between us is gone. Did you think you could leave Mama and me alone, and I would forgive you? After the debt Mama paid to wipe your slate clean?"

"Izzy!" Mama hollered, but Izzy raised her palm to stop her from saying more.

"Go away, Enrique. Don't come back. I never want to see you again."

Her mother gasped, staggering backward into Enrique's arms.

Izzy tried desperately not to cry, but she couldn't stop the tears from falling. She turned her back to them. Shouted for him to go. After the officials saw how little she cared for him, he wouldn't be in danger. No one would stop him at the border. He could visit Mama again. Mama should not lose both her children. Somehow, someday, she would make Enrique understand she had done this for him, for her mother, for Sammy.

"Leave me," she screamed.

People around them began noticing. She fought the urge to turn and run to him. She wanted to throw her arms around him, so he could hold her, pat her back, and say, "Muchacha, don't cry."

Tears streamed down her face. When she finally mustered the courage to turn, he still stood staring, holding Mama.

Her eyes met his, and he made a simple, subtle gesture. The movement would look like the sign of the cross to anyone watching. He touched the tip of one finger to his ear lobe, lips, head, and chest.

Her heart leaped. He understood. Of course, he did. Enrique knew her better than she knew herself. And she knew him. He had to go. For now. Because now he must protect two of them, Izzy—and Sammy.

She did not hear his voice, but in her mind, she heard him.

*I won't say the words, but I think them and feel them in my heart. I'll always love and protect you, Isabelly. Always.*

## Chapter 12  Rachel

The newspaper never mentioned the attacker killed anyone, but three days ago Lisa ran crying to Rachel. She claimed two girls had died. For well over a year, the police had been searching for a man attacking women in the Erie area. In the beginning, his attacks were sporadic, but in recent months they had escalated. He'd assaulted and bloodied several women—girls, really. The newspaper now gave weekly updates on the assaults.

Lisa, in a fit of panic, told Rachel that the man had murdered two of his victims. Their bodies were lying in shallow graves. Lisa had talked to one of the girl's spirits.

*Oy vey.*

Rachel fanned out her fingers and covered her eyes with two flat palms. She concentrated. She had clairvoyant skills herself, but for the life of her, she couldn't see where the two girls were buried. Lisa's dreams were so much more vivid than hers.

Rachel's hands slid from her face.

She, Lisa, and Gee had been born with a so-called gift. The skill, embedded in their bloodline, had skipped only a lucky few generations. The degree to which individual family members "dreamed" varied. Gee said not many kin had keener insight than Rachel, but none had the acuteness of Lisa.

*Figures.*

Isn't that the way life went? You got what you didn't want, and you didn't get what you wanted.

She grabbed the newspaper. Read the notes one last time. Memorized them. Then she tossed the paper on her desk, finished dressing for school, and fell back on her bed for a few minutes of peace.

She rolled onto her stomach and bent her knees, swinging her feet back and forth in the air behind her. Her mattress squeaked as her legs swayed and her mind wandered.

She wished she hadn't heard Pops's and Gee's conversation about their finances. Knew that they worried Gee might have to be moved to the county home. Imagining Gee curled up in a strange bed without Mom at her side, without LeeLee charging in every day after school, and with Pops reduced to visiting rather than sleeping on the cot beside her bed, weighed on her.

At thirteen years old, she should be thinking of boys and summer and going to high school next year. Instead, her family crowded her even when they weren't in the room.

Dad had taken a second job. Lisa talked about babysitting. Pops heard they needed help at the corner hardware store.

Rachel could solve their financial woes. Lisa could, too, but clearly, she should stay with Momma and Gee. She was the kinder, gentler soul.

Rachel stopped swinging her legs and rolled onto her back. She was going to miss LeeLee.

*Stop.*

She sat up, grabbed the newspaper, and tucked it under her mattress. She stood and glanced into the mirror, straightening her cross tie.

Today was Officer Appreciation Day at school. She was going to tell the handsome officer whose picture had been in the paper—for being a war hero—what LeeLee had dreamt. The bad man lived only fifteen miles west of Erie. LeeLee had jotted down an address.

Rachel took a step back to glance at her entire body. She looked older than she was. The officer would pay more attention to her than Lisa. Older guys usually did.

A boy at the pharmacy down the street invited her to go to a movie last summer. She said maybe, knowing for certain her mother wouldn't let her. When the boy found out she was in grade school, he never talked to her again.

She tossed her dark brown hair over her shoulders, watching herself. People often commented on her beautiful face. In the grocery store. At the doctor's office. Under the playground canopy where neighborhood kids smoked cigarettes and made out when they snuck out at night.

Of course, neighborhood boys were too immature—or maybe too short—for Rachel. They begged her to bring her petite, goody-two-shoed sister along. Lisa seldom went.

"I can't believe you guys are sisters. Lisa is gorgeous," one neighborhood bully, Rob Robby, said one night. "Your face is pretty. Your body is dynamite. If you were just a blonde and nicer, you'd be perfect."

"You want to see how nice I am?" she replied. Then she knocked the crap out of him. She wondered how he explained his split lip and black eye to his mother in the morning.

Yet, truth be told, Rachel would have killed for Lisa's blonde hair and Caribbean blue eyes. Her gaze rose from her own blue eyes to the top of her head. Maybe for Lisa's dainty frame, too.

Being a half a foot taller than Lisa, she appeared older. People were aghast when they heard her age. They commented about her height. Her long legs. She stood at least two inches taller than every boy at her school. The pesky grade-school boys liked petite, little girls, not her.

She didn't care. She liked high-school boys. She could keep their attention until they found out her age. Yet therein was the reason she had no boyfriend, unlike most of the eighth-grade girls.

"Maybe at the next school." She straightened her shoulders and headed out of her room with her bookbag.

At the bottom of the stairs, she stopped short of entering the living room. Her mother's soft voice flowed in melodious thanks. Rachel peeked around the corner. Her mother hugged

LeeLee. Said something about her being sweet. How LeeLee shouldn't have spent her money on the pretty scarf.

*Dang.*

She had forgotten her mother's birthday again.

Annoyed, she leaned back so they couldn't see her. Impatiently, she waited for them to stop gushing over each other. She shifted her weight. Inspected her cuticles.

When, mercifully, they finished, she headed toward the front door, calling over her shoulder, "Hurry up, Lisa, we're going to be late."

"I'm coming, Sissy. I love you, Momma." Lisa's sugary sweet voice shot vinegar into Rachel's morning.

Rachel barreled out the door without saying a word to her mother. Not happy birthday, not have a nice day, not even goodbye. When Lisa caught up to her halfway down the street, Rachel shoved her onto the ground.

"What was that for?"

"Thanks for telling me it was Mom's birthday."

"I did tell you." Lisa picked herself up and brushed the dirt off her uniform. "Last night when you were at the window. You weren't listening."

"That's because you're always blah blahing about stuff that isn't important."

"We can stop at the store on the way home from school. I'll help you pick something out."

"No thanks, little miss priss."

Rachel didn't buy anything for her mother after school. Not even a card.

For the rest of her life, she would regret it. She'd never spend another birthday with her mother again.

## Chapter 13  Ben Morgan

Ben Morgan slept less than three hours a night in the fall of 2003. His wife hounded him to make a doctor's appointment. To get her off his back, he did. But at the scheduled time, he was up to his elbows filing reports. He forgot and missed the appointment. She warned he was headed for a heart attack.

Ben was too young to have heart problems, but when chest pains immobilized him, he stopped at an immediate-care facility to be sure. The verdict? Stress. Cold, hard, police-officer stress. He had the heart of a bull.

He relaxed. Cut his sleep to two hours a night.

Ben Morgan also made a promise to himself. He wouldn't lighten his load until a judge sent the man who raped his niece up the river to a state penitentiary, preferably Muncy, where the worst of life's human beings kicked and shoved each other, treading the waters of time.

Today he and his partner, Eddie Kallen, sat at a long folding table in a Veterans Hospital office with no windows. Two hundred manila files with the names of any veteran who ever committed a crime in the tri-state area, and some who hadn't but seemed suspicious, sat in front of them.

"I don't think this guy is a vet," Kallen said.

"Me either. But I'm going to eliminate this question mark from the chief's list and move on." He tossed another file on top of his finished stack.

"How's your niece?"

"She's coming along." Ben's throat tightened as if he'd swallowed a chunk of a meatball sub, and the bread was lodged halfway down. "She's tough, but finding this guy will be her best medicine—the whole family's elixir."

"The fact he shows up every few months and then hibernates gives people a hope he's gone."

"Then he wakes." Ben pulled his vibrating cell from his pocket. "This time with a vengeance."

He pressed the cell to an ear. "Yeah, Chief, what do you need?"

"Gehrlein is out sick." The chief's gruff voice reverberated with angst. "You and Kallen at the Veterans Hospital?"

"Yeah." Ben guessed what was coming. His eyes searched out Kallen's for help. "We're up to our neck in files."

Kallen leaned across the table and raised his voice to make sure the chief could hear him. "We have to get to the Mission Center by five to talk to the dinner walk-ins."

"Chief, Kallen and I—"

"I heard him, but there's nothing I can do. You're going to have to cover for Gehrlein. Go over to St. Luke's and give a ten-minute speech. It's the school's Officer Appreciation Day."

"Can't you send—"

The chief cut him off. "Get your asses over there and give the speech, Morgan. As fast as possible."

Ben heard the phone click. He leaned back in his chair.

"What the hell? Why us?" Kallen slapped a file shut.

"Because we are five minutes away." Ben stood. "Let's get in and out as quick as we can."

He slipped a hand into his pocket and pulled out his keys, tossing them to Kallen. "You drive. Let me make some notes."

Five minutes later, Ben and Eddie strolled up onto the auditorium stage, Ben's imposing frame stalwart, Kallen's average stature square but lacking next to his partner's. Ben Morgan's physique along with his purple-heart tour of duty in Iraq won him a great many public-eye engagements.

Ben approached the mic. "Good afternoon."

A shrill metallic sound exploded into the auditorium. The principal ran to adjust the sound. When the shrillness vanished, Ben continued.

"Thank you for honoring us with your Officer Appreciation Day. I've been many places in my lifetime, but the city I love most is Erie, Pennsylvania. The reason Erie is so near and dear to me is because I have the privilege of speaking to kids like you. Good kids. Some of you will grow up and become doctors, teachers, engineers, or scientists. Some may even hope to be police officers. I encourage you to work hard, study, and go after your dreams.

"One of the greatest aspects of my job as a City of Erie police officer is having a brotherhood of men and women, most of them born and raised here, coming together to protect the streets around you. We grew up here. We know many of you. How many of you know a police officer? Raise your hand."

Arms with fluttering fingers shot up around the room.

"Lots of you, I see. Those are the men and women who keep you safe. So you can learn, play, grow, and dream. Over a hundred officers walk and ride our streets…"

He continued and when he finished, the children and teachers rose from their seats, clapping and cheering. The principal approached with a glass, flame-like memento that had words etched in its wood base: The St. Luke Student Body Appreciates Erie Police Department Officers.

Ben glanced at the words, struggling to look touched. He shook the principal's hand and raised the piece in the air toward the teachers and students. He started toward the stairs.

"Nice speech." Eddie stepped beside him, smirking. He raised his voice to compete with the applause. "Brought tears to my eye."

Ben clomped down the stage steps, ignoring him. When his feet hit the gym floor, he realized the students had formed a line that extended all the way to the auditorium exit sign. The first boy in line held out his hand to shake Ben's. Eddie sighed behind him. Ben shook the boy's hand.

"Thank you so much, officers." A teacher, sandwiched between the first and second students, said.

Again, a handshake.

"You're welcome." Ben smiled and moved on, leaning down to shake child after child's hand.

"It was our pleasure." He heard Eddie say behind him.

Ben nodded and smiled and shook more hands.

"Thank you, Mr. Officer." "Are there bullets in your gun, Mr. Officer?" "You have big hands, Mr. Policeman." "Is your cruiser outside?" "Can you turn on your siren when you ride away?"

He neared the doors, and actually, the littlest ones' remarks coaxed sincerity into his smile. In his last few steps, probably three kids away from the big doors, he slipped his fingers around the slender hand of a quite attractive teacher.

Wait, he took a second look. She wasn't a teacher. She had a uniform on.

He drew his arm back. His stare moved to the next person. A tall boy, most likely an eighth grader, held out his hand, gazing eagerly toward him. But Ben stopped and turned his gaze back to the girl.

Eddie bumped into him and glanced at the girl himself. Something in her eyes caught them both off guard.

"Is there something you need?" The girl wouldn't release Ben's hand.

The girl with the dark hair, blue eyes, and perfect face leaned toward him.

"I know where he buried the two girls."

Ben did a double take to see if she was serious.

"What?" Eddie leaned toward her.

She appeared not to hear Eddie. She held Ben's hand firmly. Tightened her grip. "Right over the border. Geneva on the Lake. His name is Kevin somebody."

"Holy shit," Eddie let slip out.

"What's your name, miss?" Oddly, the girl stared right through Ben. After a few seconds, her vacant daze melted away. Her face reddened.

"Her name is Rachel." The boy beside her, a shadow of hair growth over his lip, spoke up. "Rachel Callahan."

The girl let go, and Eddie pushed Ben out the door and toward the car.

"Shit, what was that about?" Eddie commented.

Later that evening, Ben Morgan and Eddie Kallen visited the home of Rachel Callahan to inquire as to how she knew one of the suspect's names. Rachel acted lackadaisically. Halfway through the conversation, she told her mother she had to go to the bathroom and excused herself.

"Hurry along, Rachel," her mother said nervously.

Rachel ran to the stairs and took them in twos and threes. Ben wondered why she hadn't used the bathroom by the front door.

Five minutes later, Rachel returned with the front page of an old Erie newspaper. Someone had drawn a map and penned notes in the margins. A trail wound down the page next to the words "Ohio border." The sketch was mediocre but discernable. The path wound beside what appeared to be a stream, a chicken coop, and a barn. The squiggly line snaked down a hill toward an old well. The figures were labeled for clarity. A street name, Garden Lane, was penciled in the forefront. Something that began with an L had been scratched out.

"They're in the well. The two he killed."

How the hell did this kid know the disappearance of two girls might be related to this case? That they suspected the same man attacked them? He stood dumbstruck, staring. Eddie stared, too. As did the girl's parents.

"His name is Kevin. Kevin Reeves."

Two days later, two bodies were fished out of a well on Kevin Reeves's cousin's property. The plot of land sat twenty-five miles past the Ohio line in a town called Geneva On the

Lake. One week later, Kevin Reeves was arrested for the murder of two women and the rape of many others, including Ben Morgan's niece.

Five years later, Ben Morgan, the desert storm hero and solver of Erie, Pennsylvania's most heinous crime, would be named the youngest police chief ever to serve Erie.

# Chapter 14  Rachel

Rachel didn't like the man named Bart, who visited their home often and bragged about the prodigy military school in Arizona.

"He's scary." Lisa didn't like him, either. Her voice trembled when she spoke of him. She ran and hid in her closet when his car pulled into their driveway.

"Don't be such a sissy," Rachel said one Friday afternoon when he sat downstairs chatting with their parents. Rachel stomped out of Lisa's bedroom. "It's not like he wants to take me away or anything."

Shortly after she uttered those words, she found out she was wrong. From the upstairs hallway, she heard their voices. She slowed her step and stopped at the stairway to listen to the heated conversation on the first floor.

"We've told you, Mr. Conrad. We aren't allowing Rachel to go to school in Arizona."

"You don't understand the quality of the school she has access to, Mrs. Callahan."

Rachel sat down on the top step. This wasn't the first time her parents had refused Bart Conrad's proposal, but Rachel hoped it would be the last.

"Mrs. Callahan." Conrad cleared his throat. "I understand your mother is ill."

"How did you—"

"She lives around the corner."

"Now wait a minute," objected Rachel's father. The couch cushion made a springy noise. He must have jumped to his feet.

"Hear me out, Mr. Callahan. I realize this has been a long ordeal for your wife's parents. I know the nursing money from the lawsuit has run out."

"I'm going to ask you kindly to leave, Mr. Conrad." Her father's voice plummeted. He was probably stabbing a finger toward the man. "In other words, get the hell out of my house."

Rachel heard the springs beneath her mother's chair release, too. She wished she could see their expressions.

"How do you know about my parents' finances?"

"I work for the government, ma'am. We investigate all candidates thoroughly."

"Candidates?"

"Yes, ma'am. This Arizona school is highly classified. White House officials accept recommendations from educational facilities, psychologists, and police departments. The board must approve candidates. Your daughter isn't assured a spot in the school until she's been there three months."

"What does that have to do with my parents'—"

"Finances? Everything. The government will take over the in-home nursing-care payments for your mother."

Rachel covered her mouth with a hand.

She had eavesdropped on several of Pops's phone calls and conversations. The money for the nursing staff who visited her grandmother's home each day was due to run out within six months. Pops wanted to sell the house, but Gee said no, she would go into the county home before doing that. Pops had become indignant. "I'll be damned if I let them take you to a home. Those bastards said the money would never run out. Now Medicare issues an investigation, and our attorney says there's a problem? What the hell is going on?"

Rachel had a regurgitating feeling this Bart person was at the root of her grandparents' financial woes.

The floor squeaked behind her. Lisa, rheumy-eyed and shamefaced, stepped into the hall. Rachel turned away and continued to listen to a conversation that increasingly let her know, if she didn't go to this military school out West, Gee would go to the county home.

After several loud minutes, Rachel's parents ushered Mr. Conrad out of their house. Once he was gone, Rachel's mother pressed her back against the front door with relief. She tipped her head back and noticed Rachel sitting on the top step.

"Rachel." Her voice shook. "You were listening?"

"Yeah, and what's the big deal?" Rachel stood. "Guys go in the service all the time. I was going to join the ROTC next year, so why can't I go to a military school?"

Her mother placed her hand on her forehead and began to cry.

"Oh, for God's sake, Mom, don't start crying again."

Her father slipped an arm around her mother's waist. "Come down here, Rachel." He led her mother out of the foyer and into the living room.

"Rachel?"

Lisa's voice startled her. She'd forgotten she was there.

"What?" She yelled nastily.

"We need to tell them I'm the person who found the girls in the well."

"Are you crazy?" She walked over to Lisa and forced her back into her bedroom, wrenching the door closed behind them.

"First of all, it would kill Gee if you went away. Second, didn't you hear what they said?'

"I did—"

"They said physical superiority. What physical superiority do you have? You're a puny little pip-squeak. And third, maybe I want to go. I told you I wanted to be a Navy SEAL someday."

Lisa's expression melted into shame. Rachel couldn't take it. She wrenched the door open and lowered her voice. "I'm going downstairs. Go ahead, come down. Tell Mom and Dad it was you, and I'll tell them you want to go to the school. That you're lying, and they'll believe me. You know why?"

Lisa shook her head. Tears rolled down her face.

"Because they'll want to believe me. They know you would never survive in a military school."

Rachel stomped out of the room and down the stairs. Lisa followed and, being the sickeningly honest person that she was, she admitted she had dreamed of the girls in the well. Rachel called her a liar. A fight broke out between the four of them. Lisa and her mother held each other, crying, while Rachel and her father flung their arms and screamed until their voices were so hoarse, they could no longer yell.

One month later, Rachel sat down in the back seat of a black limousine. The door locked behind her. She didn't reach to open it. Her destiny was set.

Her parents, sister, and PopPops stood at the back of City Hall, waving goodbye. Her mother and sister sobbed uncontrollably.

Rachel swore she wouldn't turn around, but as the car began pulling away, the loneliness of the limousine grabbed her. She screamed, "Wait." The driver couldn't hear her. A thick glass separated them. She turned and rested her forehead against the dark-tinted window.

She watched the vision of her family fade into the past. She didn't cry.

# Chapter 15  Izzy

Izzy remained hopeful Project Dream would end. Instructors hinted that if they met their goals, students would be released at age eighteen, at which time they would be enrolled in the military branch of their choosing.

Clearly, they exceeded their goals. The training techniques worked. Kids were meditating. Dreaming. For once, Izzy found herself at the top of the class. She attributed her success to the white people, who seldom let her down.

From the first to the last step, Izzy outdid her classmates. The hardest factor of remote viewing for many kids included the "cleaning their slate" or "wiping their minds clean" phase. Ms. Sherman called this clearing, step one. Mastering this step was essential to accomplishing step two, the "probing" phase.

In probing, Izzy excelled. When she cleared her mind and called in the white people—they came.

She prayed. The angels painted foggy pictures in her mind, and Ms. Sherman taught her how to handle the pictures.

"Don't interpret them. Simply accept the pictures," she told the class. "Stifle your conscious mind. Work through your higher mind."

They used paper and black pens with liquid ink to draw what they saw. They practiced telepathy, each of them taking a turn sitting in the front of the room, thinking a thought repetitively, while the rest of the class attempted to enter their mind and grasp their thought.

Some kids were exceptional at telepathy, some automatic writing, and some at remotely viewing objects in the desert. They were advancing in aggregate. No one failed. A few fell behind in a task or two, but every project dreamer successfully identified objects on their own.

The program was working.

Instructors couldn't conceal their excitement when several of the kids proficiently completed step three, "delivery." Annie Sherman said delivery was Project Dream's most critical phase.

Kids meditated, probed, and delivered the location of objects with unprecedented accuracy.

Instructors placed objects, "targets" teachers called them, within a one-mile radius of their compound. They asked students to locate those objects in their minds. Within two months, kids began identifying where the targets were hidden. Instructors widened the radius to two, four, eight, and ten miles away within the next six months.

Four months after that, instructors gave them no objects. They asked dreamers to meditate for an hour, probe the geography of the ten-mile area in their heads, and identify anything out of the ordinary.

Izzy's angels showed her guns, ammunition buried three feet under sand, pointy weapons that shot arrows, and a myriad of other items. Through the visions the white people provided, she managed to locate a small set of files hidden in a mountain alcove two miles away. She and Lenny Emling accomplished that feat in month ten.

"You two are progressing nicely," Annie Sherman told her.

"But what are we doing this for? I mean, I know the government wants us to work for them. But how?"

"Eventually, after college, you'll be assigned to a city somewhere in the United States. You'll meet once or twice a month and practice using the remote-viewing skills you've garnered here."

"But what will we be looking for?"

Ms. Sherman hesitated. "Izzy, you'll be using your minds to search for terrorists."

"Terrorists?"

"Military officials hope you will be able to avert another 9/11."

"Oh my God, we aren't that good!'

"You will be. Trust me. This is the first program of its kind. And you're one of our best students. You are remarkable."

Yes, clearly, she had emerged as one of the best dreamers. Yet, while she excelled in her afternoon remote-viewing classes, she slipped in her morning academic lessons. Project Dream's courses challenged her far more than St. Mary's had. A girl, Marva, was forced to tutor her in English. A boy, Marcus, had to help her with math.

She also failed to make friends in the evening. While kids formed groups and friendships, Izzy wrote letters to Mama. She lived for the once-a-month visit with her mother.

During the visits, Mama brought pictures of Enrique's baby, who had wide eyes and a head full of shimmering black hair. Samantha, Sammy for short, walked a week before she turned nine months and began running at ten months. Izzy begged her mother to bring Sammy for a visit, but Ricky's wife would not allow such a thing. Escort a baby across the border? Too dangerous. So Izzy pumped Mama with questions.

"Tell me again how she danced when you visited."

"Well." Her mother clasped her hands together. "A man your brother works with played his guitar, and she moved her feet like a little angel."

"And she sings?"

"Yes, she sings and laughs and plays like a little boy who feels no pain. Oh, and she can swim," her mother said. "She's going to be better than Enrique. She'll be as good a swimmer as you were."

Her mother gasped, realizing she had referred to Izzy's swimming in the past tense. She covered her mouth with both hands.

"It's okay, Mama."

Her mother's hands fell from her face. "But I sent you here, and now—"

"You can't feel guilty over something out of your control. You had two choices: Project Dream or reformatory school." Izzy stroked her arm. "When I come home, we'll go visit Sammy."

Her mother drew a tissue from her purse, dabbed her eyes, and wiped her nose. "Yes, when you come home, we will go to Mexico. I'm saving the money the government is sending me. All of it. It's yours, Izzy. Every cent. I won't spend a dime."

"You should spend the money, Mama. Spend some on Sammy, too. I have everything I need. My closet is full of lovely things. Look." She stepped back, twirled around, and lied. "See? Don't be sad. I have friends. We have tennis and basketball courts. A lake nearby where we swim. There is an observatory that sits at the edge of the mountains, and I'm learning about the constellation. Some nights we lie outside under the stars."

"Really?" Her mother sniffled. "You truly like it there?"

"I love it, Mama," Izzy raised her hand and brushed a strand of hair off her mother's forehead. "Everything happens for the best. That's what you say."

"I do, don't I?"

Izzy hugged her gently. She could manage anything for her sweet Mama. Even refraining from admitting her greatest fear—that they may never allow her to go home.

Even before the end of the first year, more kids arrived in the desert, their faces joyful and dreamy. Officials may have recruited the second wave of students by coercing or blackmailing parents into enrolling their children but, obviously, the kids had no idea they had stepped in a glue that imprisoned them in a cageless hell.

As the months passed, the number of students rose to thirty, then forty, and Izzy's dream of going home began slipping away.

"I thought this joint was supposed to be in Arizona," a new girl, Sonnie, said one day when she took a seat at Izzy's table. Other tables had filled.

Izzy knew better than to talk in the cafeteria by then.

None of the newly enrolled teenagers had juvenile records or were transferred from detention centers. Government officials had learned their lesson. Kids with records caused too much chaos.

Like the original twenty-five, however, each new student had a sixth sense and superior physical quality. Recruited from churches, schools, and police precincts now, all of them had experienced some type of psychic phenomenon. Some saw apparitions. Some had premonitions. And some simply reported having seen ghosts. A few born to spiritualists had deep-meditation experience and advanced rapidly. Others were clairvoyant before they arrived and swiftly caught the original children in delivery. Some were artists who could draw what their mind's eye showed them proficiently. All were fast on their feet, lean, and muscular. Certainly, Izzy fell short on this last trait. That inadequacy sparked a glimmer of hope.

Maybe she'd get kicked out for size.

Eighteen months into the program, one hundred children filled the cafeteria tables each morning. Repetitious days bored them. The daily routine included breakfast, academic school work, a silent lunch, meditation, probing, and dreaming. Evenings included dinner, two hours of recreation or study, reading, and lights out. They lived this way six days a week.

Occasionally, instructors added a Saturday afternoon tracking session that involved travel. Kids fought for that brief liberty. Sundays offered a modified daily routine with optional academic study, remote-viewing practice sessions, and extra recreation. Because she had so few friends, Izzy wasn't particularly fond of Sundays. Too much time alone often resulted in downheartedness.

Izzy did talk to some kids during the Saturday travel days. None of them had told their parents the main facility wasn't in

Arizona. Teachers persuaded students that if they revealed the truth, their families would suffer. Again, no one defined suffer but it was safe to say, by now they all understood the details of the program must remain secret.

This was the United States government.

Izzy watched the smiles and hopes, once so evident on new students' faces, slide into a mellow, somber realization. This was no elite high school prodigy program. This was a disciplinary, national-defense military institute.

Seven children didn't pan out and were removed from the program. No one heard from them again. Six were replaced by kids who trained in the wings somewhere in Arizona. Kids in the program referred to those replacement children as "benchers," for bench warmers. The benchers attended classes in the desert twice a month. None of the one hundred were permitted to associate with them.

When the last didn't-pan-out student set her bags in the limousine and rode away, Izzy expected one of those bench kids to show up as the final replacement, but two days later a new girl stepped out of a limousine. Rachel somebody. She was tall and beautiful. She turned heads as she walked by. She had to be older than the rest of them.

Some kids alleged this last girl was a mole, placed there by the government to see which kids talked. Nevertheless, the girl with the long legs and perfect face had sealed spot number one hundred. Rachel was faster, smarter, and pushier than all of the girls and most of the boys. Project Dream's team was complete. Counselors announced recruiting had ended.

Up until now, Izzy had made only one real friend: Sonja, Sonnie for short. She and Sonnie were the sole girls rubbing elbows at her cafeteria table. In addition to Lenny and Todd, now John Michael, Marcus, and some Sam kid sat with them. So when Annie Sherman assigned the last vacant seat at their table to the new girl, Izzy hoped she and Sonnie would gain a comrade.

Quickly, she realized that wasn't going to happen.

"So what's your story?" the Rachel girl said on the Sunday evening of her first week there. Kids congregated in a makeshift game room.

"What do you mean?" Izzy rolled her neck around in her shirt uncomfortably.

"Well, you're puny. Tinier than my little sister. They said everyone accepted had to have some physical strength. What could yours be?"

"Well." Rachel had caught Izzy off guard. "I can swim."

The Rachel girl grinned. "And that will do you a lot of good in the middle of a desert."

Izzy watched the girl turn her long legs around and head toward the pool table where several boys played eight ball. Rachel snatched a pool stick from a boy, leaned down, and set the stick softly between her index finger and thumb. She sank a solid-colored ball. Then four more. And the eight ball, at which time she tossed the pool stick on the table and said, "When you boys learn to play, call me." She walked on to another table.

"Did you see that?" Sonnie whispered. "Maybe we can be friends with her. She sits with us."

"I kind of doubt it."

"But didn't she say she was from the same hometown as Lenny?"

"Yeah, she did. I wonder how that happened. There are no kids from the same town except Richard and Alex, and they're brothers."

"Well, statistically there is a chance of two people coming from the same city, not a high probability but a probability."

"Sonnie, stop with the math."

Of course, the only friend she could attract would be a math nerd. There was no way the new girl would hang with the two of them.

"Sorry." Sonnie's thick glasses slid down her nose. She pushed them back on her face and took a seat on the couch in front of the big-screen TV.

"It's okay." Izzy sat down beside her.

"You should talk to Lenny, though. He protects you. I overheard him talking to Rachel about her little sister. You remind him of her."

"I'm sure I don't."

"Why not?"

"She's blonde."

"How do you know?"

"I just know."

Suddenly they heard a rustle, and the cushions shook. The new girl reappeared, hopping over the back of the couch and plopping between them. They both jumped.

"Know what?" Besides her utter beauty, the girl's voice had a unique natural rasp.

"Nothing." Izzy's face reddened.

"She says your sister is a blonde."

"Shut up, Sonnie." Izzy glanced past Rachel, widening her eyes at Sonnie.

"How do you know anything about my sister?"

"I just do."

Rachel sized her up from her shoes to her headband. "You are the littlest kid here."

"I know. You pretty much said that already." Izzy scratched her upper lip, hoping her hives hadn't surfaced. "Like I said. I'm fast."

"You didn't seem so fast in the four-hundred run on Friday."

"I fell down." Izzy fumbled with the collar of her shirt. "I'm a little clumsy."

"A little?" Sonnie laughed so hard she snorted.

Izzy glared at her.

Rachel sniggered. "So how do you know Lisa is a blonde?"

"Who?"

"Lisa, my sister."

"Oh, well." Izzy wiggled in her seat and straightened. "There's this thing we do, where we try to see things in other rooms. And I sorta' saw the picture of you with a blonde girl. I figured it was your sister. The picture on your bulletin board."

"Get out."

Izzy offered some short crisp nods to say she meant it.

"You must have passed by my room and looked in.

"No, I didn't."

"She's really good at remote viewing." Sonnie chimed in.

"Yeah, well, what's the other picture of?"

"Your grandmother."

"No, not the one on the bulletin board. The one in my closet. That no one can see."

"Oh." Was the new girl testing her? They weren't permitted to use excess energy on anything other than what their teachers allowed. "I'm not supposed to—"

"Yeah, right." Rachel smirked at Sonnie.

Sonnie snickered and something inside Izzy clicked. She couldn't be left out. If Sonnie ganged up against her with Rachel, she'd have no one. And despite this Rachel being a bully, there was something charismatic about her, too. A charm. She had an alluring magnetism. You couldn't wait to see what she would do next. The boys would like her unpredictability.

She thought of Enrique. How everyone loved him and consequently, accepted her. Izzy was smart enough to recognize one of her true abilities was grabbing hold of someone's coattails and holding on for dear life.

"Okay," she conceded, leaning down, and placing a finger over her lip to quiet them.

Her head snapped left and right. No one was within earshot. She closed her eyes. Spent a minute or two trying. After too much time lapsed, she opened her eyes disappointedly. "I'm sorry. I can't get anything other than stars. A constellation."

Rachel kept staring blankly at her.

"I told you I'm not proficient." Izzy bent forward and shot a scathing glance toward Sonnie. "See, I'm not so good at this."

"Orion. It's Orion," The Rachel girl said after a while.

Izzy looked at her, confusedly. "What?"

"The picture in my closet. It's of Orion."

"See, you are good," Sonnie said, loudly.

Izzy shushed her.

"So this works?" Rachel lowered her voice. "You can learn this remote-viewing stuff?"

"Yes," Izzy responded, glad for a simple question.

"Izzy is excellent at it. She's Sherman's pet," Sonnie chirped in. "And McDaniel throws her abilities at the rest of us."

"No, he doesn't." Izzy waved a hand at Sonnie. "And I'm not Sherman's pet."

"McDaniel? Is that the hot director? Wavy brown hair. Blue eyes?"

"Yeah, he's got a thing for Izzy."

Rachel's gaze snapped from Sonnie to Izzy. "As in you're sleeping with the director?"

"No!" Izzy squinted her eyes and shook her head appallingly. "My God, no. He's old. Older than my brother. Not that I wouldn't like an older guy. But Mr. McDaniel? How could you even...I mean...no, he's not for me."

"Well, how old could blue eyes be? Thirty? Maybe thirty-five?"

Quite unintentionally, Izzy snapped her neck to the side. "But ah, well, how old are you?"

Rachel appeared pensive for a moment. She smiled. "Old enough to know a good-looking guy when I see one."

She turned on her heels and left them.

Izzy raised her eyebrows at Sonnie, and Sonnie shrugged.

"I'm happy hanging out, just the two of us." Sonnie leaned back in her seat and resumed watching TV.

"Me, too." Izzy glanced over her shoulder and watched the Rachel girl's long legs stroll back toward the pool table. Boys crawled out of the woodwork to watch her. Izzy watched her, too.

Rachel watched no one. She existed in a world of her own.

# Chapter 16  Rachel

Rachel wished she had half of her sister's compassion. She would trade all her beauty for a portion of Lisa's calm, gentle ways. A fragment of her kindness could have helped in those first months in the desert.

Up until the government shuffled her off to dreamland, life had come easy to her. Her family lived in a nice neighborhood. She had lots of friends. A pleasant face. People considered her smart and fast on her feet. She could eat what she wanted while maintaining her thin waist, didn't require much studying to get As, had money to buy clothes, and beat the boys in basketball or soccer without exerting much energy. She had grown up in a decent middle-class family and attended a safe Catholic elementary school located three blocks from her home.

Before Project Dream, that school presented her biggest conflict.

She spent eight and a half years exposed to religious education. Swore she hated every minute of the proselytizing. The nuns and lay teachers had failed with her. Not a morsel of Catholic guilt stuck. She hadn't succumbed to their brainwashing as Lisa had. The potential guilt of an action often prevented Lisa from an escapade more so than the act itself.

Rachel wiggled her feet into the sand, fell back onto her blanket, and stared up at the stars, wondering how Lisa was doing. The Project allowed family meetings at a resort in Arizona after a dreamer—kids called themselves dreamers— had been there six months. Next weekend would be Rachel's first visit with her family. She and four other kids were the last to arrive. Rachel, the very last. For the past five months, she had remained behind on family weekends to endure Project Dream's "catch-up" training.

Rachel tucked a hand under her head and made a grunting noise. She sifted sand through her toes. "Training my ass."

She struggled with every ounce of her being not to let them get to her psychologically. This "for the good of the country," "military child prodigy," and "you can't tell anyone the true intent of Project Dream" was hogwash.

She was glad for her Catholic grade-school experience. Circumventing the nuns' attempted evangelization had been an inconvenience. But she had rather easily averted absorbing their beliefs, which now relayed the confidence she needed to do the same at Project Dream.

All was for the good of the country and their families, she had been told.

"They'll cut family members' tongues out," she mimicked Ms. Merryman's voice.

Maybe those weren't the words the propagandist used, but she implied some grueling, undisclosed punishment would befall Rachel's family if Rachel leaked Project Dream information. Full disclosure of the penalty would have been kinder. Leave something to the imagination and ideas grew like wisteria, strangling anything within its reach.

She raised an arm straight up in the air, touched the tip of her pointer finger to her thumb, and closed one eye. She moved her arm slowly until she found the North Star. She and Lisa would open her bedroom window and gaze at the stars when they stayed up late.

She let her hand fall to the sand. She missed her family terribly. Lisa had written a letter saying Gee was coughing more, and Pops was forgetting to take his pills now. Rachel hoped they lived until she got home. She hoped she lived. She could use a shot of Gee's encouragement right now to help her get through this nightmare.

"The others aren't as strong as you and me, Rachel," Gee would say when Lisa wasn't within earshot, which was a rarity.

Lisa clung to Gee like a bee to a black-eyed Susan. Sometimes their closeness made Rachel jealous.

Gee understood that, too. She had X-ray eyes that sized up people's emotions as if they wore their mood on a name tag. When Rachel's mother helped Lisa with her math homework or braided her hair, Gee sometimes called for Rachel to come to her room.

"Life is tough," she would say.

One time she patted the bed and said, "Come sit by me a while. I won't keep you long, I promise."

Rachel hadn't been born with Lisa's patience. Lisa could read or talk with Gee for hours. Rachel couldn't. When she was forced to sit for long periods of time, her blood gushed through her veins like electricity. Her heart thumped like a sneaker in a dryer. Every inch of her skin itched.

Her mother refused to put her on medication, so her behavioral reports in middle school suffered. She simply couldn't sit still. She was bored. Her mind needed something to muse on, and with a classroom full of students, there was always someone doing something so hilariously stupid that she found it funny.

But on one of the few days she managed to quiet her soul and spend an entire afternoon chatting with Gee, Gee talked about herself as a teen, about her sisters and brothers, and how often her siblings got under her skin.

Gee appreciated her big family but said a person only needed one loyal sister or brother. Rachel and Lisa were lucky because they would always have each other. There would never be another sibling to nose in between them.

"We fought terribly," Gee said that day. "I bossed my brothers and sisters around. They were younger, so I had to help my mother take care of them."

"Who was your favorite?" Rachel loved learning about Gee's family.

"Well, now if I tell you, you promise not to tell anyone?"

"I promise."

"Because, you know, you are a lot like me. I have a hard time keeping a secret. I get mad sometimes, and my secrets spew out of my mouth. Before I know it, something someone told me not to tell is out in the world like a skyscraper for everyone to see."

"I do that, too," Rachel hung her head, then snapped it upward again. "But I won't tell. I promise."

Gee laughed and coughed and tightened her grip on Rachel's hand as best she could. "I loved Bennie the most."

"Uncle Bennie?" That surprised Rachel because Gee talked so much about her sisters. "You liked him the best?"

Gee nodded and gazed toward the ceiling. "I wish you could have known him. Uncle Bennie was a gentle soul. So sweet, kind, and loving. Shooting a gun nearly sent him to his grave. When he came home after he served in the army, he was troubled. I worried for him after that war."

"The Vietnam War?"

"Yes, the Vietnam War. The helicopters would fly low, and he and the other soldiers would jump into the rice paddies."

Here she made clicking sounds with her mouth. "That war did him no good. He had to go away for a long time and be counseled afterward."

"That's when he met Aunt Wendy, right?"

"That's right, darling." She squeezed and shook Rachel's hand. "You are so smart. You surprise me every day."

She leaned and kissed Rachel on the top of her head. Rachel still remembered the sweet lemon scent fading in the air as she pulled away. Rachel's own mother took good care of Gee. Bathed her, spread lotion over her skin so bed sores didn't form, lifted her into her wheelchair every night, and rolled her out into the living room, so she could have dinner in front of the TV with PopPops.

"Uncle Bennie was the kindest soul I've ever known."

"Like Lisa," Rachel said, even though at the time she was furious with Lisa for losing her favorite horse pin.

Lisa had worn the pin to school, and when she came home, she found it missing from her coat. Devastated, she cried and apologized, but Rachel shoved her anyway. Kicked her bookbag across the room and hoped something broke inside.

Later she apologized. She wouldn't have felt an ounce of remorse for shoving anyone else, but Lisa was so pitifully kind. Oddly, that made Rachel both lenient and tough on her.

God, how she missed her.

"Like Lisa," Gee had repeated. "The way I figure life is, we choose which person we want to be before we are born."

Rachel agreed with that concept. She once told a Catholic nun she believed everyone existed before they were born, and the nun almost had a heart attack screaming. That nun was one of only two nuns in her school who still wore a habit. Her arms flailed so wildly that she knocked her veil off. Rachel picked it up and put it on her head, prancing around the room. Kids howled. Rachel spent that afternoon in the principal's office. Her mother had to come in for her disciplinary meeting.

"I think Bennie and I had a hard time deciding who we would be. The only two souls left in our family were Gee and Bennie. I decided being in bed for years would be worse than being in the army for a few. Bennie thought being in the army would be worse than being in bed, so we each sacrificed for the other. We loved each other that much."

Rachel tucked her other hand under her head and gazed up at Orion. She wondered if Gee had told Lisa that Uncle Bennie was her favorite sibling. Maybe she had and maybe Lisa was at home thinking about that same story.

She probably had dinner with Gee and Pops, watched *Jeopardy* with them, went home to study, and spend time with Mom and Dad before going upstairs to bed. She could be restlessly gazing out her window at the stars right now.

And Rachel was here watching those same stars—alone.

Being apart from her sister allowed her to understand Gee's words better. She had come to the desert because leaving Gee and her mother seemed the harder task to her soul. Lisa stayed behind because, to her, watching Gee decline was far worse.

So in the end, even though Lisa's gifts of seeing were so much grander than Rachel's, each of them sacrificed for the other.

The part of the conversation Rachel hadn't understood at the time was the ending.

"We float down the river with those we love," Gee said. "But the river has a mind of its own. The current separates people. And when it separates you and Lisa, keep swimming. Keep reaching your arms out. Keep swimming."

She hadn't liked that advice. And what Gee said next she liked even less.

"Sometimes, the current sucks the strongest of people to its rocky bottom. If that happens to you, Rachel, when your knees are wedged in sand and rock, and your eyes stare death in the face." Here Gee's voice fell into a full whisper. "Remember your old Gee's words. Fear not. You are going to live."

At the time, she thought she might have to endure some death-defying moment. But now she wondered if the story had been figurative.

Gee continued, perplexing her more. "But you and I, Rachel, we love the feel of the current."

At that moment, Lisa ran into the bedroom with a dumb smile on her face because she and Momma had found the same exact horse pin at the corner store. Lisa bought it for Rachel with her own money.

And Gee never had the chance to explain herself. Were Rachel's knees actually going to be lodged in rock? Or sand? What an odd conversation it had been. Rachel hated how Gee talked in riddles.

But now rock and sand surrounded her. She and Lisa were apart. Rachel had no one. Is that what Gee meant? Did she know how alone in the desert she would be?

*Keep swimming.*

She rolled over on her side. Looked away from the stars.

She was friendly with a few boys at Project Dream: John Michael and the small boy, Todd, who was faster than everyone except Lenny. And she liked the big lug of a Lenny, felt comfortable around him, but he wasn't exactly a conversationalist.

She picked up a fistful of sand, turned her wrist, and allowed gravity to drag the grains through her fingers.

She needed friends. Maybe she could befriend Sonnie. Or Chase.

Chase was handsome. She could go for a boy like him despite having gravitated toward older guys in the past.

Last summer she had flirted with a college boy at the beach. He had no idea how young she was. He attempted to lead her off into a nearby woodsy area to make out. She resisted, but only because her mother had drilled it into her head that she should never allow herself to be lured into a compromising situation.

But since she had come to the desert, one of her virtues—that her parents had so incessantly harped upon—had slipped to the wayside. Chastity. She no longer had any qualms about making out after the sun went down. She'd lost her virginity her second month in the desert. And, for some reason, whenever she thought about those first months, Gee's voice crept into her head.

"Anger is like dirt under your fingernails," she used to say. "Doesn't matter how pretty your face or nice your clothes, that little bit of dirt will bother you. You'll constantly have to cover up your hands until you dig it out."

Had she slept with those boys because she was angry?

*Covering up that dirt?*

She'd blamed her parents for not fighting harder to keep her out of Project Dream. But after so much time stewing in the hot sun, she'd stopped blaming them. She realized her parents hadn't had the clout to fight the American government. Rachel, like most of the kids, came from a small, powerless family.

Her mind considered that lacking element. She needed power. The kind of power Chase Finley had. Everyone loved him—even the teachers. More favors befell him than the other students.

Yes, she needed to garner the kind of friends and clout Chase had. She wouldn't roll in the sand with any other boys. She was going to hold out until Chase noticed her. Or Jerry McDaniel. Whoever came first.

She rolled over and stood, stepping into the sand, and rumpling her blanket into a bunchy mess in her arms. As she did, she caught a glimpse of John Michael in the shadows. She gave him a half-hearted wave, and he staggered toward her. Surprised by how slow and unsteady his gait was, she stopped. It was past curfew. The other kids had gone in long ago.

She squinted her eyes to see him. He weaved toward her. Obviously, he'd had too much to drink.

Most of the kids drank alcohol. One of the younger instructors, someone Swarthy, handed miniature bottles of tequila out like it was candy corn. Homesick kids sucked it down. What harm could a little drunkenness do? They were stranded out in the middle of nowhere with no parents to remind them of right and wrong, and they were desperate to fit in. But maybe John Michael had drunk too much. He reeked of alcohol as he neared.

Her glance caught his, and his eyes relayed something not quite right. He ambled forward, his steps becoming short and quick. For a moment, she thought she was going to have to fight him off, which she found odd because she had made out with him several times. He was one of the nicer boys. She had probably spent the most time rolling in the sand with him.

So why did he look as if he was about to attack her? He could have come with his tequila as he'd done before. They could have shared a good time. Usually a fun guy, right then, the fun in him seemed gone.

"What are you doing out so late?" Instinctively, she turned her left shoulder toward him in case she had to swing with her right.

He took another step in her direction, and as he did, the clouds opened up, and the moon cast light around them. They noticed a third person. Lenny Emling stood off to one side, his long arms nervously scratching his thighs. The only sound in the night was the faint itching of Lenny's fingers against his legs.

"Hi, Lenny," Rachel said.

Lenny said nothing. After an uncomfortable moment, John Michael stepped back, turned, and casually made his way toward the dormitories. "See you tomorrow, Rachel," he slurred over one shoulder.

"Yeah, see you tomorrow." Rachel watched him stagger away and disappear into the dorm. She turned toward Lenny. "What's up?"

"You g-gotta be more c-careful, Rachel."

"I'm fine. John Michael and I are friends. We've hung out before. But thanks for watching out for me."

She started walking back toward the dormitories.

"Rachel, you have to be careful out here."

She turned around and looked at him. That was the first time she had heard Lenny Emling complete an entire sentence without stuttering.

# Chapter 17  Jerry McDaniel

Jerry McDaniel's family had money. He grew up an aristocratic, privileged kid who spent summers caddying at a D.C. country club frequented by politicians. His career with the CIA began there, on the sixteenth hole.

Jerry had two advantages over other bag rats. One, he could play golf. Man, could he play. And two, he excelled in math, especially statistics. After seventy-two holes, he had ascertained how far on average a player hit the ball with each club—and not only the men he caddied for but his player's opponents as well. He kept notes in a small notebook, which he hid inside his shirt pocket.

"What you got there, kid?" a senator once asked.

"Notes." Jerry meant for the guy to see him writing. He had removed the small pad from his shirt pocket, set it on top of the scorecard, and conspicuously scribbled numbers on its pages.

"Let me see that."

He handed him the names of sixteen senators, ten congressmen, and three cabinet members. Below each of their names, two-digit numbers filled columns. Those numbers represented the statistics for every golf club they used in the prior three-months of tournaments. The senator's name itself was number thirteen on that list.

The guy sifted through the pages, glancing around sheepishly. Then he, the high-profile senator from Virginia and possible future presidential candidate, handed the notebook back and asked Jerry for his three iron.

Jerry pulled out a four. The man hesitated.

"You think I'll overshoot the hole with a three?"

"I don't think you will." Jerry handed him the four iron. "I know you will. Your ball will land on the back edge of the green. Roll eight, nine yards into the woods."

The senator sized Jerry up then turned his gaze to the coiffured green circle with the flag in the middle. Jerry would never forget that hole as long as he lived. How the cut grass smelled thick and wet from the prior night's rain. How the birds sounded spooked in distant trees. How the skin on the back of his neck felt tight under the hot sun.

Everything about that tournament weekend was tense. The Republicans and Democrats had some big stakes they wouldn't reveal. The Virginian turned pensive.

"If you're wrong, this will be the last time you caddie at this golf course, son," he said. "Are you willing to take that chance?"

"I am, sir."

The sweat slithered down the back of Jerry's golf shirt.

The senator walked away, the club in hand. He teed up and smacked the ball with a swift, smooth swing. Jerry held his breath. The ball landed inside the green, rolled three inches to the left of the hole, and stopped about a foot beyond.

The senator set the head of his club on the ground and rested a wrist on top of the grip. One of his opponents swore, another laughed, and the caddy closest to Jerry released a long, relieved breath. Jerry himself stood shaft straight. The senator paused, hiked his club upward with one quick, fluid motion, and tipped the hand grip toward Jerry. Jerry slipped the club back into the bag without sentiment, his face stone cold.

"What's your name, son?"

"Jerry McDaniel."

"Well, Jerry McDaniel, how would you like to caddy for me the rest of the summer?"

"I'd like that, sir," he said, and with that twist of fate, Jerry accelerated onto every caddy list in the country until he was old enough to enter the tournaments and beat the good old boys he'd caddied for.

On the other side of the street, Bart Conrad, Jerry's direct supervisor, grew up in middle-class suburbia. He had deviously clawed his way to the top, coming up through the ranks the only way he knew how: eating everyone who got in his way. And despite his ravenous appetite, superiors sidestepped him several times on those first few rungs up the ladder by selecting country-club boys whose daddies sat on club boards. He worked eighty hours a week for six years to get where he was today. He had a big, weighty, I-hate-rich-boys chip on his shoulder. Conrad was never going to relinquish his hold on Project Dream to a rich kid like Jerry McDaniel without a fight.

Jerry may have been assigned direct supervision in Nevada, but Conrad was tugging on the reins from D.C., and no one could pry those straps from his hands. Only a hair's width in authority above Jerry, Bart lectured him at length about what he could or couldn't do with the program.

"I don't give a damn how badly these kids want to go home. The sooner they learn they're in the military, the better. Take control of the situation, McDaniel. Do what you must but make them understand."

So Jerry did. He told the instructors Bart Conrad, who oversaw the entire operation from D.C., was being investigated for the poisoning of Everett Sparks, the first of those seven children to be removed from the program.

Rumors swirled about the rejected seven. No one could locate six of them. But because Everett's mother had a set of vocal cords loud enough to compete with the pipes of the Boardwalk Hall Auditorium organ, word got out that Everett landed in a graveyard.

Everett's throat closed from a hard-shelled-fish allergic reaction in a small seaside restaurant on Ocean Isle, North Carolina. On that Saturday afternoon, vacationers clogged the only bridge in and out on the Isle, and every single EpiPen on that five-mile stretch of land suddenly disappeared. His mother swore he was intentionally poisoned.

Jerry McDaniel had another talent. He recognized an opportunity. He used the Sparks boy's demise to end his pissing match with Conrad.

He referred to the death as suspicious and hinted to Annie Sherman that Conrad was to blame. Annie riled up instructors and personnel. Workers complained on their monthly assessment sheets, reporting Conrad had made unreasonable demands on them and the kids. They asked why Conrad refused to relay information about the other six children removed from the program.

Unnerved, Randall Scott and Steve Larson reviewed the assessments and called Jerry to Washington. Jerry brought someone to represent Project Dream's workers.

"This worker is as straight, clean, and unwrinkled as a hot dollar bill off the press. You'll get the truth from her," Jerry told Scott and Larson.

"Her?" Larson's voice strained.

Jerry opened the door and beckoned a hand toward Annie Sherman.

When Annie walked through that door, Bart Conrad's party was over. Jerry sat beside Sherman and listened as she judiciously shoved Conrad underneath the presidential motorcade. For once Jerry didn't say a word.

In the end, of course, Larson agreed to Annie Sherman's demands.

Finally, Conrad's hold loosened. Jerry's modest, little Area 51 office felt cozier, remoter. Bart retained some authority, but McDaniel was in charge now. Teachers referred to Conrad as Bye-bye Bart.

With Larson's absent hand, instructors thought Project Dream's take-to-your-death element was quashed, but the truth was the government had amassed a substantial pay-off package to keep families of fallen dreamers quiet. If the money didn't work, well then, they were forced to take other measures. Jerry was perfectly willing to overlook what those other measures entailed.

Anything for the good of the people. As long as it was for the good of Jerry.

For a while, Jerry McDaniel settled in contentedly. Then Annie Sherman knocked on his door and confided in him. Student morale had become so low instructors were forced into suicide-watch status.

Jerry gave orders to keep them out of the mountains, halt target practice, and lock the guns away. Whispers of this or that kid's impending suicide persisted.

"These kids are starved for affection. Most of the instructors, maybe all of them except me, have no regard for them. They're teenagers and they have no role models. No parents. No religion. Very little recreation. Everything has been ripped from them, and so they're groping to find love in anything and everything. Each other, alcohol—maybe death. There is going to be a problem. I worry about suicide and sex."

"It can't be that bad."

"How would you feel, Jerry, if you were taken from your family at thirteen? What was your life like when you were fifteen? God help us when they turn sixteen or seventeen." Annie implored McDaniel to take action now.

He did. He recalled his own teenage years when golf, girls, and grades were his only concern. He put himself in the shoes of the dreamers. He stepped away from his desk for a week and watched them. Morning through late evening. He grasped the doldrums of their existence.

Sherman was right. He had to do something. This was the military, yes, but they were kids, too.

He pulled the head instructor aside.

"Lighten up at meals, Merryman. Let them have some fun. Stop chasing them in at curfew."

"Yes, sir." She was reluctant but obedient.

"We are placing an order to bring in some marihuana."

"Marihuana?" Her mouth widened into a big, fat circle. Jerry could have chipped a ball into it.

"Yes, marihuana, maybe some coke. A little dope never hurt anyone. Cocaine boosts dopamine in the brain. You ought to try it once in a while."

"I don't think that's a good idea."

"Well, Bart does. He still has some control."

That everyone hated Bart Conrad held so many advantages.

Merryman objected again but eventually accepted, and McDaniel pilfered drug supplies from intercepted Mexican cartel planes—lots of programs did.

Six weeks later, morale still low, McDaniel lightened their weekly schedule, gave them Sundays completely off, and upped their supply of cocaine. For some reason, the cocaine heightened their clairvoyance.

"We can't give them more, sir," Merryman said.

"I don't think we have a choice. Their results are staggering. The cocaine seems to have opened parts of their brain they never accessed before."

"But they'll become addicted," she argued.

"If you're worried about addiction, pull some back. But." He squinted and raised his chin. "Then it's on you, Merryman. Their successes must continue to rise, and I better not hear of one single dreamer killing themselves because they couldn't go home. The drugs seem to relieve them of their depression."

"We can help them through this," Swarthy chimed in. Jerry had begun inviting him to sensitive meetings. Swarthy's ruthlessness made Jerry seem like a nanny. "We have a plethora of coke. They love it. I say give them as much as they want."

Coming from Swarthy's mouth, McDaniel quickly realized that might not be the answer, either. They couldn't have a bunch of cokeheads roaming the desert.

What would he want, other than drugs, if he were a teenager in the middle of the desert?

"Let's bring in some sod and let them play a few holes of golf."

"A golf course?" Merryman's jaw dropped so low you'd thought he'd suggested a brothel.

"Not an entire course. Three holes. Get them the best clubs. Hire the firm that installed the basketball courts to construct three holes. And purchase some Jeeps. Swarthy, you teach them to drive. You're a driver, correct?"

"Yes, sir, I raced cars during high school on a mud track in upstate New York."

"Fine. Teach them to drive. The girls, too."

McDaniel thought of the Callahan girl. How fine she would look behind the wheel of a Jeep.

"Can we open the shooting range?" Swarthy interrupted the picture McDaniel had of Rachel Callahan driving a Jeep through the mountains. That girl was becoming the talk of Area 51. "The kids love target practice even more than the observatory."

"Wait until morale is up. Then restore it." Jerry shook Callahan from his thoughts.

"Jeeps?" Ms. Merryman looked as if she'd witnessed a death. "Are you crazy?"

"What are they going to do, Joanne? Ride away? Get them the damn Jeeps and let them have some fun. They're in Phoenix this weekend, but have the Jeeps here by the following Sunday."

"How many do you want?" beamed Swarthy.

"Let's say twenty. Get them from the army."

"It will take longer than two weeks."

"Well, lighten up on the rules and have the Jeeps here by the end of next month. We have to engage these kids somehow, or we'll have a mutiny on our hands. Turn your back on their sneaking out at night. They're kids."

"But, sir—"

"Joanne Merryman, you must have had one dull childhood." He waved a hand and the meeting ended.

## Chapter 18  Rachel

At roughly five feet ten inches tall and one hundred and forty pounds of solid muscle, Rachel had no problem keeping up a tough front. Winning a down-on-the-ground scuffle with a Minnesota farm girl nearly twice her weight had awarded her the title of camp bully.

Clearly, the friend thing wasn't going well.

She stood sideways in front of the mirror, eyeing her figure. She wore her clothes tight, so the boys—and teachers—noticed her. In this prison of a place where money had no value, and cigarettes and booze passed freely from hand to hand, Rachel had to find another bartering tool.

Done right, good looks could spoil a person.

She ran her hands over her flat ribcage and gathered her shirt in back, so the material tightened around her. A pin or two ought to impress Chase Finley.

Or Jerry McDaniel.

Rachel cared little about appearance until she realized that weaponizing her looks could save her from wanting anything in the desert. Jerry McDaniel had taken an interest in her. He'd summoned her to his office several times, and she'd flirted with him willingly. She might get anything from that guy in exchange for a wrestle under the covers.

Almost anything. As the days passed, it became clear going home would not be an option. She'd spent time with a bunch of kids in the evening—because Chase hung with them—and their cynicism had worn off on her.

They said she would never go home and live with Lisa again.

Rachel frowned. She refused to miss her sister today. Instructors had announced that, academically, everyone passed their classes and, in aggregate, they exceeded their remote-viewing expectations. As a reward, Jerry McDaniel had relaxed the rules, stretched the curfew, sealed plans to install a three-hole golf course in the near future, and planned a celebratory race into the mountains on the new Jeeps he had purchased.

She snorted. Two months ago, during a meeting with Jerry, she had suggested more Jeeps might boost morale. In addition to flying planes, she had heard Chase Finley raced cars. When the Jeeps arrived, Rachel garnered a few extra driving lessons. She hoped those lessons paid off.

For the first time since she secured that last spot in Project Dream, she had something to look forward to.

"The last will be first," she said out loud.

At that same time, Izzy Jimenez passed her doorway. The girl backed up. "And the first will be last," she said.

Rachel rolled her eyes. The girl stepped gingerly into her room.

"Hi, sorry to barge in, but you are going, right?" Izzy's nervousness was one of her many annoying qualities. Her ability to crawl out of the woodwork when you least expected her was another.

Rachel eyed her up and down. Since day one, the clumsy girl had been as underfoot as Lisa. She even had the nervous habit of picking her fingers like Lisa.

"Why are your fingers bleeding?"

She had picked one finger raw. Blood ran down her hand and dripped onto her shorts.

"Oh, gosh." She stuck the finger in her mouth and sucked.

Rachel cringed. "That is disgusting."

Embarrassedly, Izzy removed the finger. "Sorry."

"Please tell me you are not going today."

"No. I mean, yes. I want to go. I told them I was going." She scratched the side of her face and as she did, blood from her finger stained her cheek. "So I was thinking I would."

"Well, are you or aren't you?"

"Yes…yes. I am." Izzy nodded her head.

"Oh my God." Rachel turned back to the mirror. "Are you, like even a hundred pounds?"

"A hundred and two."

Rachel stopped managing her hair. Shot a hateful stare. The girl's stupid face turned red. Like Lisa's used to do when she said something dumb and couldn't take it back.

"I mean, I don't know, maybe a hundred and five," Izzy stammered.

A wave of sympathy washed over Rachel. She hated this girl, but she was so pathetically pitiful you couldn't help but feel bad for her. She cursed herself for what she was about to do.

"I suppose you aren't going to drive a Jeep yourself."

"Oh, no." Izzy snapped her head and shoulders backward and wrinkled her forehead. "No, I couldn't."

A big, heavy, regretful sigh whizzed over Rachel's bottom lip. "And I suppose no one has asked you to ride along with them."

"No, but I'm hopeful one of the boys at our table will let me."

There was more chance of a tidal wave obliterating Project Dream in the middle of the desert than any boy asking Izzy to ride with them.

*Pitiful.*

Izzy stood gazing off in the distance, scratching her face, looking as if she was realizing the same. A long red line of blood streaked her right cheek.

Why did everything about this girl piss her off?

"You're still bleeding."

"What?"

Rachel gestured toward her face.

"Your cheek has blood all over it from your finger."

Izzy wrapped a hand around her bleeding finger, applying pressure.

"Oh, for the love of—here." Rachel snapped a tissue from its box and handed it to her. "You can ride with me today. I'm driving."

"I can?"

"Yes, get out of here. Go change into jeans or tights or something other than whatever the hell kind of shorts you have on. I don't want you coming back burnt."

"I'm Mexican. I rarely burn."

"Well, cover your legs so you don't get scraped up. Put on something casual. Don't show up like you've been invited to tea."

"Oh, okay." Izzy's cheeks grew embarrassingly red. It was sad.

"Get out of here, will you? I'll meet you at the garage."

She hurried away hastily, smacking her shoulder against the door jam. She stopped a second to moan then rushed off, her shirt torn.

Rachel slammed the door shut behind her and leaned against it with crossed arms. She stood for a second before busting out into a laugh.

"Total dork." She pushed off the door and moved toward the mirror in a better mood.

Despite her distaste for Izzy, that girl's continual mishaps made for a good laugh. Scaring the hell out of her on a Jeep ride would be fun. Besides, taking the awkward Izzy would make points with Chase. He loved sheltering the weak.

She removed her shirt, doubled the fabric over in back to form a pleat, inserted a tiny safety pin to hold it in place, and put the shirt back on. There. The adjustment made her waist appear thinner, her chest bigger.

"Let's see if I can't coax a kiss out of you tonight, Chase Finley."

She straightened her shoulders, lifted her chin, and sashayed out the door, strolling toward the garage.

Twenty Jeeps queued up in line. Each faced the mountains. Rachel hung a straight, flat palm over her sunglasses, so she could better see the crags and ridges. The hills of the first range hung low. The second range towered over the first, its peaks clearly set against a pale-blue sky.

Halfway up the largest mountain of that range, a band of black metal spikes embedded in rock lined up twenty feet apart. From the garage, she could barely see the black pegs, but they were out there. They served as a boundary. A sharp reminder of Project Dream's spatial limitations. If kids passed those markers? That arrogant instructor—the one almost as good-looking as the director but nowhere near as cute as Chase—said the consequences were simple. They'd be shot.

No one believed him, and no one cared much about the second range, either. Climbing the first hill was task enough. So much rock and loose sand clung to it that instructors cautioned the kids driving to stay on the switchbacks.

Rachel sauntered toward the Jeeps, lifted the hood of one and then another. She inspected the radiator and engine, slammed the second Jeep's hood shut, and jumped in the driver's seat. She closed her eyes. Sifted the steering wheel through her fingers.

"Think you can handle her on your own?" A voice caught her off guard. She opened her eyes.

Russet-colored sunglasses rested on the top of his dirty-blond hair. He hadn't covered his eyes with them yet. He stood so close she could see the little white lines cutting into his ocean-blue irises. The two colors together made his eyes match the clear Nevada sky. Who was that old actor with the sky-blue eyes whom her mother loved? Paul somebody. Yes, she was sure Chase's eyes must be as blue as Paul somebody's.

"I know I can."

He placed a foot on the rock rail of her Jeep, crossed his arms, leaned over a bent knee, and moved into her space. She noticed his five o'clock shadow then. The scruffy face she loved on a guy. She wondered if he shaved with a dull blade for the effect.

The sun beat down on him. He inched his face farther inside the Jeep, so the roll bar blocked the sun from his eyes.

For a moment, the air stifled her.

"Are you confident in everything you do?" He smirked.

"I don't know as I'm confident in anything I do."

He laughed, dropped his gaze to his boot, picked up a foot, and kicked sand off the rail. "Most of the time you're pretty cocky. For a girl."

"For a girl? Okay, I see how this is going to be."

He set his foot down into the dirt and took a pair of gloves out of his back pocket. "How many times have you driven one of these?"

"A few. And you?"

"I grew up driving them. Colorado. My father taught me."

"The big pilot?"

Kids said his dad had more purple hearts than any pilot in the history of the United States. Rumors circled that Chase, too, had made a name for himself in the aviation world.

"Yeah, the big pilot."

"Well, then." She intentionally blinked her eyes slowly. "You must be good."

Pops once forced her to watch a western movie with a wickedly dumb plot. The scene where the woman sexily blinked her eyes at the big strapping cowboy stuck with her. The man lunged forward and kissed the girl instantly. Rachel thought that woman with the lovely eyelashes could finagle anything she wanted from a guy.

Her own eyelashes were longer than that actress's lashes. She jutted her chin and blinked. "You'll be bored racing the rest of us, won't you? I better get my helmet. I'm frightened."

"Funny you should mention. They're making the girls wear them."

"Then I'm sure they'll hand you one, too." She fluttered her lashes.

His face lit up; a simper stuck on his lips.

"I don't think I've ever met a girl as sassy as you, Rachel Callahan." He pulled his gloves over his wrists. "Or one as— good-loo—"

"Hello!" Izzy ran up alongside him.

Rachel's smile fell off her face. She closed her eyes.

*Perfect timing.*

This girl had every last annoying quality known to women.

"Hi." Rachel opened her eyes, unable to mask her annoyance.

Chase's smile widened.

Rachel took a long breath in. Her chest swelled up as if it might bust.

"Hi, Izzy," Chase said. "You're not riding with Danica here, are you?"

"Ha-ha." Rachel squinted her eyes.

"No," Izzy responded. "I'm riding with Rachel. Who's Danica?"

Chase grinned.

"Are you for real?" Rachel turned the key that was lodged in the ignition. "Just get in."

In the distance, Sonnie hollered to Rachel as she ran toward them, a girl named Marva trailing on her heels. Rachel waved a hand to them, they jumped in the back, and Izzy circled to the other side of the Jeep.

"All girls, nice," Chase said. "See you on the mountain."

As he trotted off, a man carrying helmets approached Rachel's Jeep. Chase nodded at the guy and turned to salute Rachel, a cheeky grin sweeping across his face. He walked away backward, smiling.

"Here you go, girls." The man dropped four helmets into the Jeep.

"You can't be serious."

"Girls have to wear them, Rachel."

"The girls? Not the guys?"

"Let's not make this Roe vs Wade, Callahan. Put your helmet on and get ready to ride."

"I'm ready."

"You don't look ready," the instructor said, backing away. "Put your helmet on."

She glanced down the line of Jeeps and watched Chase Finley jump in one. He smiled at her from behind the steering wheel. She grabbed a helmet and put it on her head without breaking eye contact. "Put your helmets on girls. Let's show these boys what we're made of."

"But we're not—" Izzy started to say.

"Put your fricken' helmet on."

"Well, okay," Izzy said, fumbling with the helmet straps, still standing on the side of the Jeep.

"Get your ass in here," Rachel screamed.

Izzy flung herself into the Jeep. Rachel reached across her and buckled the seatbelt for her in one swooping motion. Ken Swarthy began a little starting-line speech, but Rachel had no intention of listening. She pushed the gas to the floor and headed toward the mountains. Behind her voices raged, and a roar of engines taking off sounded.

By the time she made her way to the bottom of the first mountain range, three Jeeps, including Chase's, nudged toward her back bumper. They scrambled for a place in line and climbed the switchbacks up the hill easily. Those first paths were well worn. The Jeeps kept their positions to the top of the first range. When they hit the highest peak, everything changed.

There were no clear passages on the way down the other side of the hill. A less-cut path eased back and forth, forking at different spots. Some forked trails headed around the side of the hill in a longer route, and some dead-ended into piles of rock. One led straight down the hill over the rocks. Rachel hesitated at the top to decide the lesser of the evils. She turned right, taking the longer route. The two Jeeps behind her charged straight down over the rocks. They slowed to a crawl.

She kept close to the unkempt switchbacks, edging into the sand where the road narrowed. Chase's vehicle managed to pass her on a parallel pass. A second Jeep passed her on another. By the time she made her way to the small valley between the two mountain ranges, several vehicles behind her had dead-ended into rock barriers. Their wheels flung sand and pebbles as they backed up the hill out of their impasses. Rachel could hear their tires squealing. She gave her own vehicle more gas.

Chase, still in front of her, headed straight toward the small watering hole in the valley. He bore to the right and skimmed its edge. Rachel turned her wheel to pass him on land.

"No, no," Izzy pushed the wheel in the other direction. "Follow him."

"He's in the water."

"He knows what he's doing."

Against her better judgment, Rachel straightened the steering wheel and followed.

"No, go around the pond," Sonnie wailed. "We'll get stuck."

"No, go through it. Cool the engine." Izzy's voice competed against grinding engines and wind. "Pass him on the inside. It's shallow."

"We'll sink."

"It's rock." Izzy hollered.

"Are you sure?"

"I'm positive."

Rachel drove through the water and cut Chase off, averting the first switchback by driving straight up the least steep path on the hill.

"Hold on," she shouted, and for a moment she thought they'd tumble backward, but the wheels held ground. She turned onto a switchback, cutting off a Jeep that had forgone the water and jumped ahead.

Chase's Jeep followed alongside her on a parallel trail. When their paths converged, Rachel slowed for the switchback's ninety-degree turn, and Chase's vehicle bounded onto the path in front of her.

He led the entire way up the hill, and at one point, the switchback disappeared and, expeditiously, each driver judged which rocks held the least decline. Ascending on rock taxed even the army Jeeps.

"Turn your heater on," Izzy screeched.

"What?"

"You're overheating." Izzy freed one hand's death grip on the seat and hit the heater.

"What are you doing?"

"Trust me." Izzy grabbed Rachel's hand, stopped her from turning the heater off. "My brother had a car that overheated."

A rugged bounce forced Rachel to grab the wheel once again, and she moved upward.

Long, bumpy, sometimes death-defying minutes later, Rachel managed the Jeep toward the flags.

"Get ready," she hollered. There were flags for them to grab at the turnaround point.

Izzy leaned out her side of the Jeep and swiped a flag into her hand.

"I got it," she squealed.

Rachel turned the Jeep around and selected a descending path. Jeeps dappled the mountain below her. Some crawled like too-fat animals on a staircase. Others were wedged in the sand, exhaust dissipating into the air around them.

A vehicle passed her as she climbed back up the first hill. By now the number of Jeeps still moving had plummeted to nine. So much space separated them that the drivers had time to think, evaluate, chart their course ahead.

As she mounted the last peak and began her descent, she jockeyed from fourth place to third. She approached Chase, in second place, until he was a mere car length in front of her.

She couldn't allow him to beat her. She made a gut-wrenching decision to abort the switchback. The Jeep jolted back and forth over rock. Two wheels left the ground. The girls screamed, and when they had less than a quarter of the mountain left to descend, Rachel decided to go straight down the mountain and cut him off.

"Hold on, girls." With one last surge, Rachel pulled up alongside his Jeep, nudged its side and forged ahead.

She glanced at him for a second. He wasn't looking. When she turned back, a boulder appeared out of nowhere, she steered to the right but two of her wheels bounced over rock. She held the steering wheel tight, but her grip slipped. The wheels skated rock, and her Jeep plummeted sideways.

Rachel's body jolted to the right. Her seatbelt held her, but because of the slope of the hillside, the Jeep tipped onto two wheels, toggled, and then toppled over, once, twice, three times, slicing through sand and rock. On the fourth somersault, the Jeep hit the flat gulley and sunk into the sand.

A few seconds passed before any of them spoke.

Rachel glanced at her passengers. Everyone sat upright, gripping odd parts of the Jeep. She smiled.

"You nearly killed us." Marva, her soft-brown face bloodied by a brush against a rock, unbuckled her seatbelt and jumped out. "Are you crazy?"

The first-place Jeep descended the last of the switchback paths and sped by them just missing Marva. She screamed and jumped to the side. The second-place Jeep slowed.

"Are you all right?" Rachel recognized his voice, Chase. "Everyone alive?"

Rachel's Jeep made a grunting noise, jolted, and Rachel turned the ignition off before the Jeep could hiss.

Sonnie and Izzy jumped out. When they trudged out of the sand and their feet hit solid ground, Izzy began running in circles. Her shrill scream was so high-pitched the two boys with Chase covered their ears.

A third Jeep sped down the mountain. Then a fourth. The other still-functioning Jeeps bounced downward, carefully avoiding the stalled Jeeps. Instructors and a few kids standing at the distant finish line began running toward Rachel's vehicle.

Izzy's screams escalated, rebounding off the mountains.

"Oh my God. Oh my God," she screeched.

"Izzy." Rachel unbuckled her belt and stood inside the Jeep. "Calm down. Are you all right?"

"Am I all right?" She stopped circling but jogged in place, unable to still her legs. Her eyes roamed over the desert. "Yes, I'm all right. I'm…I'm wonderfully all right."

"Huh?" Sonnie took a step away from her.

"That." Izzy put a hand to her chest and leaned over to catch her breath. She removed her helmet and then straightened, wiping the sweat from her forehead. "That was the most fun I've ever experienced in my entire life."

Rachel felt her mouth widen. "You…liked that?"

"Liked that?" Izzy stomped her feet in rapid succession. "I loved that. Can we roll it down the hill again?"

Chase, standing in his own Jeep, laughed and sat back down. Sonnie sidled to the Jeep and jumped in. Marva stomped away mad.

"You people are crazy," she wailed. "For as long as I live, I will never again get in a Jeep with you, Rachel Callahan."

An instructor arrived in a Jeep, chastising Rachel. Chase buckled in and took off toward the finish line, passing an oncoming Jeep carrying Jerry McDaniel. Everyone wanted to know whose vehicle tumbled over the edge of the mountain and what the damage entailed. McDaniel shifted into park, grabbed his windshield, and stood inside his Jeep to inspect the mishap. No looming injuries prevailed.

He sat back down, shifted, and drove away, grinning.

Rachel sat down, too, turning the key. The engine throttled and spit before starting up like the military vehicle it was. Eventually, the sound slowed into a perfect whir. She gave the engine gas and rocked the wheels back and forth to break free from the sand. Izzy put her helmet back on, jumped in, and buckled her seatbelt.

Rachel looked blankly at her. "You want more?"

Izzy raised and dropped her chin in short, abrupt nods. "Yes, please."

Rachel stepped on the gas and headed toward the garage.

Laughing so hard she could barely see, Rachel hit a rock and the Jeep jolted, tossing everyone to their left. One of Rachel's hands dislodged from the impact, and she found herself half in and half out of the vehicle. She nearly fell from the Jeep, but at the last second, Izzy held a hand toward Rachel.

*Keep reaching your hand out.*

Rachel lifted her arm and grabbed Izzy's hand. Izzy pulled her inside.

People jumped left and right out of their way as Rachel drove the vehicle toward the finish line. She ended up driving the seventh-place vehicle across the line, but she couldn't have felt more exhilarated than if she had won.

She suddenly understood what Gee had told her long ago.

*You and I, Rachel, we love the feel of the current.*

## Chapter 19  Izzy

On a Saturday evening, four weeks after Rachel Callahan's infamous ride, Izzy succumbed to the loosened leash of Director McDaniel. She had a drink of tequila.

More than a month of the new less-stringent rules had passed.

The mellow, depressed mood of the one hundred kids had concerned instructors. For months before the rule relaxing, rumors of a suicide pact between six kids dominated hall whispers. Not Izzy's, of course. She had no friends to whisper with, save Sonnie.

Which was why when the director originally issued the order to relax the rules and allow the kids more free time, Izzy had worried. What if additional cliques formed? Whom would she and Sonnie hang out with? To Izzy, having more downtime to spend with other kids meant having more rope to hang herself.

Then Rachel Callahan waltzed in. Invited her for a Jeep ride. Izzy joyously celebrated that girl's unbridled courage behind the steering wheel.

Suddenly, Izzy had an alliance.

Now kids slept in on Saturdays and Sundays, ate at their leisure, played basketball or tennis, rode Jeeps, and exercised free reign under the evening stars with friends. More alcohol passed from hand to hand, and kids showed up with marihuana and cocaine in their backpacks. Where they got the stuff, Izzy wasn't sure. Sonnie said the younger instructor, Ken Swarthy, doled it out like chewing gum. Not that Izzy would ever hold her hand out for any, but she accepted the tequila when Todd Kennedy graciously offered to share some with her. Since Rachel Callahan was her friend, life had grown easy. She dared not do anything to risk that new friendship.

So, despite her better judgment, she drank tequila, smoked marihuana, and even tried snorting cocaine, although most of the powder ended up in her hair and down her blouse.

Boys from another cafeteria table hung around with them now in addition to the boys from their own table. Marva hung on their heels, still complaining about Rachel's wild drive. Dawn Davis, who had emerged as the girl's leader and spokesperson up until Rachel took over, tried nosing into their group. Thankfully, Rachel quickly nudged her out. Izzy didn't trust that girl. And the cool kid, Chase Finley, began sitting with them in the evening, too. Every girl just about melted at the sound of their name crossing his lips.

So, naturally, Chase ended up on Rachel's blanket. The pecking order had been set. Rachel's drive had distinguished her, and rumors of Chase's past had exalted him. Someone said his father piloted Air Force One for a while. Others said when Chase was eleven years old, he himself had flown solo across the Pacific from Pasadena, California to Maui, Hawaii.

She didn't believe that one.

Still, Izzy agreed. There was something more than stellar looks about Chase Finley. He had an air about him. He acted older. Izzy glanced at the other boys. Even in her slightly drunk state, they looked younger.

Kids tossed frisbees and congregated on lit-up basketball and tennis courts. Dozens traipsed in and out of the desert. Izzy and Sonnie sat on their blanket, which abutted the edge of Rachel's. Several boys joined them. One boy, Marcus, pulled a bottle of tequila out of a knapsack. He drank some and passed the bottle to Izzy, who took a small swig and handed it to Sonnie. Sonnie drank and passed the bottle to Todd, who always took two or three nips to everyone else's one.

Izzy studied him. Todd had come out of his shell since those first days. Kids liked him. The more he drank, the funnier he became. And the more the kids laughed at his jokes, the more Todd drank. Now he was snorting cocaine. A sea of partiers began following him around.

Izzy leaned into the center of the blanket and grabbed the tequila. Maybe alcohol could boost her popularity. She took a swig. A real gulp, not a sip. She choked it down and took another. Then she handed the bottle to John Michael, coughing and trying not to belch.

The bottle passed from hand to hand and when Todd drank the last of it, he reached into his own bag and pulled out another. The passing resumed and as it did, Izzy spotted Lenny Emling walking alone in the distance. Rachal saw him, too.

"Lenny," Rachel hollered. "Come over here and sit with us."

Todd stopped laughing. John Michael stopped breathing.

"N-no I'm headed to the observatory," Lenny said, not raising his eyes.

He sat at their table for meals but did little else with them. Sometimes he hung out with two quiet kids who didn't drink and also had trouble making friends, but mostly he kept to himself. No one teased him. After the big fight in the first week, everyone steered clear of Lenny. Only after Rachel Callahan showed up and said she had grown up with him did the kids begin to at least say hello to him.

Izzy listened admiringly to Rachel's raspy voice. Rachel had a soft spot for unpopular kids like Lenny—and Izzy— whether she admitted it or not. Somewhere underneath her rough surface and gravelly voice, she had a mushy heart.

"Oh, come on. Sit with us. You deserve a drink after the run you had yesterday," Rachel yelled. "Just this once."

On Friday instructors timed their mile. Lenny had sprinted in front of Chase Finley and Todd Kennedy at the last moment. No one had seen that coming. Todd was made for running with his lean frame, and no one could believe Lenny had beaten the star athlete, Chase Finley.

"She's right. Come sit with us," Chase called. "I owe you a celebratory drink."

Moonlight hit Lenny. He smiled.

"Where'd you learn to run like that?" Chase inched toward Rachel as if creating a place for him.

Lenny put his hands in his pockets, took a few steps toward them, and shrugged. For some reason, Chase liked Lenny. Izzy presumed that made Rachel like Chase even more.

"Sit down."

"N-no thanks, Chase. I'm going to the observatory."

"No, sit with us." Rachel laid back on the blanket and patted a spot beside her. "You can see the stars from here."

Any other boy would have jumped down beside her so fast the ground would have shuddered. But not Lenny.

"Orion is out t-tonight." He pointed upward. "S-s-see Rigel? I want to take a closer look."

Rachel tucked an arm under her head and gazed upward.

The single, best quality of the desert was its darkness. The black nights were perfect for star gazing.

"I see it. Come name the stars for us."

"I can name the stars," Todd said. He jumped from his own blanket to Rachel and Chase's, began naming them. Another boy crept over, and quickly, the open space around Rachel disappeared.

"T-talk later, Rachel," Lenny said.

He tipped his hand slightly, waving timidly, and headed toward the small domed building, where a row of high-powered microscopes hid inside. A girl, the quiet one, rose from another blanket and followed him. Several other kids had already made their way there. The observatory coaxed constellation lovers. With the touch of a fingertip to the control panel's red button, one-third of the roof opened, and the stars and galaxies lit up against the magnificent sky like grains of salt on black agate.

"Okay, man, see you later." Chase fell back beside Rachel.

After a few minutes, he rolled over on his side and propped his head in his hand. He pulled out a silver flask, drank, and offered Rachel some. Izzy watched Rachel drink eagerly and hand it back.

Izzy reached for the bottle of tequila on her own blanket to try again. She took another drink and passed it. She laid back and closed her eyes, thanking her lucky stars Rachel Callahan had decided to be her friend. Within minutes she fell asleep. A soft, simple snore whirred over her lips.

# Chapter 20  Rachel

"Is she snoring?" Rachel pinched Izzy's nose. Izzy squirmed and Rachel let go.

Laughter rumbled from both blankets.

"Leave her alone." Chase chuckled. "She took a terrible spill today on our hike."

The others sniggered. There was something cute and funny about the little girl who always fell down and never knew when to shut her mouth. If anyone else fell asleep and snored, kids would wake and taunt them, but not Izzy. Kids were quickly taking a liking to her. For some reason, that made Rachel happy.

"She is her own worst enemy," she said. "If she lives through this it will be a miracle."

"Nice thing about having her around," Todd Kennedy said, "is no one has to worry about finishing last in anything."

"Her Jeep beat yours," Rachel jeered.

"Yeah," Sonnie added. "And she can swim like a fish. You'll never beat her in the water."

"She didn't seem so fast at the lake last week," John Michael grunted.

"Did you see what she does?" Sonnie's face lit up.

"Not really." John Michael snorted the long line of cocaine he had formed on his small round mirror.

"She dives low and floats at the bottom. She can hold her breath forever. She's toying with us."

"I saw that, too." Chase sat up. "And no one yelled at her for taking her time."

"I know." Rachel sprang up beside Chase. "What do you think is going on around here? Why do you suppose they lightened the rules?"

"Because everybody's too depressed." Sonnie pressed a tequila bottle to her lips again.

"So what?" Todd said. "It's not like they'll ever let us out of this program. We'll go to college, but we'll have to do our remote viewing, protect the country, and who knows what other shit."

"I'm not." Chase took a swig from his bottle.

"Yeah, right." Rachel nudged him with her shoulder. "Like you have a choice."

He became sullen. His gaze, distant. She liked the way the lights from the courts and buildings and stars reflected in his eyes.

They had virtually spent every day together after that Jeep race. He'd kissed her the day after, and they'd made out the next weekend and the weekend after that. Last Friday they had snuck out in the middle of the night, and he'd made love to her under the stars.

He told her about growing up in Colorado, how he loved to fly planes, missed his family. Rachel told him about Lisa and Gee and even admitted she had considered sleeping with Jerry McDaniel in an attempt to go home.

She trusted Chase that much. It scared her how quickly she had spilled her secrets to him.

He told her he had never met a girl as fearless as her and made her promise never to sleep with Jerry McDaniel. She liked the way he had pulled her close last Saturday and said he never wanted her to sleep with anyone else ever again. She promised not to.

It was funny how drastically life could change in a few weeks.

For the first time in the desert, she felt content, happy.

Chase took the last drink from his flask and lifted the bottle of tequila off the blanket. He drank and passed it to her. She took a swig and passed it to Todd. When she leaned her hand on the blanket, Chase placed his hand on top of hers. Chills rose through her.

Todd gulped the remainder of the bottle down and crawled to Sonnie's blanket after inspecting his own backpack and realizing he'd consumed his own alcohol. The others followed suit, leaving Rachel and Chase alone.

"You know if anyone tries to get out." He leaned close and spoke low so that no one else could hear. "They'll kill them."

She only half-heartedly paid attention. She sat wondering if her eyes were reflecting the stars like his. "I doubt they'd actually kill us, but I suppose they won't let us go after all this training."

He leaned closer. His breath warmed her cheek. She shivered.

"That boy Lenny beat up the first week?"

What was he saying? She couldn't concentrate.

"They pulled the plug on him."

"What?"

"They killed him."

Suddenly, she reentered the conversation. "The kid Lenny knocked into a coma? He died?"

Chase grabbed another bottle from his bag and took a swig. She drank from it, too.

"A few weeks after the fight, he came out of the coma. He started talking about Area 51 and how there was this remote-viewing program for kids. He told his mother he had been in Nevada, not Arizona, and he never wanted to go back. He wanted to go home and they—" He made a clacking noise inside his mouth and a gesture as if he'd sliced his throat with a knife.

She burst out laughing, her head swirling from the tequila. "You're crazy. They wouldn't do that."

He looked away and drank again, swaying on the blanket. Was it her or him? Was she drunk or was he?

"Give me that. You drank too much."

"I'm not drunk, Rachel."

But he was. His normal happy demeanor had changed.

"Yes, you are. You don't know what happened to that boy Lenny beat up."

"My father does. He heard about it from—" He tipped the bottle against his lips again and drank. "A friend."

"You're talking foolishly."

She ripped the tequila out of his hand, screwed its top on, and tucked it in his backpack. She crept closer to him, tugging him down onto the blanket.

She melted into his arms, set her cheek against his chest, and listened to the thump of his heart. Its soft, steady beat soothed her. She fell asleep and awoke around one in the morning when Ken Swarthy flashed the floodlights, signaling they had a half hour before they had to come inside.

Chase took Rachel's hand. He helped her to her feet but didn't lead her toward the building. He tugged her toward the mountain range, away from the others. She followed willingly. They passed by the observatory and kept walking. When they were deep enough into the black desert where no one could see them, they began running.

They ran toward the mountain range as fast as their inebriated legs could take them and when there were no more lights but the moon and the stars, they fell to the ground. Rachel ripped her clothes off, and Chase made love to her as if he already knew every inch of her body. When they rolled over exhausted in each other's arms, sand caked in every fold of their skin, he kissed her again, softly.

They lay there for a long time before he spoke. "This is not a good time for this."

"Not a good time for what?"

"For me to be falling in love." He thrust his mouth onto hers, and they made love a second time.

For the rest of her life, Rachel would recall that night as the first time she made love to someone she truly loved. She felt remorse for having slept with other boys in the desert before Chase.

Perhaps she had not been as strong as she thought.

## Chapter 21  Lenny

Exhausted but content, Lenny fell into his bed at about 2 a.m. that evening. Rachel had gotten the notion of sleeping with Jerry McDaniel out of her head. Her wanting to go home held no uniqueness. What separated her wants from the others', however, was she had the tools to make her desires come true.

Every man at Project Dream, students and teachers, wanted her—except Lenny.

Four months ago, before the curfew had been lifted, before Chase had fallen in love with her, Rachel had snuck out and became so inebriated that Lenny had to carry her back to her room before Swarthy or Merryman found her. In order to do so, Lenny implored Ms. Sherman to turn off the cameras for two minutes while he carried Rachel into the dormitory. Sherman was the single person in the entire compound whom Lenny trusted.

When he tucked Rachel into bed that night, Rachel drunkenly spilled her plans to him.

"I'm going to get Jerry McDaniel to send me home," she muttered.

"D-don't be foolish," he'd cautioned.

"No, I'm going to do it. I'm getting out of here. I'm going home to Lisa."

He had known what she meant. She was going to sleep with the guy.

"I'm going to get you out of here, too. I know you want to go home and help your mother."

"That's n-not a good idea."

He pulled the covers up to her chin, knowing he only had a few seconds to get out.

"Yes, it is. You'll see. We are both going home."

He stroked her forehead until she fell asleep, then he dashed away. Sherman had kept the cameras off for a full five minutes, once again saving his neck. He made his way safely to his room. Later, Lenny heard Sherman tell Swarthy there had been a power surge.

After Rachel's middle-of-the-night confession, Lenny devised a plan himself. He talked to Chase Finley about Rachel Callahan. The real Rachel Callahan.

Chase was a good guy, and Rachel had her eye on him. So Lenny did a little matchmaking. He told Chase the truth. How Rachel appeared so much tougher on the outside than she was on the inside. He acknowledged girls steered clear of her, and boys used her. In some ways, life was tougher for Rachel than even for Lenny.

That hint of vulnerability in her grabbed Chase's attention.

Lenny proceeded to tell him about Rachel's life in Erie, Pennsylvania. How she defended people. Loved her grandmother. Took her sister's place at Project Dream. Chase seemed impressed. Lenny watched him. Chase looked at Rachel differently. After the race with the Jeeps, Chase and Rachel were falling in love.

Lenny thought of Kiera, the quiet girl. Maybe someday…

He wouldn't think about that now. Now his only goals were to keep Rachel out of trouble and find a way home. Once home, he could take care of his mom and watch over LeeLee.

Being born with the ability to concentrate and read a person's mind had been such a blessing in the desert. The skill had literally saved his life.

But his other gift? What he saw when he looked into a person's eyes? No other person on earth could see what he saw.

Rachel, Chase, Kiera, and Lenny would make it through this god-forsaken program.

Lenny hit the light switch near his bed. His room darkened, and for the first time since he carried Rachel into her dormitory months ago, Lenny slept peacefully.

# Chapter 22  Rachel

After Chase Finley fell in love with Rachel, life in the desert became tolerable. She and the others snuck out nearly every night with fewer consequences. No one chastised anyone for missing the 1:30 curfew on the weekends. Several other relationships began in the dark hours.

Drinking became the norm. Drug usage accompanied both depression and dreaming troubles. Lots of kids, even some of Rachel's friends, realized coke stimulated the brain and inspired dreams. So snorting cocaine became the favored vice. Remote viewing became easier. Morale improved.

One by one, homesick kids replaced the love of their family with sex or drugs. Ken Swarthy distributed ample alcohol, an average amount of marihuana, and a small amount of cocaine. Kids quickly found a cafeteria worker who would sneak them more if they paid him cash. So they asked family members for money on their weekends in Phoenix.

The surmounting addiction fed promiscuity. As fifteen- and sixteen-year-old adolescents with no parental influence, they found solace in each other. Some fell in love. Others pretended to fall in love. Having someone to confide in and spend evenings with proved critical—even life-saving.

Rachel had Chase. She drank some and partied, but she didn't need alcohol or drugs like the others. Chase was enough for her.

Izzy fared well. Rachel had begun to think she was stronger than she appeared. Marva's headstrong ways kept her sober, also. Sonnie immersed herself in math and computers. But their other friends, Todd, John Michael, and Marcus, fell heavily into the drugs.

She doubted the director and instructors knew about the cafeteria worker who came every other weekend with a new supply of cocaine and occasionally OxyContin. Or maybe they just didn't care. Meeting goals mattered, not emotional stability.

Gradually, the task of identifying objects stored in the miles of desert became elementary. Instructors hid items far beyond the mountains. Kids identified the location of objects with precise accuracy. Some could state the latitude and longitude of their targets.

Twice, men flew in from Washington D.C. to spend a few days watching the top dreamers. Rachel heard the reports they took back to Washington dumbfounded White House officials. Project Dream's funding skyrocketed. Chase said with that sort of success, they would never get out of the program.

"But when we go to college, we will. I'm hoping they send me to Erie," Rachel told him.

"They won't," he replied. "This program is doing too well. They're going to hand the reports over to the President earlier than originally intended."

"That doesn't mean we won't go to college.

"We'll go, but they'll lump us together in groups of five, ten, or more."

"You don't know that for sure."

He clammed up. His expression sobered. He was keeping something from her.

"What is it?"

They were alone, far from the dorm, long past curfew. Not that anyone cared any longer.

He took her hand in his and drew her close, breathed lightly into her ear. "I'm getting out. Come with me."

He set a finger against her lips so that she wouldn't respond.

She inched backward, away from him, gazing into his eyes. He couldn't be serious.

He leaned in. "My father is coming for me. You can come with me."

Instantly, once she grasped his seriousness, a euphoria swept through her. Could they get out of this god-forsaken desert? The two of them? She could spend the rest of her life with Chase. Live a normal life.

"Where would we go?"

"Far away, so no one can ever find us."

No one? Did he mean she couldn't tell anyone? Not her mother or Gee or—Lisa? She could never leave Lisa behind. She whispered into his ear, "Can I come back if anything happens to my grandmother?"

He shook his head.

"But if something happens to my parents?"

"We could never come back."

She loved Chase, yes, but did he expect her to leave and never see her family again? Lisa?

"Could my sister come to live with us?"

"No." She felt his arm tighten around her shoulder. "No one can."

"Could I come back and see her? Someday? In a few years?"

"You don't understand the gravity of our situation. We can never come home. We can never tell a soul where we are."

"But your father will know."

"My father is the reason we have this opportunity. People owe him favors. Important people from other countries."

She loved Chase. But she couldn't leave Lisa forever.

"No." She wrapped her arms around him. "I can't go. And you can't leave me. I love you. Please don't go."

He talked again a week later about leaving. She argued they should stay. They could go away to college together. She would convince Jerry McDaniel to send them to the same school. Chase grew angry. He warned her to stay away from McDaniel. He was dangerous.

"When will you go?"

"I don't know. My father's making the arrangements."

She begged him to forget the idea.

"How can you leave me?" she asked over and over.

Chase stopped talking about it. Rachel prayed daily he would forget the idea. Whenever he brought the subject up, she refused to discuss it, but every night when he kissed her goodbye, she pulled him close, murmuring, "Don't leave me. I love you."

As the months passed, he talked less about leaving, and she pushed the thought to the back of her mind. Selfishly, she prayed his father had been unable to make the arrangements. She made up her mind to convince McDaniel to send them to the same college. She wouldn't tell Chase, but she was prepared to do whatever she must do. She was desperate to be with him. Determined to remain in McDaniel's good graces so that they could be together. She must also stay in the top ten.

Yet, with this, she struggled lately. The harder she tried to remain in the upper echelon, the further down the ladder she fell.

For some time, a few kids jockeyed for the tenth remote-viewing position. Until recently, those competing had not included Rachel. Her feet had landed solidly within the top five. But now, Swarthy and Sherman occasionally took the top ten out of Area 51 to prove they could perform in any location. Kids began battling for the coveted tenth spot to escape for a day.

Rachel began having trouble concentrating in class. Her conscious mind distracted her higher mind. Falling in love with Chase had affected her dreaming. She flitted in and out of the top ten, along with John Michael, Marva, and Todd Kennedy. Izzy's, Lenny's, and Chase's spots at the top firmed up while as more kids meditated, trained, and learned to open their minds, Rachel found staying above fifteen difficult.

One novelty of being eleventh was Swarthy slipped you an extra dollop of coke. He, unlike other instructors, totally believed the cocaine augmented dreaming. Rachel thought

Todd Kennedy aimed to be number eleven for that bonus. Seesawing back and forth between ninth, tenth, and eleventh place made for an endless supply of cocaine. No one brought more coke to their midnight excursions than Todd Kennedy.

By the time high-ranking officials placed Project Dream's reports into the President's hands, several kids were snorting cocaine daily to increase their clairvoyant capacities. Many others used casually, but was there a growing number of teenagers becoming hooked? No one cared.

Officials reinstituted the listening to tapes at night. The new tapes brainwashed them while they slept. Each teen wore high-tech earbuds that once again played soft voices warning them not to reveal secrets to family members. Military-sounding men chanted patriotic slogans in the background.

Sometimes when Rachel woke in the middle of the night, she listened with her conscious mind. The number one mantra, never speak of Project Dream, played over and over. Instructors said tapes were individually designed for each student according to their needs. Of course, Rachel confided in Chase what her tapes said. He confirmed his relayed identical information.

They could recite verses verbatim: *tell no one of Project Dream. Duty, loyalty, and averting another 9/11 are paramount. The safety and livelihood of the American people depend on the strength of the government's military. You are a member of our military family. You shall protect America.*

"It's bullshit," Chase said one Saturday night in the desert.

The tapes convinced some kids they were "special," "important," "children of the moon." One night when a bunch of them had too much to drink, they dared to discuss the issue outright.

"I totally agree with Chase," Izzy said. "It's all baloney."

Realizing Izzy was not as naïve as many of the others surprised Rachel.

"We shouldn't be discussing this," Marva said after a few minutes. "I'm not getting in trouble."

She stomped off and a few others followed.

"She's right," Izzy said. "It's late anyhow. We should head in."

They gathered their blankets and backpacks. Rachel spent time saying good night to Chase, then caught Izzy and Sonnie on her way back.

"How come you're so skeptical?" Rachel stepped alongside Izzy.

"My brother knows some cartel members and Federales. He told me we are never getting out of this program."

"Your brother knows the cartel?" Izzy had totally thrown Rachel for a loop.

"A few. No big names. But they warned him we will never get out."

"We can go to college wherever we want," Rachel responded.

"Maybe you can." Sonnie sounded annoyed.

"You don't think we can?"

"No," Izzy answered. "We'll go where they tell us. Watch and see. Chase will go to the Air Force Academy. Rachel, you'll go to Pepperdine. I'm working like hell to stay at the top, so they change their mind and send me to the University of San Diego."

"Where do they want you to go?"

"Florida."

Rachel turned toward Sonnie. "And you?"

"Alabama," Sonnie grumbled.

"Well, I'd rather go to Alabama than California. The farther we get from Nevada the better we'll be. Plus, the weather's nice there."

"Sonnie wants to go to Stanford, Rachel. They're sending her to Auburn."

"How do you know where everyone's going?"

"I just do," Izzy said, and for once, Rachel couldn't pry her sources out of her.

Eventually, Rachal stopped hounding Izzy and turned to Sonnie. "Why would you want to go to Stanford? I hear San Francisco is crowded and foggy."

"Are you kidding?" Izzy stopped walking.

"About what?"

"You don't know?"

"Know what?"

"Sonnie is dying to go to Stanford." For the first time, Izzy looked annoyed with Rachel.

"Are you?" Rachel turned toward Sonnie.

Sonnie shrugged. "I am but they'll never let me."

"Why do you want to go there?"

Sonnie shot her a perplexed glance but didn't answer. Izzy answered for her.

"Rachel, what's wrong with you lately? Of course, she does. She wants to land in Silicon Valley. We think in words; she thinks in numbers."

"I suppose that makes sense," she said.

They stomped along quietly for a while. Then Izzy stopped a second time. Placed a hand on Rachel's arm to stop her, too. Sonnie followed suit. A few kids passed them. When they were the last three left in the dark, completely alone, Izzy continued.

"I have to ask you something. But I'm afraid you'll get mad."

"I'm always getting mad at you. So far that hasn't fazed you."

Sonnie cackled.

"This time it's important." Izzy frowned at Sonnie.

"Okay, what do you want? You must want something."

"I don't want anything."

"Well, what's it about?"

Rachel turned and studied Sonnie. Sonnie glanced away, averting eye contact. "What's going on with you two?"

She prayed they didn't know Chase's plan.

"It's not about us. It's about you." Izzy folded the blanket in her arms, nervously. "You've been at the top of our remote-viewing class for well over a year. You never slipped below five once, but now you're struggling to make the top twelve. You're lower than you've ever been. Someone said you weren't even in the top twenty last week."

"I was fifteen, and what's it to you?" Izzy was annoying Rachel.

"Don't get mad. Sonnie and I noticed that in the last three weeks your mind has gone downhill dramatically. You've regressed."

Rachel studied them. They must know. Had someone leaked Chase's escape plan? She tried to act nonchalant. "I suppose I've been preoccupied with Chase."

"Yes, Chase. He's who I wanted to talk to you about."

Rachel gazed right and left, over her shoulders. They were too close to the building to talk. She grabbed Izzy's arm and tried tugging her away. Izzy dug her feet into the ground and refused to move.

"No. I have to say this."

"Not here!" Rachel's voice rose. She yanked her hard, but Izzy didn't budge.

"Tell her," Sonnie chided.

Izzy took a deep breath and leaned toward her. "I think you're pregnant."

## Chapter 23  Rachel

Rachel couldn't believe this was happening to her. There were others sleeping together. Why her?

The adolescent cravings in Project Dream had skyrocketed. The eighteen boys who came in with the first crew had all slept with someone—except Lenny. And Rachel wasn't totally sure he hadn't slept with that quiet little girl. Some girls just couldn't resist a bad boy—especially out in the middle of a desert.

The boys far outnumbered the girls, too. Girls became a commodity. None were raped but not because all of the boys held higher moral standards, but because Lenny Emling did. Since his first week there when he beat the life out of that kid, no one messed with him.

And Lenny lurked in the dark, defending the girls. He averted several attempts of boys—all from the original "reformatory" eighteen—forcing themselves on unwilling participants. He had an uncanny way of showing up when people least expected.

Could he read minds? Kids said the sandstone walls talked to him, which tempted Rachel to ask if he knew if she was pregnant or not. She blushed.

"They say Indians talk to you," she told him.

Lenny's big head bounced up and down with mirth for a change.

"You know what they s-say about y-you?"

"Me?" Rachel responded. "I'm afraid to ask."

"The town of Rachel that sits at the edge of Area 51 was named after y-you."

"That's hilarious. Why do they say that?"

Lenny's face reddened. "B-because the desert looks so beautiful at s-sunset." He lowered his head and slouched his shoulders.

"That's sweet of you to say."

"Well, y-you n-need to be careful around here."

"Who do I need to be careful of?'

He shrugged. "Everyone."

"Tell me. Who?"

He shrugged again.

"Chase? Do I need to worry about Chase?"

"Nah; Chase is ok-kay. Just everyone else."

"Everyone but Chase? You think he's a nice guy?"

Lenny hesitated and then said, "I know he is."

Rachel trusted Lenny. His simple seal of approval for Chase pacified her. His words gave her the push she needed. Mulling over her possible pregnancy alone had been difficult. Her breasts swelled. She missed her period a second time. Hope that Izzy was wrong dimmed.

Though she was terrified to tell Chase about the possibility of bringing a child of his into this world, Lenny's words had boosted her confidence.

Did Chase love her? The way she loved him? Maybe. He hadn't talked of leaving lately. Regardless, she felt compelled to tell him.

So later that evening when Chase emerged from the observatory, Rachel was waiting outside for him. Despite the confidence Lenny had inspired, she shuddered.

"Hey," he said. "I thought you were going to bring a blanket?

"What? Oh, I forgot."

"That's okay, I can grab one from the observatory." He turned to go back inside, but Rachel placed her hand on his arm, gingerly. He glanced her way. "Is everything all right?"

She shook her head.

Chase slipped an arm around her. "Let's find a place we can talk."

They meandered behind the observatory where a patch of rocks lodged in sand provided makeshift benches and seats. The moon cast an eerie eggshell and gray light onto their shoulders. The color faded to black, reappeared, and faded again as clouds scuttled over, under, and around the half crescent.

He led her toward a big flat rock, his hand on the small of her back. They sat down, and he faced her. Took her hands in his.

"Rachel, you're shaking. What's wrong?"

What was wrong? She was terrified he'd ask her if the baby was his, that's what was wrong. She wasn't a virgin when they made love. She'd foolishly slept with both John Michael and Todd Kennedy early on. She was ashamed and sorry for that now. Like some of the other kids, Rachel had been desperately lonely in those early months. But she had since been faithful to Chase.

"Did something happen?" He rubbed her hands gently and then, as if an idea suddenly dawned on him, his eyes widened. "Are you thinking of coming with me?"

"Oh, Chase." She tilted her head backward and let out a long breath. "You can't still be thinking of leaving."

He spent a quiet moment staring. "Then what is it, Rachel? Are you saying goodbye? Is that what you want?"

Then when she wanted so desperately to be strong, a weakness rushed through her. She slouched, and he immediately wrapped his arms around her.

"Rachel?"

Too much time passed before she could speak, but he didn't press her. Instead, he held her until she composed herself.

"I'm pregnant," she said flat out.

She couldn't make eye contact. She buried her gaze in the sand at her feet. My God, she was only sixteen years old. Chase was seventeen. What would they do?

He tightened his grip on her so swiftly the motion took her breath away. He rested his chin on her shoulder, held her close. He sat quietly for so long she thought she'd go mad. Then she felt the soft stroke of his hand guiding her ear toward his lips. "Okay…give me a minute…to process this. You're pregnant."

"Yes."

Of course, he needed time to digest this disaster. She spent the past seven days dancing with denial and disbelief. When she realized the truth, she collected herself and faked strength in front of Izzy and Sonnie. But frankly, she wanted to go home. She was pregnant. She needed her mother. She needed Lisa.

"Who knows?" he spoke so low she could barely hear him.

"Izzy and Sonnie."

"Don't tell another person, and tell them not to say anything to anyone."

"They won't.

He pushed her away lightly and stared into her eyes.

"Come away with me."

"No, Chase—"

He shook her shoulders gently. "They will never allow you to have this baby. Or worse. They'll let you give birth and take the baby away. A child of two dreamers? They'll make our baby a science experiment."

A moan escaped her. He'd said our baby. Her tears blurred everything around her in the dark night.

"Come with me," he uttered. "Leave with me, and we'll never look back."

"They'll find us."

"My father won't let them. He'll protect us."

"How?"

"I can't tell you. I can only say this is a sure thing."

"He would hide us?"

"Yes, there is a place for us to go. They'll never find us. He's just waiting for the right moment."

"But what about my sister? And my parents? My father is ill. If something hap—"

"Sh." He put a finger to her lips and shook his head. "You can never come back."

"But, my sister—"

"She couldn't know. They will say we died. We will change our identities."

"How? Like a witness protection program?"

"The government won't be protecting us if that's what you're asking. We will be running from them."

"No one can run from this government. That's impossible." She placed a palm on her forehead. Chase was deluding himself.

"It's possible for me because of my father. And now? It is for you, too."

Voices from kids exiting the observatory distracted them. Rachel buried her face in Chase's shirt. They held their breaths, hoping no one would see them. The kids meandered toward the dorms. Chase and Rachel waited quietly as they strolled away.

During that silence, torturous thoughts flowed through her. The pregnancy. The escape. She loved him. He loved her. She wanted her mother. Her father was ill. Gee was in poor health.

Lisa would think she was dead.

The ground beneath her began to sway. Next weekend she would see Lisa in Phoenix. She wouldn't tell her, but she would know then. Know if she could leave her.

"Give me some time to think this over," she said.

Yes, next weekend she would give him her answer.

*****

On Friday evening in Phoenix, she met the national icon, Chase's pilot father. He took her hand gently into his and said he was glad to meet her at last. She surmised Chase had spoken of her.

*He knows.*

Her face reddened, but he smiled and nodded while Chase stood beside her holding her elbow to keep her from collapsing. She had never been so weak in her life. They conversed for a while. He said he'd like to meet her family, and she explained they had missed their connecting flight and wouldn't be there until the morning.

"Well, I'm glad to have met you." He nodded toward her. Chase kissed her, and they excused themselves.

Rachel watched them walk away, father and son.

She spent the rest of Friday evening with the other kids whose families weren't arriving until Saturday.

The next morning when she exited the dormitory, Chase stood in the courtyard waiting for her. When their eyes met, he hurried toward her. He pulled her aside, away from the others.

She spoke first. "You mentioned me to your father?"

"No, I didn't."

"But he said he was glad to finally meet me. How did—"

"Don't ask, Rachel. My father has lots of connections."

"How could he possibly know me without you telling him about me?"

His face strained. "Everyone knows you. Even the President of the United States. He knows every name of any dreamer who moved to the top ten. Our names are known to many."

"That's impossible." Her voice raised. "How would they—"

He pulled her close and right there in front of everyone, he kissed her lips long and hard, silencing her. When he removed his lips from hers, his blue eyes pierced her.

He leaned his forehead onto hers and whispered. "I love you."

She felt the cold rush of their two bodies separating when he removed his arms from her. He walked backward a few steps, staring at her, before turning and hurrying away. He disappeared into the oncoming crowd, and her eyes searched the throng for Lisa, her head still reeling from the words she so desperately loved hearing.

When Lisa's face peeked through the crowd, Rachel ran toward her and threw her arms around her. "I missed you. "

Rachel was wiping away tears.

"What's wrong?" Lisa asked.

"Nothing. Nothing at all. Everything's fine. More than fine." She released her and picked up a lock of Lisa's hair. Sifted the blonde strands through her fingers. "Your hair, it's longer."

Lisa's eyes roamed Rachel's face. "I decided to let it grow. Are you sure you're all right?"

"I'm great. Where's Mom?"

"She's not coming. Pops came."

"Why not? Is it dad?"

Lisa nodded.

"The cancer? Has the cancer come back?"

Lisa closed her eyes and nodded. "With a vengeance."

Diagnosed eight months ago with small cell carcinoma lung cancer, her father had only missed one Phoenix family meeting. Even throughout his chemotherapy, he made the trip—until last month.

"How bad?"

Lisa's fingers slipped around her sister's arm. "Bad, but we can talk about that later."

Rachel had seen this expression on Lisa's face before. Sheer desperation.

"I have to tell you something before Pops catches up," she glanced behind her. "You must listen to me. I had a dream."

*Oh no.*

Lisa leaned in and spoke so faintly Rachel could hardly hear her. "Someone handed you a card with your picture on it. Only your name was Sally someone. You and a boy ran to a plane, and the plane rose in the sky and exploded."

Rachel became acutely aware of the nearby people and buildings. Could someone hear a whisper? She shook her head subtly. Lisa appeared to contemplate the gesture.

In her head, she begged God to stop Lisa from saying more. "You always have such strange dreams. You hate to fly." She forced a laugh, widening her eyes.

Lisa became quiet. Her face paled. When she spoke, her voice flowed calmly. "I know. I have such silly dreams."

Lisa's grip tightened like a vice. She gave a minuscule dip of her chin, and Rachel relaxed her shoulders, relieved. They carried on glibly in conversation before Rachel realized Lisa was stroking her hand. Her fingers were forming images on her palm, letters. She was drawing words like they had done in the back seat of the car when they were little. When they didn't want Mom and Dad to know their conversation.

She concentrated. Felt the tip of her nail drawing curves. Finally, she decoded what Lisa had been marking over and over in her hand. "2 planes."

"So we have to redo the kitchen." Lisa camouflaged her true conversation by talking about a leak in their roof at home.

"I see." Rachel waited for Lisa to talk with her fingers again.

Initially, she had difficulty deciphering the words. She drew a question mark on Lisa's palm. Lisa persisted. Pressed harder as she drew. "Cargo plane 1 ok." Then, "Plane 2 crash."

"I wish you could fly home and help Pops with the kitchen. But I know you can't. You can't go anywhere."

Rachel squeezed out a smile.

"I must," she drew on Lisa's palm.

"No," she drew back.

"Yes."

"No."

Lisa drew words again. "Plane 2, crash. Foxtrot crash."

"Foxtrot?"

They drew words for quite a while. Lisa fingered the message on Rachel's palm again and again, but Rachel struggled to understand. Then right before her grandfather arrived, Rachel accurately interpreted the words. "Plane 1 good. Plane 2 Foxtrot will b shot down."

But Lisa, being Lisa, wouldn't risk her misunderstanding. Rachel watched in horror as Lisa leaned toward her ear. She backed away, but Lisa held on and faintly—Rachel could barely make the words out—she uttered, "Chase must get out soon. They're watching him. But you can't go. If he takes the second plane, it will crash."

Her nails dug into Rachel's forearms. Next, she thought she felt Lisa grab her palm, but it was Pops. He tugged her away from Lisa and wrapped his arms around her.

At the end of the day, before they parted ways, Lisa etched secret words one last time. "Plane 1 good, Foxtrot crash." She flashed Rachel a hopeless expression.

The next day, they ate breakfast together and spent the late morning and early afternoon at the pool, shoulder to shoulder with the others. There was no time for talk.

Right before they left, Pops loaded the luggage into the cab. Lisa hugged Rachel and whispered in her ear, "One light."

Rachel didn't understand, but before she could question what one light meant, Lisa spoke again, her eyes sad. "Dad is dying. They don't expect him to live out the week."

# Chapter 24  Rachel and Chase

For twenty-four hours they argued. They ran far into the desert after midnight. Climbed the first hill to the top and crammed themselves into an alcove of molten rock on the hill's backside. Sonnie named a four by four patch of rock on that ledge, the dead zone. There, because of the way the boulders sat, cameras could not pick up movement or noise.

They prayed Sonnie was as brilliant as everyone claimed.

"You have to come with me." Chase leaned his forehead against hers. His hands gripped her forearms as if nothing could pry him from her. "They'll never let you keep the baby."

"They may if they know it is the child of two dreamers."

"No, they won't," he said. "Rachel, my father was coming for me tomorrow, but he has agreed—"

"Tomorrow?"

"Listen to me. I told him you were pregnant."

"You did?"

"Yes, he can change his plans and come Thursday instead. But I need to let him know tonight."

"What do you mean he can come Thursday?"

"For you to come with us, he'll need to get you an identity."

"So he'd come Thursday instead of Tuesday?" She plopped down hard on the rock. "Dear God, no."

He knelt beside her. "What's wrong?"

She put her head in her hands. "I can't go."

"I can't leave you here."

"You have to go without me."

"I can't leave you, our baby. You have to come."

"You don't understand. I can't."

"Yes, you can Rachel." He grabbed her arms. "I'm not leaving without you."

"Chase, if you don't go tomorrow, we may never get out of here, but if you leave tomorrow, maybe later you and your father can get the baby and me out."

"That doesn't make sense. Come with me on Thursday. We'll go far away and never look back."

"I'm going to ask you two questions. You must answer honestly."

"Anything."

"Does your father have to take a different plane if he comes on Thursday?"

"Yes, but he has access to lots of planes."

"Then no, I can't go with you on Thursday," she cried.

"Rachel!" He set his hands on the back of her shoulders and drew her into him.

"My sister had a dream about two planes," she whispered. "The second one will crash. You have to take the first."

"Your sister?"

"Yes."

"You told her?" His face couldn't hide his fury.

"I didn't tell her a thing."

"Then why would she mention a plane?"

"You don't know her. Her dreams are clearer than ours. She also saw them watching you."

"Who?"

"I don't know who, but she's never wrong. You have to get out of here tomorrow."

"It's two days. Forty-eight hours. I can wait."

"No, you can't. The second plane will crash."

"Rachel, the plane won't crash."

"Yes, it will. If you don't leave on the first one, you'll die. We'll both die."

"You're wrong. You don't know how resourceful my father is."

She stood. He did the same, clutching at her. She whispered in his ear. "He names his planes, doesn't he?"

He didn't respond.

"He names them, doesn't he?"

"Yes, he does. Lots of pilots do."

"The plane coming tomorrow he calls cargo."

Again, he grew quiet.

"I'm right, aren't I?"

"He calls it his cargo plane, but that doesn't mean a thing."

Rachel dropped her head, fighting tears. "Chase, trust me, you have to go without me."

"I can't."

"You can and you will. If you wait for the second plane—a plane your father calls Foxtrot—we will all be killed."

Chase's face wrinkled. "That's the name of my father's plane. How did you—"

"Lisa. I'm telling you, she's never wrong." Rachel slouched into him, crying. He set his head on top of hers.

"Let me think," he said, but Rachel forced him to listen to her. She talked about Lisa, and he admitted Lenny Emling had told him stories about her, too. She said those stories were true. No one could see the future like her. But Chase was willing to risk their lives to get Rachel out. Rachel agreed, yes, it might be worth risking their lives.

But not their baby's.

"Time is running out. I have to let him know."

"How?"

"I have to signal him at three o'clock." Chase touched his watch. The blue light flashed 2:57. "Please say yes, Rachel."

"You'll signal him? How?"

"With a light. A satellite will pick it up. One flash, he comes tomorrow. Two, he comes Thursday with an identity for you."

Rachel closed her eyes and tipped her head backward, breaking into a sob. He held her until she composed herself.

When she did, she whispered, "Right before Lisa left, she said something I didn't understand until right now."

"What?"

"One light."

The black night closed around her. "Go for our baby."

Lisa would not be wrong about this. Rachel had to think quickly. Talk him out of staying. "When I have the baby, I'll be at a hospital, right?"

"I would think so, yes."

"Getting the baby and me out of a hospital will be so much easier."

He seemed to consider the thought.

"It will work. You have to go."

She argued fast. This plan to take her was too rushed. She reminded him that his father had been waiting for months for the perfect day. Forty-eight hours mattered. Being cautious and staying alive for their child was more important than them being together. If his father could devise a plan to get him out of the heavily guarded Area 51, then certainly he could get her and their baby out of a hospital. "As long as I know you are alive, I can do this. I can survive. Just go now. Come back for us later."

"No."

"Chase, get a hold of yourself. You have to do this. For me. For our baby."

He couldn't speak. His anguish overpowered him. He cried until no more tears could come.

Finally, at 3 a.m., she rose because he couldn't. She walked to the edge of the dead zone, flashed the light once, and fell to the ground, crying.

*****

In the morning, a nurse passed out the normal morning vitamins. Rachel thought hers was a deeper gray. Two hours later, she began cramping. Three hours later she began bleeding. By dinner, she had spontaneously aborted the baby.

Chase knelt at her bedside that evening. He buried his face in her pillows, and the two of them cried like babies. He removed a cross on a silver chain from around his neck, and he placed it on Rachel's neck. She removed her gold miraculous medal of the Blessed Virgin and placed it around his.

"I will come for you," he whispered in her ear. "It may take ten months, or it may take ten years, but never forget. I'll come for you."

Five hours later, in the middle of the night, Chase Finley disappeared.

## Chapter 25  Rachel

Rachel kept stock-still in her seat while they questioned her. Cramping from the miscarriage persisted. Pain medication eased the discomfort, but the strength also dulled her cognizance, which may have been their intent.

"Did he say where he was going?"

"Who?"

"Rachel, we know you spent Monday night with Chase. He must have said something."

What she wanted to say, "Yes, he told me you'd never let me have this baby," sat at the back of her throat.

"I told him I was pregnant and we fought," she whimpered instead.

"Fought?"

"He didn't believe the baby was his." She sobbed. Dropped her face into her hands. Pretended how she would have acted had he doubted he fathered the child.

That he didn't doubt he was the father made her love him more.

Which now made her cry harder, shielding her true feelings from McDaniel, Swarthy, and Ms. Merryman.

They released her to bedrest, questioning her off and on throughout the day, allowing her to sleep through the night, and summoning her again the next day to appear before McDaniel. She walked languidly despite feeling a bit healthier after uninterrupted sleep. She could think of nothing but Chase.

She prayed he made it out safely.

In McDaniel's office, she sat down on an overstuffed leather chair, opposite Jerry McDaniel. She tucked her knees together in front of the big desk and clasped her hands in her lap, expecting the worst of the questioning now that her health had returned. What happened, shocked her.

McDaniel's face sagged. For the first time, she witnessed sincerity in him.

"Rachel, I'm sorry to have to tell you this. I didn't have the heart to tell you last night." He swallowed deeply. Rachel watched his Adam's apple rise and fall.

She realized that he hadn't said a word to her the previous day. He'd let Merryman and Swarthy do the badgering. He checked on her late in the night, too. She saw him standing in her doorway but, exhausted, she couldn't come to.

She raised her chin, considered his mien. Yes, Merryman and Swarthy had done the coercing. Jerry McDaniel had not said a word.

"I wish I could spare you from this. It seems more than a sixteen-year-old can handle." He appeared positively disgusted. He wiped his face with one palm, and when he returned his hand to the desk, he looked tired. "There is no easy way to tell you. I'm sorry. Your father passed away last night."

The words didn't register. A numbness grew inside her. First, her arms tingled, then her legs. What had the man across from her said? Where was she? Her father had died? Black speckles blurred her vision. She felt her body slipping down the big russet-colored chair. For a moment, she thought she was in a waterpark, sliding.

No, she was at Project Dream. Her father had died, and the nice-looking man with the wise blue eyes and the frightened face was sprinting around the big desk.

She twisted and realized her knees had hit the gray Persian rug that covered the sandstone floor. She felt big arms grasping her shoulders, lifting her off the ground.

Blackness consumed her.

# Chapter 26  Jerry McDaniel

Chase Finley's disappearance was a problem for Washington. His father, the most decorated pilot in the Air Force since World War II, had nabbed his son out of a top-secret program and performed a disappearing act. No signs of him or his thirteen-year-old daughter remained at their Salt Lake City home. Their son, one of Project Dream's top ten, had vanished.

In the pitch black of night, Pete Finley had flown a single-engine plane into Area 51, skirting the desert mountain range by a matter of yards to avoid radar. There were tracks in places where he had actually landed, steered the plane across the ground, and lifted off again. He'd done that several times, in fact, to avoid surveillance. He had plotted his course perfectly.

The CIA was investigating if someone on the inside helped him locate those dead zones in the radar. Furthermore, there were points of entry into and out of Area 51 where there was absolutely no avoiding detection. Suspicions mounted. Someone in the control room had to have turned their back. Investigations had been initiated on the security officers who were on duty that night.

Area monitoring had picked up some motion, but officers said they had been preparing for the forecasted windstorm for four days. They were preoccupied. No one suspected a plane could fly so close to the mountains during a storm like that. Surely a pilot would have to fly higher above the mountains to survive the bouncing. Now government officials were researching if anyone in the bordering airport control rooms had a history with Finley.

Or anyone on the ground in Area 51. A power surge at 4:15 in the morning lasted fifteen minutes. Instructors, security, and maintenance men were polygraphed. Everyone passed. From all inspection, the storm had caused the surge.

When McDaniel entered the Washington office, he faked concern. He could be brilliant at camouflaging true emotion.

"I knew Pete Finley," he said. "I worked beside him in Washington during the general's debacle. More patriotism flowed through Pete's veins than you, me, Scott, or any of the United States presidents. Way more."

"Then what's going on?" Steve Larson looked ragged. Scott did, too. Both of their necks were on the line. The head of the CIA had peeked his nose outside the Middle East to ask what was going on in Area 51.

"My guess is Pete knew he would never get his kid out of the project through the proper channels. This sixth sense runs in families. I heard rumors about his telepathy from fellow pilots."

"Or he had access to confidential files."

"Not likely." McDaniel had debated that suspicion himself. "He's been in Salt Lake City as a civilian for quite a while now."

"Well, what about the girl?" Scott broke into the conversation, which until now had seemed exclusively between Jerry and Steve Larson.

"Excuse me?" Jerry infused incredulity into his tone.

"The girl everyone in the desert seems to be swooning over. My God, someone said they named that hole-in-the-wall city after her."

"Rachel Callahan?" Jerry fought a grin. "She was sleeping with Finley."

"Does she know anything?" Scott asked.

"He left without her; what do you think?"

"I saw that girl when I visited." Steve Larson flashed a confounded expression.

McDaniel was enjoying this.

"For God's sake, Jerry, what is she doing there? There's no way that girl is a teenager. She has to be in her twenties."

"She's sixteen, sir."

"Are you sure? Sixteen?"

Jerry took a moment to relish their disbelief before responding. "I'm sure."

"And she was pregnant?" Larson raised his eyebrows.

Jerry closed his eyes for effect, nodded, and raised his eyelids slowly. "Miscarried."

"How many does that make?" Scott groaned.

"She's the third. But we've remedied the problem. We're placing the girls on birth control."

"Three miscarriages too late." Larson sounded disgusted.

"Better than four." Jerry was having fun.

Bright sunshine filtered through the ceiling-to-floor windows of the Washington office. The room was hot. Glass covered one entire wall. In the distance, a small opening between the trees and buildings allowed Lincoln to peek directly into their room from his Memorial. Everything about the view out those windows was patriotic and stately. Yet, somehow, Steve Larson's ninth-floor office no longer seemed so high up.

Larson's head bobbed over the reports on the desk. Jerry himself had signed the last quarterly report sent to the White House. Within the last three months, a few of these kids had located weapons planted as far away as Death Valley. There was no way Larson could pull the plug on the project now.

"I can't express how impressed White House officials are with the results."

Jerry grinned. Maybe he had a marginal amount of mind-reading ability himself.

"We can't have this sex, drugs, and rock and roll obliterate what we've accomplished."

"It won't," Scott interjected. He had removed his suit coat, and Jerry noticed his shirt's stained armpits as he spoke. "Since we allowed them the marihuana, within moderation, of course, their morale has lifted. And as far as the cocaine goes, I don't know why, but it inspires these kids to dream. The best of them are snorting."

"Not true. There are several good dreamers not using. The top person never uses." Jerry was having fun.

"Who?" Scott glowered at Jerry.

"Izzy Jimenez."

Larson sifted through the reports. "Isn't she the one whose brother was asking questions around the border?"

"Yes, sir, we've taken care of that. He's no longer permitted in the country."

Quiet, again.

"Excellent. We must rid the program of outside as well as inside problems." He turned pages. "I see here a few kids locate items no matter where the birds hide them."

Larson was referring to the men who planted the weapons for the kids to locate remotely. They called those officers birds. The birds had pushed the hiding spots further and further away. Two and three years of intensely training kids had produced better results than even the Arizona professors predicted. Cabinet members worried Pete Finley was headed to Russia—or worse, the Middle East—with that knowledge.

"Yes, sir, as far away as Death Valley with four or five identifying items even beyond that."

"Who are they?"

"Rachel Callahan is one. Lenny Emling, Isabella Jimenez, John Michael Turnbull, and well, Chase, of course."

"The Callahan girl. Lately, she flits in and out of the top ten." Larson glanced over the top of his glasses.

"Since the pregnancy. With the miscarriage and Finley's disappearance, she'll be fine. I'll see to it."

Yes, he'd take care of it.

"I suppose that's the silver lining in this entire mess. I hear she's superb. But everyone had high hopes for him. Are there others as mentally and physically capable as Finley?"

"A few." McDaniel himself heard the insincerity in his tone.

Nobody equaled the golden boy, Chase Finley. His well-rounded, raw talent went unmatched, but others excelled in individual skills. No one was faster or stronger than Lenny. The Sonnie girl soared in mathematical aptitude. A boy, Todd Kennedy, stood out amongst his peers despite his size, although clearly, he fell victim to drug abuse. Who else? There were so many with individual strengths. It was a crapshoot who would turn out the best. "We are still determining their talents."

"We can't lose any more of the good ones." Larson removed his glasses and sat back.

"We won't, sir," Scott assured him. "I guarantee that."

You can't guarantee anything was Jerry's first thought. *Only I can.*

"What will stop more from attempting to leave?" Larson lowered his chin and peered at Scott.

"We'll circulate rumors Chase and his family are deceased." Jerry responded before Scott could. He almost felt the pull from him. There was an invisible rope in the room. Jerry and Randall were in a tug-of-war contest. Steve Larson unknowingly toggled the middle of that twine. "We'll say it was an unfortunate plane crash."

"They won't believe it."

"They will, sir. We turned Finley's hangar upside down for evidence. In doing so, we were able to fabricate some fairly convincing pictures."

"Just make sure they're convincing enough to let these kids understand this is a lifetime commitment."

"They'll understand." Again, Jerry responded.

His measures to circulate rumors that the kids who left the program had mysteriously died were paying off. He'd do the same for Chase. Then right before they were released to the colleges of the government's choice, he'd hit them with the "make one wrong move and your families pay" threat.

Out of the one hundred students and four remaining replacement kids training in the wings, only a few worried him. All girls. Isabelle Jimenez talked too much. Dawn Davis had the will of Angela Merkel. And Rachel Callahan was a ticking bomb.

But Annie Sherman could handle the little girl, Izzy, and he could take care of the beauty, Rachel.

"You needn't worry, Steve." It was the first time Jerry had the guts to call Larson by his first name. "Everything is under control."

## Chapter 27  Izzy

Izzy could point to the kids who would become alcoholics. Her own father hid tequila in a coffee cup every morning until his liver gave out and the cancer set in. Now all around her, kids snuck sips of alcohol in the morning and afternoon and drank heartily under the stars.

Major problems with drugs developed, too, which made Todd Kennedy rapidly climb the ladder of popularity. He held the pharmaceutical keys tightly in his hand. Proficient in poker, Todd joked and dared kids to toss alcohol and drugs—which they obtained from Swarthy or bought on the sly at the cafeteria—onto the table. Then he swept in like a vulture on a rabbit. Kids quickly learned if they wanted drugs: befriend Todd.

"Be careful of him," Izzy warned Rachel.

Easy access was a temptation, and hiding alcohol or drugs? That was always a bad sign. Besides alcohol, marihuana, and cocaine, now drugs in the form of pills made a presence in the desert. Yesterday, Izzy noticed Rachel slipping a pill under her tongue when she thought no one was looking. Izzy suspected Todd gave it to her.

She prayed it wasn't from McDaniel.

"You need to be careful around Jerry McDaniel, too," she told her. "Whatever you do, don't confide in him."

McDaniel had allowed Rachel two weeks at home after her father passed away. Such a long stay had never been granted. When she returned and heard the news Chase's plane had been shot down, Rachel didn't believe it.

Slowly, over the next few weeks, instructors circulated newspaper articles claiming the Coast Guard had recovered plane parts in the Pacific Ocean. Rachel refused to believe any of the reports.

"They're lying," she insisted.

Then one day, several pictures of plane parts floating in the water fell into the hands of Dawn Davis. Dawn grew up on the California coast as the single grandchild of some age-old actor, whom none of the kids knew. She exuded a haughty, pompous demeanor and constantly belittled others. If she could get someone in trouble or cause them grief, she did. Not many kids liked her. Some thought she was a mole. She shot her mouth off a lot, with no repercussions. Not very proficient in remote viewing or academics, kids thought they may have brought her in to spy on them.

"Where'd you get these?" Rachel grabbed the photographs from Dawn.

"Ken Swarthy gave them to us."

"No, he didn't."

"Yes, he did. He said they were still searching for bodies."

Rachel studied the pictures so long that Izzy stepped forward and glanced over her shoulder to take a peek. Rachel seemed focused on one picture in particular: a photo of the plane's side panel that had been recovered. The word "Foxtrot" spread across it.

"What is it?" Izzy asked.

"That's not the plane," Rachel responded. She hurried off. Izzy watched her traipse directly to Jerry McDaniel's office.

Later that evening, Rachel locked herself in her room and wouldn't come out. Izzy could hear her crying. She pleaded with her to open the door, but Rachel refused. She didn't come out of her room the next day, either. The following day Merryman forced her to attend classes, but Rachel kept her distance from everyone.

For the next week, despite Izzy's constant attempts, Rachel wouldn't talk to her or anyone else—only her sister.

She accepted several phone calls from home, but she even seemed angry with Lisa.

During one call, Izzy listened from around the corner, expecting to hear Rachel crying about her father, Chase, or the miscarriage. Instead, Rachel argued furiously. Something about the plane crash.

When the conversation ended, Rachel stomped to her room. Izzy followed her in.

"I told you. I don't want to talk to anyone." Rachel tried to push her out the door.

"I'm not leaving. This has all been too much for you, between losing your dad, and Chase, and the miscarriage—"

"It wasn't a miscarriage. They gave me something."

Izzy believed that. Two other girls claimed they'd been given something to abort unexpected pregnancies. Now all of the girls were forced to take birth control.

But there was something more than the miscarriage. More than even the deaths of her father and Chase. Rachel was keeping something from her. Worried, Izzy refused to leave her alone that evening. She stayed with her all night, probing. Finally, in a fit of despair and exhaustion, Rachel broke down sobbing. Izzy held her.

"I know there's something you're not telling me," she whispered.

They knew better now than to talk full-voiced. There were microphones everywhere.

"My sister said the plane named Foxtrot would crash," Rachel whispered back. "But he wasn't supposed to be on that plane. He was supposed to be on another plane."

"Then maybe he is alive?"

"No," she whimpered. "They changed planes. Jerry McDaniel showed me more photos."

She sobbed in Izzy's arms for a long time before she fell asleep. Izzy slept on the floor next to her bed in case she woke. In the morning, she helped her dress, and they went to breakfast and classes together, but something had changed in Rachel.

After that day, McDaniel summoned Rachel to his office more often. Izzy hated him taking advantage of her misery. Rachel insisted he continued asking questions about Chase's disappearance, but more and more favors befell her. Despite Rachel swearing McDaniel was a fatherly figure, Izzy's suspicions mounted.

Rachel began hanging out with Todd in the evenings, too. He had grown taller. Friendlier. Because of their time spent under the desert sun, a cute spray of freckles crossed his nose. Those speckles, amalgamated with his black hair and deep brown eyes, made him handsome. Rachel enjoyed listening to Todd talk about Las Vegas, the constellation, and his detestation of religion. Although Izzy didn't approve of Todd's constant drug use, as the weeks passed, his presence at least lifted Rachel's spirits.

He had grown up the only son of an ardent Catholic mother. Todd sometimes brought out his childhood Bible and initiated philosophical discussions. He quoted passages proving seers existed.

Of course, his mother had made notes in the margins regarding devils and spirits. Todd would read those, too, and laugh. Kids gathered to listen to his deep but comical views. His Bible debates both taunted and delighted kids.

"The Almighty gives us our sight," he said.

"I believe the devil whispers in our ear," John Michael debated.

"There is no such thing as a devil," Todd countered. "Only positivism and negativism. I choose to call positivism the Almighty. Others maintain that phenomenon is Buddha."

Kids chose sides to debate issues on those dark nights. Todd emerged as a leader. Naturally, that leadership impressed Rachel. His talons inched deeper into her skin.

Izzy hoped their relationship at least prevented Rachel from sleeping with anyone else.

Shamelessly, Rachel had told her, "Don't be a prude. I've slept with Chase, Todd, John Michael, and hmm, who else?"

*And Jerry McDaniel?*

Izzy didn't ask, but she did ask about Swarthy.

"You aren't sleeping with Swarthy, are you?"

"Hell, no. I can't stand him," Rachel said. "But he'd take me on a vacation if I did."

"Oh, Rachel don't." Izzy quickly said.

"I won't. But does it matter? Does anything really matter anymore?"

"Everything matters," Izzy told her.

Rachel simply shrugged. A stone-cold expression set on her face. The rumor that Chase and his family had died in a crash dimmed the last of Rachel's hope. Her personality changed. She became subdued. Todd Kennedy led her around like a lost kitten.

"She hasn't come to terms with Chase's death. She loved him. Everyone did," Sonnie said. "When Swarthy showed us pictures of pieces of Chase's plane floating off the coast, lots of kids' dreams of getting out died, especially Rachel's."

The story perpetuated the notion that leaving was impossible. Questions surfaced about the other dreamers who left. Rumors circulated that their records had been obliterated.

Some kids wanted to find out if that was true.

Next to the observatory, three connecting buildings, flat-roofed and with sandstone walls like the other buildings in Project Dream, were being erected. Security cameras flanked all three. Military trucks thundered in and out of the garages of one. More soldiers arrived. McDaniel announced plans to move the infirmary and central records to the new buildings.

A construction crew erected a tower on top of the second building. Kids with binoculars could see men pointing guns at them when they hiked the valley between the first and second mountain range.

One evening, Todd Kennedy tested them. He convinced several kids to take their evening party to the other side of the smallest hill, to the dead zone. They arrived early, the sun high in the sky. After they laid out their blankets and Todd snorted his cocaine, he stood up, laughing. "Let's see how close we can get to the line."

He took off running. Kids watched as he traversed the rocky patch of land beneath their hidden spot. He went straight down the hill, avoiding all paths.

Todd was lean and agile and jumped from rock to rock as if he'd been practicing. He made his way to the bottom of the hill and disappeared from view only to reappear minutes later in the valley. There he sprinted around the water hole toward the second mountain range. Within ten minutes, he was running up the switchbacks. The sun had begun to set, but a shadow of light still grazed the spiked boundary line above him.

Three switchbacks down from the spikes, Todd turned toward them, cupped his hand, and let his voice echo over valley and rock. "Come over. No one cares."

Suddenly, a noise whizzed to Izzy's left, and she heard a pecking sound, metal nipping rock. The noise reverberated from the second mountain range to their hiding spot. Everyone turned toward Todd. He took off running down the switchbacks. Through his binoculars, Marcus said it appeared a spray of bullets had etched a perfectly straight line in the rock about six feet above where Todd had stood.

They waited for what seemed an eternity until Todd found his way back to the dead zone.

"Did you see where they came from?" Todd asked, as if he had expected gunshots.

"What's going on?" Izzy tugged Rachel aside.

"Lenny thinks there are more snipers than those in the tower," Rachel explained.

"What do you mean snipers?"

"Izzy, you are so naive. They brought snipers in to detain us."

"Don't be ridiculous."

"It's t-true." Lenny confirmed. "They d-don't want k-kids trying to leave like Chase."

"Then why would Todd go up there?"

"We want them to watch us out here." Rachel beckoned to everyone with the wave of a hand. She sat on the blanket, and they crowded around her. Even Lenny.

"Why?"

"We're going to break into central records," Marcus confided.

Izzy's eyes widened. "Why in God's name would you do that?"

"To see if they are really killing kids that leave."

Izzy stood. "I want no part of this."

"Izzy." Marcus hurried to his feet, grabbed her hand.

"We need you." Rachel stood. "Todd can distract the men in the tower. Now that he's gone up once, they'll be watching him."

"There are cameras around the campus that aren't connected." Sonnie spoke up. "But there are blind spots. They have orders to revamp security. Once that's done, we have no chance."

"Are you people crazy?"

"That's w-what I told them." Lenny threw his two cents in.

"I want no part of this." Izzy began walking again. Rachel yanked her back.

"You are Annie Sherman's favorite student. We need you to ask her for help some night."

"I will not."

"Izzy," Marcus crept closer. "If we create a night of distraction, one of us can sneak in. The best day would be a weekend when Sherman is here, and Swarthy and Merryman are gone."

"You can't distract everyone."

"If you take care of Sherman, Todd will distract the tower guards," he muttered.

"What about everyone else?"

"If Lenny creates a disturbance, everyone else will come running. Sonnie can send out a short power surge that brings down a few more cameras."

"Lenny?" Izzy turned to him. "You'd do that?"

He shrugged. Of course, Lenny would do anything for Rachel.

"Well, what about McDaniel? He stays if Swarthy leaves."

"I'll take care of him."

Izzy gazed directly into Rachel's eyes, and for the briefest second, Rachel's eyelids flickered and Izzy knew.

Rachel was already sleeping with Jerry McDaniel.

# Chapter 28  Ken Swarthy

Ken Swarthy didn't like Randall Scott or Joanne Merryman, but he hated Jerry McDaniel. That guy had eyes in the back of his head. He showed up digging around and sinking his teeth into everything Swarthy did or wanted to do at the most inopportune times. Especially concerning Rachel Callahan.

That girl was movie-star beautiful. Her dark hair and blue eyes, enticing. And her lips? Swarthy couldn't decide what would sink a man first, her eyes, her long, shapely legs, or those full, red lips.

And she was what? Seventeen? How old had she been when the golden boy had planted his seed in her, and they had been forced to exfoliate? That girl had rested her head under every hairy armpit in Project Dream—except his.

That infuriated him.

Swarthy closed his eyes and batted down the pressure climbing the veins in his neck. McDaniel had the gall to order him to stay away from Callahan. Swarthy could only imagine her legs wrapped around him, every luscious curve of her pressing against him.

He shook off the carnal longing and opened his eyes.

And what was up with this Lenny Emling dude always hanging around her, too? If the commander didn't have big plans for that kid after dreamland, he'd slip a bullet in his back. Every time McDaniel wandered two feet out of dreamland, Emling hovered around Rachel like a hired bodyguard.

He decided to approach Annie Sherman about the ogre.

"What's with that Lenny kid?"

"What do you mean?" Annie glowered. She tended to defend Lenny.

"He's a lurker, creepy. Hangs around in the background and watches everyone."

"He keeps to himself and if I were you, I wouldn't make him mad. No one wants a repeat performance of the first week when he beat that kid to death. McDaniel says they need his strength and speed in the Marines."

"Did that kid die?" Swarthy wasn't sure. Never cared to find out.

"He did."

"So Lenny Emling killed a kid with his bare hands."

"And a cafeteria tray."

"While the security guard stood five feet from him."

"That's right."

"But he tamed down after that. Before the second crew came in."

Annie folded her arms and studied him.

"Right," she said. "Before the second crew arrived. Before Rachel Callahan completed the one hundred."

Swarthy's face reddened. She had read his mind.

"She barely made it in, I hear." He attempted to appear nonchalant. "I heard they considered enrolling one of the backup kids from Phoenix instead of her."

"She was better than them. Lucky her." Annie Sherman's high hopes for Project Dream must have dampened. Her tone held a disgust never present in those first days.

"Well, it's a waste if you ask me."

"What do you mean?"

"Her in the army."

Annie looked at Swarthy as if he had a third eye.

"What?" He held his hands out.

"You're kidding me, right?"

"Kidding you about what?"

"Her going to the army? You think they're putting her in the military?"

"Aren't they?"

She sighed with astonishment. Her shock ended with a chuckle. "They're sending that girl to Hollywood when this is over. Big plans to use her for PR. Grab the attention of elitists."

"You're crazy."

Annie chortled.

"What's funny?"

Annie herself was nice looking. Her dimples surfaced when she laughed. Swarthy wouldn't mind slipping beneath the covers with her, but the love of her life lived fifty miles away, and she made the trip home to see him every weekend she could. Word about her was "hands off." Her father was a general. However, that hadn't discouraged him from trying once.

She'd shut him down as if he'd offered her an ice-cream cone in a snowstorm.

The coldness in her still showed. She shrugged and grinned. "Rachel Callahan will do what she wants, so y'all better be nice to her."

"She'll do what we tell her."

She shot him a long stare. "You have no idea what she is like, do you? Rachel Callahan may be confined to this place, but she's no man's doormat and never will be."

Something about Annie Sherman's smug smile annoyed him. "She'll cave."

"If anyone could spark more defiance into that girl's spirit, it wouldn't be you, Swarthy." Her eyes twinkled like stars in a black night. "Leave her alone. She'll never go for you. She's too smart."

"Don't be so sure. I can be very convincing."

"A girl like Rachel Callahan picks a guy. They don't pick her."

Briefly, Ken wondered if they were still talking about Rachel. "Maybe back in Erie, Pennsylvania, but now? She's in the middle of the desert."

"That's the thing about a tough broad. She can spot a worthless jerk of a guy in a big city, small town—or the middle of the desert."

The sting couldn't have hurt more if she had slapped him across the face. He understood. She hadn't been talking about Rachel.

"We'll see," he said under his breath.

"Yeah, well," she said over one shoulder right before she left the room. "You better look under the covers before you jump in bed. There's someone else there."

When the door slammed shut behind her, he didn't know who he hated more: Annie Sherman or Jerry McDaniel.

## Chapter 29  Izzy

Izzy flew so low under the radar, even nesting birds in trees couldn't see her.

The other girls flaunted their looks. As their time in the desert grew closer to graduation, they tested beauty and fashion trends enthusiastically. But makeup caked on a girl's face or expensive cleansing oils didn't impress Izzy. She declined testing night facial masks. Girls swore they made their skin creamy soft, but a vigorous cleansing with a washcloth and scented soap did Izzy fine.

Since they would be released to colleges in less than eighteen months, most had stepped up their game. They showed up to class with manicures, personally tinted makeup bases, fake eyelashes, and eyebrows trimmed so finely they looked painted on. Most owned hair extensions, all were tanned, and none left their room without a whiff of expensive perfume trailing behind them.

As long as their dreaming flourished, officials rewarded girls with the latest fads no matter how eccentric or costly. They could have any luxurious item they wanted. In a way, they were spoiled. Outwardly, the girls appeared trendy and content.

Inwardly? They suffered—especially Rachel.

"She's going to get into trouble." Izzy talked to herself as she gathered her hair back into a ponytail, plucked a few hairs from her soft eyebrows, not too many, and rubbed sunscreen into her cheeks.

Rachel still talked of breaking into central records, but not as much. With Ken Swarthy breathing down their necks about their placement in the program, Rachel, along with the others,

seemed hard-pressed to perform. Their factfinding plans fell
to the back burner. Izzy hoped they'd forget the whole dumb
idea.

She stood back. Stared at her pale face.

"You look fine. Don't let their glamorous looks or
ridiculous plans tempt you. Stay in the top ten. Out of the
limelight."

She nudged her chin left and right to inspect her face.
"And out of the sun."

On one cheek, she spotted a streak of sunscreen. She
rubbed in the white line and applied more, as if the lotion
could protect her from more than the sun. Then she spread
the cream over her neck and exposed limbs.

Sometimes, Rachel's arms were darker than Marva's, who
was African American. But Izzy doubted the sun would harm
Rachel. Izzy had met Rachel's mother. Not a wrinkle marred
her. She looked thirty. Rachel said her grandmother was young
looking, too, despite spending years basking in the sun.

*Figures.*

Izzy had no idea if the women on her father's side of the
family were wrinkled or not. None of them had lived to see
sixty.

Annoyed, she snapped her head back and forth,
inspecting for more streaks. From every angle, life challenged
her.

"I'm not giving myself to just anyone, either." She slipped
into a blue and white bathing suit cover-up. "Just because a
girl is lonely doesn't mean she has to sleep with a guy."

She had crushes on boys. Samuel at one time, John
Michael, at another. Marcus. Steve. She even admired Todd
Kennedy before he and Rachel hooked up. None of the boys
seemed even remotely interested in her. Marcus had once
called her too skinny.

When in grade school she had worried about her belly fat,
now she had trouble keeping weight on, which of course
wasn't good. Her timing forever failed her. Toggling the

hundred-pound line at Project Dream hurt. Here strength was key—both mental and physical.

Having seen spirits and future events as far back as she could remember, Izzy remained one of the strongest dreamers. Every afternoon, she sat in her space in the sandstone building and concentrated, tapped into her higher self, and located weapons hidden all over Nevada, Arizona, and California, and last week she had identified objects in the state of Washington.

They referred to militia personnel who hid weapons or "seeds" as birds. Recently, the birds had tucked away explosives in a secluded forest. No one located the woodland area except her and Lenny. Even Rachel guessed the munitions were hidden somewhere in Oregon.

Izzy and Lenny both said the eight four-by-four packages sat in hollowed-out ground in the middle of pine trees. Instructors had afforded them a few clues, and some kids dreamed of boxes in the woods, but only she and Lenny placed them near Seattle.

"The forest is near Seattle for sure, but why do I keep seeing a storm? A hurricane," she asked. The angels showed her gale-force winds. In the end, Sherman informed her the explosives were a hundred miles northwest of Seattle in a place called Hurricane Ridge. Izzy hadn't even heard of any Hurricane Ridge.

Lenny, of course, narrowed in on the latitude and longitude. He was that exceptional.

But Izzy's mental abilities didn't matter if she couldn't keep up physically. In the end, only those who excelled in both areas would make the final top ten. Rumors swirled those on the bottom would be expelled.

What the heck happened to you if you were removed from the project? That was the million-dollar question. Izzy didn't want to find out.

So today they were swimming, and she wasn't going to skim the bottom of the lake and take it easy floating in peace and quiet like she normally did. She planned on staying near the surface and swimming hard.

But naturally, because she hadn't swum to her potential in over a year, Swarthy had assigned her position ninety-three. She would begin the race next to the worst seven swimmers. That meant she had nearly the farthest to swim to the first turn when, this time, every second counted.

That would teach her to dog it.

And as if her position at the end of the line wasn't unfortunate enough, she had started her period this morning.

"I'm not only a klutz. I'm dog-down unlucky."

She may enjoy flying low under the radar, but now she must expose her true capability. Disclose her extreme speed in the water. Annie Sherman said the top dreamers might be permitted to select the college of their choice, and Izzy wanted, no, she had to go to San Diego.

Living near Friendship Park where Americans could meet their Mexican kin on Sunday afternoons would allow her to see Enrique and meet Sammy. Federales stopped Enrique at the border these days. He wouldn't risk taking Sammy across illegally, so Mama visited him there now.

Hence, getting into the University of San Diego was paramount. She couldn't have it any other way. She had to prove to them she was Navy SEAL worthy, whatever that meant.

She bent her elbows and lifted her arms, examining her developing biceps. Maybe she had only worked her way up to benching seventy-eight pounds in the weight room, but her consistency in lifting those darn dumbbells had afforded her some strength. She may linger at the bottom in athletic points, but she could climb the fifteen-foot wall in the obstacle course and pull herself up more easily while mountain climbing now. Although she did drop her pick and nearly take Marcus's eye out on that test. And she sucked at cycling and jumping out of planes. Weaponry challenged her, too. Her bullets barely grazed the target, let alone hit the bull's eye. And a bow and arrow? Disastrous. Twice her arrows had nicked bystanders.

Her only hope was swimming.

She stuffed her swimming apparel, tampons, and extra clothes into her backpack, took one long, last look at herself in the mirror, and headed outside toward the other kids.

Sonnie beckoned to her from one bus. She tossed her gear inside that bus's cargo area and climbed in the bus. She took a seat near Rachel and Sonnie and told them she intended on swimming hard today.

"What do you mean, swim hard?" Rachel asked.

"I haven't shown them my true potential."

"You did the first six months you were here," Sonnie reminded her. "Then you backed off."

"Yeah, I did. I wanted to make sure I could go to Arizona to see my mother and Enrique when I first got here, but then I quit swimming hard. Annie Sherman advised me to show them how fast I was a while ago, but I didn't want to. I like taking my time."

"Why?" Rachel asked.

"Because I don't want the swim to end. I love floating under water. I'd stay down there all day if I could hold my breath long enough. Everything is so quiet and peaceful at the bottom of the lake."

Rachel scoffed. "I hate swimming under water. Especially in that lake we swim at. It's suffocating."

"Yeah, like being entombed," Sonnie agreed. "All you see is black."

"I've never felt that way. I love the blackness."

"Weird," Rachel said.

"Yeah, weird, and you can't do that today, anyhow," Sonnie added. "We are going to the ocean."

Yes, the ocean.

She was at home in the ocean. At age three, she had stood at the water's edge and begged her father to take her surfing with him. He bought her a surfboard on her fourth birthday. Mama screamed at him for months afterward.

"You'll kill her," she said.

But Izzy had no fear of the water. She loved paddling out over the waves, straddling her board to watch the dolphins swim by, hollering "I'm okay, Papa," after catching a wave and an upsurge plummeting her into the water. She fell incessantly in those early years, her lung capacity expanding with each tumble. By the time she turned eight, she could hold her breath for over three minutes.

She had ached to surf like her big brother. Enrique's age gave him such an advantage, but their age difference helped her, too. She worked twice as hard to stay on top of her board.

Izzy settled back in her seat, recalling her first real breakthrough. One marvelous wave crept up behind her just days after her ninth birthday. The surging water broke a few feet behind her, and she skimmed the coast, sailing along, trimmed in white wave for more than twenty-five glorious seconds. Her tiny body embedded in wave coaxed the surfers on shore into wild applause.

Then the wrath of the water consumed her. A rage of waves tossed her. She whirled in white bubbles until her board bashed her head. Knocked senseless, she spun in the ocean's fury. She lost her bearings. When at last she poked her head out of the water, she saw men on the beach dashing into the ocean. As she slipped underneath the waves, she knew the men would never reach her in time. Then she felt her head jerk upward, and Papa pulled her out of the ocean by her hair, tugging her onto his surfboard.

"Izzy," he cried when they finally managed to float ashore. "I thought I lost you."

"Papa," she said. "Can I go again?"

Those twenty-five seconds had been her proudest moment.

"Wasn't she remarkable?" he would say when he drank tequila and spoke of that ride. "Only nine years old. She's special, that little spitfire. She's going places."

How she loved piling surfboards in the holey bed of Papa's rusted, old truck. The smell of board wax, tequila, and cigarettes. The sound of the crashing waves as his truck neared the ocean. How wonderful it had all been until the fights began, the money problems, the divorce, the cancer.

The sweet memories faded.

She glanced out the window and saw the reflection of herself in the glass. What would Papa say about her now? She closed her eyes. Oh, how she hurt. Such dreams he'd had for her. Deep down inside, an almost unbearable hurt gripped her. Where did that ache hide?

"Feel the sensation," Ms. Sherman had taught in her pain-blocking class. "Close your eyes. Concentrate. Find the point of pain. Block the nerve endings around the discomfort."

Izzy concentrated. Searched her body trying to locate the pain raging within. Where was it?

*In my soul.*

She opened her eyes.

That's why she had lingered at the bottom of the lake during those swims. In the water, the pain subsided. Your body twisted and snaked and the cool smooth sea rushed over every inch of you, caressing each fragment of your being. When she swam at Project Dream, she dove into the black lake with outstretched arms feeling for the bottom. Down there, she controlled her direction. Floated. Remembered. Forgot.

Today would be different. Today, she would soar.

She said a rosary in her head while the bus wheels rolled. She counted the Hail Marys and Our Fathers on her fingers.

"Hail Mary, full of grace, please Mary Mother don't let me blow it. This one time, don't let anything go wrong."

Past Project Dream tests had been disastrous. Her gun had jammed at the shooting range. She had to deploy an emergency parachute when her main parachute bunched on the solo-jump test. She had gotten lost on the timed trail run and suffered two flat tires on her hundred-mile bike ride.

"Get me out from under this gray cloud, sweet mother of Jesus. This is my last chance."

By the time the bus pulled up to the ocean, she had recited so many rosaries she couldn't count them. So nervous she shook, she ignored Sonnie's and Rachel's calls to come and join them as they readied. She grabbed her gear, stripped down to her bathing suit, and realized she didn't have her bathing cap.

She swore under her breath and tightened her ponytail. Wound her long hair into a bun behind her.

"It doesn't matter. I'll be fine," she told herself.

She secured her goggles, shook the numbness from her fingers, and took her place on the beach. She glanced down the long forming line. Kids stepped into assigned spots. In the distance, Tim Sackett stood, swaying his arms, limbering up in the number-one spot. He had the shortest distance to the turn. Spot number one hundred had the furthest.

Izzy glanced toward the big orange ball in the ocean that signaled where swimmers would turn and head down the coast, back toward land. Her gaze raked the coastline to her right. In the distance, she could see the dock that served as the finish line. She glanced back at the orange ball.

Once she rounded that turn, the playing field equaled. Everyone had the same distance to swim from the ball to the small, jutting dock with the bell. Officer Swarthy said each swimmer must ring the bell when they finished. Hearing that ring would help swimmers still in the water count their place. Make them swim faster.

*I must finish before the tenth ring.*

She returned her gaze to the dock. She studied the surrounding area. A tremendous white home on the edge of a cliff towered over that dock.

From her experience of swimming in the ocean, she knew seeing the dock while immersed in waves would be impossible.

Once she rounded the turn, she must swim toward the white house high up on the hill.

She did her stretches, planted her toes in the sand, took a deep breath, made the sign of the cross, and waited.

When the instructor blew the horn for the race to begin, Izzy ran through the sand and dove into the ocean. Immediately, her goggles dislodged and fell down around her neck. She couldn't see a thing.

# Chapter 30  Annie Sherman

Annie Sherman was a girl's girl at heart. She spent half of her thirty-two years competing against and getting beat up by four extremely athletic brothers. Until recently, she wanted no real commitment with any guy.

Born into a military family, Annie joined the Air Force out of college. She excelled in flight school. People called her the girl who flew with the angels. No one knew she flew with them in more ways than one.

How she became an instructor in the desert was about that secret. Her crazy mind had inspired her to apply for an instructor's position at Project Dream. She believed life on this earth was not reality. The next life signified true reality. Angels from the next dimension surrounded us here, listening to and helping us. Only a thin line, a breath, separated us from the angels, this life from the next.

In other words, Annie Sherman saw angels. And consequently, death had no hold over her, which showed in her wild living

Her free-spirited ways extended to her love life. In selecting boyfriends, she had not discriminated. She dated military personnel flaunting White House credentials and privates scrubbing floors. Names on that list included a senator, Steve Larson, an officer, two privates, and Danny Morris, her roommate and now fiancé.

Project Dream would be history for her in less than a year. Danny had been awarded an embassy job in the Middle East. There would be a position for her, too, if she wanted it. Until then, her sole task was ensuring the Project Dream girls flourished. And under her direction, most of them had.

At times, she pulled strings to keep girls in the desert. She spent Sundays personally training those who fell behind. Meditation, dreaming, shooting, running. She excelled in it all. A proficient marksman and athlete, she had advice to give every girl with a problem.

Now they were getting down to the wire and only a few worried her: Rachel Callahan, Dawn Davis, sometimes Marva Edwards, and most of all, Izzy Jimenez.

In the combined categories of mental and physical superiority, Rachel Callahan ranked at the top. Her biggest problem? She was her own worst enemy. She may have unwisely jumped into bed with the director, thinking he could get her out of Project Dream. Clearly, that would not end well. If she had, and if her latest sand-wrestling partner, Todd Kennedy—that kid had a serious drug problem—found out, he'd go berserk. Annie couldn't control the boys, too.

Annie herself wasn't privy to the confidential information some of the other instructors were. Jerry McDaniel had brought her in as a ploy to blackmail Steve Larson, whom she had slept with. And yes, she had known he was married. She was young and stupid back then. One rendezvous with him had led to pictures now locked away in some safety deposit box, to which only Jerry McDaniel held the key.

If her father saw those, she wouldn't have to worry about surviving her time in the Middle East. He'd kill her.

Well, what was done was done. She had told Danny about the photos. He loved her anyway. Thank God Danny never dwelled on the past. She wouldn't, either.

But what of the future?

What would happen to the girls when she left, and Ken Swarthy held free rein? Merryman was useless. If she'd had her way, Rachel Callahan and Izzy Jimenez would be gone. Maybe dead.

A shudder ran through her.

Today was the day the final testing began. Twice a month for the next six months, the kids would compete against each other in some physical or mental challenge. These final tests were meant to weed out last-minute failures. The final one hundred students who would be accepted into one of Project Dream's military branches would be set one year before college.

Kids had to excel in at least one physical test. First up was the ocean swim.

Annie stood on the dock where the swimmers would finish and shook the post with the bell secured on top, testing its stability. Swarthy had cleared the path from the edge of the dock to the bell post, so swimmers didn't trip over anything as they ran. The finish line set, Annie held a hand over her eyes, gazing toward the beaches where the kids had formed a line.

She thought about swimmer number ninety-three.

Izzy had to make this swim memorable. All the psychic abilities and clairvoyant skills in the world wouldn't help her if she lagged in this test, too. Randall Scott didn't like Izzy's brother. Continually, Enrique Jimenez wreaked havoc at the border. Everything about him spelled trouble. Their informants said he had cartel connections.

"We don't need that problem," Scott had said at their last meeting.

"But she can swim, sir." Annie defended Izzy. "Like a fish."

Annie hoped Izzy's grade-school swim coach hadn't inflated her talent. Izzy hadn't swum as fast as he said she would.

"Well, unless she's a female version of Michael Phelps, she's out."

Worried about Izzy, Annie broached the subject with her own father. Requested a favor in anticipation Izzy failed.

"Can you talk to Randall?"

"If the girl can't at least swim," he said, "then maybe she doesn't belong there. I hear every single one has been promised to the military. Maybe it's time for her to go home."

Annie held her tongue. She wasn't sure anyone who left Project Dream went home.

A horn blast in the distance stole her thoughts from that conversation with her dad. Her stomach turned. She gazed down the coastline, watched the kids run toward the water, and repeated to herself what she had told Izzy last night.

*Swim like a fish, Izzy. I can't help you anymore.*

Whether Izzy knew it or not, she was on her own.

## Chapter 31  Izzy

The instant her goggles dislodged, a numbness swept through every ounce of Izzy's hundred pounds.

In times of extreme stress, Annie Sherman had taught her to breathe deeply—okay, she couldn't do that under water, but she could wait for the numbing sensation to fade. In a few gut-wrenching seconds, Annie said, the immobilizing fear would pass, and a person could catapult forward.

Izzy stretched her arms above her head, gliding through the water. She flapped her feet and concentrated on the cool ocean washing over her hot skin.

*I didn't need goggles in the black of the lake. I certainly don't need them in the Pacific where I grew up.*

After the longest glide of her life, she surfaced to take a breath and could not see a thing.

All around her she could feel the others. She took four strokes between breaths because that was her optimum breathing pattern. A coach at Saint Mary's had told her to take two when she swam for her grade school's swim team, but Izzy had such powerful lungs she took more.

Now she reconsidered.

*Annie said world-class swimmers take two.*

She decided on the fly to take two strokes between breaths and look for the orange ball on the tenth stroke. Probably not a good idea to change her breathing pattern, but she was desperate. For a good three minutes, other swimmers boxed her in. They kicked and scratched her unintentionally. She swam harder, hoping to remove herself from mid-pack. Slowly, the spreading out of swimmers hit her. She had room to open up.

Here was her test. This was the point in her swim where she typically fell behind. Where she dove and resurfaced like a dolphin playing. This time she kicked and stroked, and the space around her completely opened up. No more swimmers bumped and slapped her. She felt nothing but the smooth water.

Each time her head rose, she saw the orange ball and nothing more.

*How many are in front of me?*

She had a naturalness in the ocean the others didn't have, but today her mind played with her. She fought the temptation to stop and pull up her goggles—prescription goggles. She kept stroking. She'd never get them on without water bubbling inside. Her vision would worsen. The time to clear them of water and defog them would be lengthy.

*Just keep swimming.*

Last night, Annie Sherman had reiterated the importance of this swim. How every second counted.

*Swim like a fish, Izzy.*

She forged on. Lifted her head out of the water every tenth stroke and swam toward the large orange ball. The ocean waves posed no problem. They surged averagely today. Turning and seeing the dock in the distance would be the problem. After a turn to the right, the dock with the rope and the bell would sit a quarter of a mile away.

She inhaled a bit of water but coughed through it. That mistake, that slight intake, boosted her adrenaline, and she stroked faster, kicked harder. She rounded the orange balloon and turned sharply right. Often at the ball, a congestion of swimmers struggled against each other trying to come as close to it as they could to turn.

Today? No one.

*My, God, am I last?*

She pushed harder and swore at herself for swimming leisurely in the past few years. Where was everyone? She couldn't see. Were the boys far ahead of her?

*Their lungs are larger. Their hearts pump faster.*

Fear erupted in her chest. She couldn't understand where everyone was. They couldn't all be ahead of her. Where were the girls?

*Am I swimming in the right direction?*

Panicking, she lifted her head out of the water and fixed her eyes on the white blur on the hill. That had to be the house. It was the only one within miles. She plunged her head back into the water and swam toward that fuzzy white spot, kicking and stroking vigorously. She listened, afraid to hear the sound of the bell. But instead of a bell ringing, she heard her Papa.

*Swim fast, Izzy. The ocean is your home.*

She pulled palms full of water with each stroke. Her hands flowed from outstretched arms to the back of her thigh in a perfect S formation. In the distance, she spotted a small brown patch beneath the white of the hillside. She dipped her head back into the water and prayed the brown speck was a dock with a rope and a bell.

She listened. Nothing.

She dug deeper with her right arm. The water's current pushed her left. She fought. Held steady.

Why was no one ringing the bell? She lifted her head. The brown patch had transformed into a dock. Was she swimming toward the right dock? Had there been more than one?

*No bells. No bells. Why hasn't Tim rung the bell?*

When she could clearly see the dock, she took a deep breath, dipped her head, and propelled through the water. She expected to feel the kick of a foot or the brush of an arm as other swimmers converged toward the same point. She listened for a ring or cheers from the instructors.

*Nothing.*

She stoked and pulled and stroked and pulled. The dock neared. She rose for a breath and dove one last time under the water, gliding with outstretched arms until one finger touched wood. She lifted herself out of the water and slithered onto the dock like a salamander onto rock. Her foot landed flat. She glanced and could see it. The rope. The bell. She ran.

My God, there was no one. Was she last? Had she not heard the bell? Had she deluded herself into thinking she could keep up with the boys?

She grabbed the rope and pulled. Heard the twang. Then she fell to her knees, swirled around, and landed on her buttocks, dropping her hands behind her.

When she pushed her goggles onto her eyes so she could see, she found herself staring into the face of Ken Swarthy, his mouth agape. No one cheered or shouted. She glanced around. Found Annie Sherman. Annie stood paralyzed on the deck. Why wasn't anyone saying anything?

She glanced over her shoulder and all around. Not one single kid sat on the dock. Where was everyone? She breathed deeply, returning her gaze to the water. Arms and legs flailed through the waves. Kids were still swimming. She folded her legs beneath her, sucking in the ocean air.

No one had finished? She was alone?

Wait. Had Annie Sherman just shrieked?

A thudding noise captured Izzy's attention. A hand surfaced and slapped the end of the dock. A swimmer hoisted himself up onto the wood. With a thud, his feet hit the ground and he began running. She recognized him. It was Tim Sackett.

He reached the post, pulled the cord, and the bell rang. He ripped his goggles from his face, glanced down at Izzy sitting on the dock, and said, "Are you fucking kidding me?"

# Chapter 32  Annie Sherman

Six months later, instructors reviewed the results of the final Project Dream tests, and Jerry McDaniel set up a meeting with Randall Scott. When they stacked the results in front of him, they saved the swim times for last.

Scott grabbed the report. "What do you mean a woman broke the record? Project Dream's or the Navy's?"

"Neither," McDaniel responded.

"She broke the world record, sir." Annie Sherman couldn't contain herself.

Izzy Jimenez breaking the women's fifteen-hundred-meter world record at a dinky, hidden opening on the California coast, during a half-assed swim in a covert operation called Project Dream, breathed new life into Annie. She hadn't liked her job this much since—since never. For the first time in her military career, she felt alive. After years of trying to prove herself, always fighting men for jobs, working twice as hard as they worked, ignoring their rude comments, here came little Izzy Jimenez to give her a shot in the arm and boost her confidence.

If ever again an officer inquired if she needed someone to hold her hand until the firing stopped, like one had done seven years ago in the middle of combat, she would hold her head up and answer, no, she didn't need double coverage. Then she'd give him the finger.

Her four brothers had more than prepared her for a military career. Growing up, they had beaten the crap out of her.

Why did men, particularly military men, feel a need to demean women?

"Take that, you self-absorbed egotists," she wanted to say to Scott, McDaniel, and Swarthy. "Take that you filthy, rotten, men-are-better-than-women morons. A hundred-pound, seventeen-year-old, pip-squeak of a girl beat your bigheaded superstar."

But instead, she said, "Sixty-one degrees, waves, no wet suit, no bathing cap, goggles around her neck, and she finished a minute before our best male swimmer."

She should have stopped there, but pride egged her on. "She beat the great Tim Sacket, your future Navy SEAL superstar."

The commander raised an eyebrow. His expression hardened.

Her outspokenness would someday end her military career, her father had warned. But then Randall Scott was a family friend, wasn't he?

*You scratch my back. I'll scratch yours. And we'll all scratch the president's back.*

Scott's mien softened. He owed a pack of favors to her father. He must have realized that, too. He let out a long breath and overlooked her comment.

"Well, who is she?" He turned toward McDaniel.

"Izzy Jimenez, sir."

"Enrique Jimenez's sister?"

Scott's face turned red. He slapped the report in his hand onto the table.

"These Jimenez kids will be the death of me. Enrique's still shooting his mouth off down in Mexico."

"Well, we have to keep her, sir," Annie said quickly.

He poked his elbows onto the table, removed his glasses, and wiped his face with his hands. "I'm getting too old for this. Where did you say she wanted to go?" He directed the question to McDaniel.

"Home to San Diego," Annie interjected.

The commander's head bobbed backward. "Another one. Tell me something, Sherman. Why do the girls in Project

Dream want to go home? The other one, Callahan, she wants to go home too, correct?"

"Yes, sir, Rachel Callahan."

"She wants to go to—" He picked up a different report. Paged through it. "What is this Mercyhurst?"

"It's an excellent school, sir. Has several academic programs that feed Washington programs, including the CIA."

"Erie, Pennsylvania?"

"Yes, sir." Annie had done her homework. "A small city with a population of 100,000 people. Located two hours from Pittsburgh, Cleveland, and Buffalo. Four hours from Toronto and Columbus. Six hours away from Baltimore and Washington, D.C. Eight hours from Chicago and New York City and, on a good day with light traffic, Boston, Massachusetts, sir."

The commander stared straight at her.

"But, sir, Rachel Call—" The commander raised his hand and silenced Swarthy's attempted interruption without looking his way.

After a long moment, Scott spoke, his tone softer. "This isn't our first discussion about Erie. The Emling kid wants to go there, too, correct?"

"Yes, sir." Annie refrained from saying Lenny wanted to go home to care for his mother, and Rachel was desperate to live near her sister. She had no desire to give them more ammunition to finagle their way with the two. "Many of the dreamers want to go home. The Jimenez girl included. As I'm sure you know, her father's entire family lives in Mexico. In San Diego, she can visit them at Friendship Park."

That, she could discuss. Everyone knew about Enrique and his family.

Again, a long silence.

"And you're going to tell me why we should grant her request, aren't you?"

Was he asking her advice? The blood in Annie's veins sped up. She waited for the numbing sensation to subside before answering.

"Yes, sir. I am." She inched forward in her seat. "She can make the swim to Mexico. I hear the Navy is looking for someone like her."

"What swim?"

"The swim from San Diego to Tijuana."

Ken Swarthy shifted in his seat, sending a faint creak into the room. She, McDaniel, and Scott sat dead still.

"The Navy—" Here Annie cleared her throat. "Or Central Intelligence could use her."

"You think this girl could swim past the radar and border control?"

"If you swim out far enough and have the equipment to stay beneath the water, you can swim to Mexico, yes, sir. There are spots where no one can detect you."

Ken Swarthy and Jerry McDaniel turned toward her.

"And you know this, how?" Scott asked.

"Because I swam across the border myself, sir."

Again silence.

"You?" he said. "You swam across the border?"

"Yes sir, me, my father, and all four of my brothers."

Annie spent every morning before school in the ocean once her father transferred to San Diego.

He taught her to swim and surf like a California-born kid. She fit in nicely—except for her obsession with guns and eager desire to shoot one. That didn't sit well in the golden state.

"There's always a way around an obstacle." Annie's father had taught his children. "No matter how closed in you are. Trust me. There's a gray spot where you can slip by."

During their teenage years, she and her brothers had begun doubting their father. So he took them on a swimming excursion. If their mother had known, she would have shot him. But that single night would become her life's biggest inspiration. They swam out into the ocean, broke through the international barrier, nearly drowned on the exhausting swim back, returned home to sleep, rose in the morning, and traipsed to school.

No one spoke in the quiet room. Everyone allowed the commander his thoughts.

"You went ashore? In Mexico?"

"No, sir, we did not. For obvious reasons. But Izzy Jimenez? She could swim out of the water and walk onto the beach without anyone questioning her. She speaks the dialect. She doesn't look Mexican; she is Mexican. Through and through. The Federales wouldn't give her a second look."

He thought about this.

"She'd swim back the same way," Annie added. "She'd be picked up by the border patrol, but they'd release her to you. She could prove valuable. Especially with the recent calls about the wall the president wants to build."

After a long silence, in which Scott rested his back against his chair and fingered his mustache unconsciously, he picked up the final report and leafed through it.

"You say you have plans for the top ten?" He addressed McDaniel.

"Yes, sir."

Again, a piercing silence.

"We have our cities set?"

"The four years after college, we do."

"After that?"

"We arrange changes when we see which cities have the best reception and where transmitters prosper."

"Are there any?" He paused here. "Controversial cities? Places we aren't sure will be beneficial?"

"A few."

"Any in the Pennsylvania area?"

"Cleveland, Ohio." Annie blurted. She wasn't sure if the commander had finished his sentence or whether she had cut him off.

After another nerve-wracking silence, the commander spoke.

"Send the Jimenez girl to San Diego." He gathered his reports. "I'll grant your requests, Jerry. All of them. Edwards, Kennedy, Emling, the tech girl. Send them where you said. And don't let anyone know we are moving the Cleveland unit to Erie in year four but make the arrangements. This is contingent upon the Callahan girl staying in California for college and the first four years of the program, of course. I'll sign the papers now to send her to Erie in year nine. You make sure she keeps her nose clean."

"She will," Jerry said. "She understands."

Randall Scott stood, leaned across the table, and shook Jerry McDaniel's hand.

Confused, Annie's gaze darted from Jerry to Randall and back to Jerry. Had she misunderstood? Hadn't she been the one pushing to send Izzy to San Diego and Rachel to Erie? Why had Scott acted as if Jerry had made the request?

Scott left the room, and Annie stepped toward Jerry. She gazed directly into his eyes. His face blushed slightly.

"I'll be damned." Her words mixed with a chuckle.

All this time she had only half believed the rumors.

# Chapter 33  Izzy

Honestly, she didn't like the attention. Not one bit.

For three years, boys flocked around Rachel Callahan as Izzy sat enviously in the shadows. Now boys Izzy barely knew dropped their blankets next to hers on those dry, hot desert nights. In the past nine months, her popularity had grown from who's-the-clumsy-little-girl to what's-the-world-record-swimmer's-name.

Not only had her fifteen minutes and thirty-nine seconds of fame cemented her feet in Project Dream's foundation, but that swim had also sensationalized her date-worthy status.

"They want a roll in the sand," Rachel said. "If you'd give up those Catholic morals of yours once in a while, you'd have some fun. There's nothing bad about it."

Rachel was wrong. Sleeping with a boy while you were intoxicated or high or just plain bored with life wasn't good. No one should sleep with anyone unless they were in love. If they ever got out of there, the promiscuous kids would regret their acts. All that rolling in the desert sand might be fun, but it wasn't love. It was sex. Purely primitive, visceral, carnal sex. Rachel didn't love any of the guys she slept with, including Todd Kennedy. Sadly, she may have loved Chase but none of the others.

Izzy glanced across her blanket to see Rachel and Todd snuggled together and found Rachel staring back at her, lips moving. Rachel leaned forward, perturbed.

"Izzy, are you listening?"

"Not really." She said without thinking. The others on her blanket laughed as if she joked. She bounced her stare from Rachel to the boys around her.

"Why do you guys like being high?"

"Huh?" Marcus grunted.

"The cocaine," she responded. "You're all getting out of hand."

They laughed more. Annoyed, she stood.

"Oh, come on, fish girl, stay. We're having a fun time."

This new nickname had stuck, also.

"I'm going to bed." She grabbed her sandals but didn't take time to put them on. She kicked sand with the tip of her toes and stamped off, ignoring Marcus's plead to come back.

As she passed Lenny Emling, off by himself, he said, "They want to d-deaden the pain."

She stopped and stepped toward the odd character. Lenny barely talked to anyone other than her, Rachel, and a few others.

"Well, I don't like it here either, but all that cocaine isn't good for them. I mean, an occasional snort might make someone feel better, but after a while, everything runs together. They can't tell the good feelings from the bad. I like to feel misery now and then, so I can appreciate happy."

She nodded her head as if she agreed with herself.

Lenny smiled. He actually smiled. He said nothing.

She stepped closer.

"You're not strung out all the time like everyone else. How come? Don't you like to deaden the pain?"

Lenny leaned back, propping himself up with his arms and crossing his feet at his ankles. "I guess I'm used to f-feeling pain. Been feeling it all my life."

A realization shot through her. Kids must have called him names as they had her. She searched for something kind to say.

"Well…you…you did well in our athletic testing. They're over now, so you'll always have that. Your name will go down in the books. You were first in almost every competition."

Lenny glanced toward her. Smiled a second time. "Not the s-swim."

"Oh, who cares if Tim Sackett beat you. You have so much more body mass than him, he looks like a toddler next to you. It's a miracle you finished second."

"Third. I finished third."

She noticed he hadn't stuttered. He smiled a second time.

"You shocked everyone with your swim, Izzy. I never congratulated you. I was glad you won."

Embarrassed, she turned slowly away before the thought to ask struck her.

"Lenny? Why are you so nice to me? I mean, here I am in a bad mood and still you're nice. And, well, you don't talk much to anyone else besides me. And Rachel."

"I grew up with R-Rachel."

"What about me? Why are you so nice to me? Sometimes I feel like you watch over me."

Lenny uncrossed his ankles and sat straight. He appeared to ponder this question seriously. She stopped herself from saying more. She stood staring, wondering what thoughts swirled in that big head of his.

"You remind me of someone."

"You mean, Lisa? Rachel's sister?"

He lowered his eyes. His shoulders slumped. "Yeah."

"Rachel says that, too, but I don't see the connection. We're both little, but other than that, totally different."

Lenny stood, tugging his blanket with one hand. He flicked his wrist and sand flew in all directions.

"You're both little but have b-big hearts." He started walking away.

"Lenny, are you in love with Lisa?"

She couldn't believe she asked. Bad moods always inspired her impulsiveness. She tried to recover. "I'm so sorry. I shouldn't have asked. That's none of my business."

He lowered his gaze.

Did he chuckle? Had he laughed mildly? After a few pensive seconds, he responded. "I'll always l-love LeeLee, but I'm n-not in love with her, no."

He sounded sincere. She glanced upward, trying to see into his eyes. He raised his head and glanced off into the distance toward a dark space. Muffled, tittering voices came from that direction. Three girls sat on a blanket. Izzy squinted to see who they were. She thought the quiet girl, Kiera someone, was one of them.

Not able to decipher which girl Lenny stared at, she turned back. Looked straight at him. Which highlighted another of his oddities. He barely ever looked anyone in the eye.

"Lisa used to stick up for me when I was little," he said, eyes still staring at the blanket in the dark.

"Lisa?" She tucked her chin. "She stuck up for you?"

"I was little back then."

He began walking toward the dormitory, his large head turned sideways, his gaze still fixed on the blanket in the dark. Once he was a good distance away, he stopped.

Soft but hurrying footsteps cut through the dark. Anne Sherman strutted toward them. Instructors seldom ventured out into the desert at night because of the fear of what they might find. So what was Annie doing? Izzy watched her walk straight to Lenny and ask where Rachel was.

And Izzy knew.

# Chapter 34  Rachel

For the first twenty-four hours after Gee lost consciousness, Lisa called sporadically to update Rachel.

Just because Gee was old didn't mean Rachel was prepared for her to die. So many times in the desert, she had wondered what Gee would do in her situation. Where Rachel's mother and sister may have boo-hood her actions, Gee would have understood. She would have said, "Rachel, darling, you did what you had to do to survive."

She desperately needed to hear those words cross Gee's lips.

At ten-thirty in the evening of the second day, Lisa called to say Gee's organs were failing. Losing her was only a matter of time.

"Please, let me go home," Rachel begged, when Annie stopped to check on her.

McDaniel was out of town. He had left Ken Swarthy in charge.

"I'm trying to get hold of McDaniel. He's not answering."

"Please try again," Rachel pleaded.

"I will." Annie rushed away.

Two hours later, she was once again summoned to the office. Her legs could barely carry her down the hall. When she heard her mother's voice, she knew. Gee was gone.

Rachel sunk to the floor. She cried for a long time before Ken Swarthy lifted her off the ground and carried her to her room. She collapsed on her bed. Todd came, and she set her soft face against his firm chest. He wrapped his arms around her. Stroked her hair and rocked her. Nothing eased the ache.

By two in the morning, Rachel still hadn't slept. She'd taken several pills during the day, and now Todd coaxed another one into her. Relief washed over her, and she dozed. Then she awoke and dozed again, glad to see someone there each time she opened her eyes.

In the few fleeting moments of sleep, she dreamed of her mother, Lisa, and Chase. Then she opened her eyes to Todd. Her hand clasped the cuff of his shirt as he slept. She fingered the frayed ends of one sleeve.

Todd had saved her from herself after Chase died. She loved Todd, but she wasn't in love with him. She had never been in love with anyone.

Except Chase.

She thought of Chase's blue eyes. His warm smile. His gentle touch. If he were still there, she could bear this. That she lay beside Todd but still loved the memory of Chase Finley sent her spiraling into an uncontrollable sob.

Todd awoke, sat up, and prepared two powdery lines on Rachel's nightstand, coaxing her to snort the cocaine with him. She did. The pain lightened. They dozed. Dreams of Chase tangled with slumber.

She woke.

For a moment she confused Todd with Chase. She even called Chase's name before she realized it was Todd beside her. Then she remembered. Chase was gone. Gee had died.

She forced herself up and searched Todd's pockets. Found a pill. Her need for drugs to dull the pain superseded her desire to remain cognizant. Todd's arms fell to his side. A slight snore escaped his lips. She stood, but her knees buckled, and she slid to the floor.

Someone knocked on her door, and Izzy and Sonnie entered. She slipped the pill into her pocket.

Izzy knelt beside her and removed a suitcase from beneath her bed. "They're going to let you go home. Annie got a hold of McDaniel."

Rachel's shoulders sagged with relief.

"They're sending a car in the morning." Izzy went to the closet and removed a simple, black dress, folded it neatly, and set it in the suitcase.

As she and Sonnie sifted through the clothes in Rachel's dresser, news of Rachel's grandmother's death spread. Kids woke each other and snuck to her room.

Lenny came first. He lifted her off the floor and onto her bed next to a sleeping Todd. John Michael sat down on one corner. Marva on another. Steve and Sam lingered in the doorway. A drug-woozy Marcus wandered in and knelt on the floor beside the bed.

When Todd awoke and saw the others, he became outraged. He flailed his arms at Marcus and John Michael, yelling unintelligibly.

"What is he saying?" Sonnie glanced at Izzy.

"I don't know." Izzy turned toward Lenny. "Maybe we should get them out of here."

He nodded and helped Marcus to his feet. "We better g-go so Rachel can sleep. She's l-leaving in the morning."

Lenny gestured for the others to make their way to the door and set a hand on Todd. Todd jerked his shoulder away.

"Let go of me, you flunky junky. She's not going anywhere."

"She's g-going home, Todd."

"Get out of here." Todd stood. "You, too." He flung an arm at Marcus. Kicked at John Michael, but he lost his balance and fell back onto the bed.

"Please, Lenny, let Todd stay," Rachel cried.

Lenny hesitated but nodded. He lumbered toward the door. John Michael and Marcus attempted to give Rachel one last hug, but Todd swung at them again. "Don't touch her."

A struggle ensued. Punches flew. Both Marcus and Todd ended up on the floor. Lenny stepped in and stopped the brawl. He ushered Marcus and John Michael out of the room. Then despite Rachel's pleading, he returned, grabbed Todd by his shoulders, lifted him up while he kicked and screamed, and carried him away.

"You sleep now." Izzy's soft, warm hand stroked Rachel's face. "You're going home."

Rachel fell back onto the bed and closed her eyes.

Home. She was going home.

She slid two fingers into the tight pocket of her pants and held the pill in her hand until Izzy and Sonnie closed the door behind them. Then she slid the pill under her tongue, and a black haze crept over her sight. Sleep relieved her pain.

# Chapter 35  The Incident

Rachel stood in the foyer next to the front office. The dark sandstone walls seemed to close in around her. She set her suitcase on the floor and sat down on a stiff, brown chair, clicking her heels together. She folded her hands in her lap and stared out the door's long side window, watching for the car.

Gee was gone. Nothing else mattered. She must get home to LeeLee.

LeeLee would need her now.

She had crashed from the drugs around six that morning, but at seven Annie Sherman had brought her breakfast. She managed to keep down water and plain biscuits. Her exhaustion was so debilitating, and her head pounded so horribly that she was forced to snort more cocaine at eight. Now the throbbing pain at her temples had somewhat subsided, but her mind once again experienced the fogginess of the drugs.

She didn't hear the approaching footsteps.

"You have feelings for him, don't you?" The skewed voice startled her.

She turned abruptly, her vision blurred. Now the coke, not simply tears, distorted her world. She barely recognized him. "Todd?

"You care for him, don't you?"

"Who?"

"You know who." He sounded breathless.

She rose.

"I don't—I don't know what you're saying." Unsteady on her feet, she clutched his forearm, then pulled a tissue from her pocket and dabbed her face. "I want to go home. I don't want to come back here—ever."

His arms encircled her, and he rested his forehead on hers. "I'm sorry, Rachel."

His tight grasp steadied her. She felt safe in his arms. "Why don't I know when the people I love are sick? With all my dreams, why can't I tell when someone close to me is dying? First my dad, now Gee."

"Rachel—" Todd swayed back and forth, rocking her in his arms. "I'm sorry. It was seeing you cry and the cocaine. I had too much. I didn't know what I was doing."

She didn't understand his words. They'd both had too much.

Her gaze stretched over his shoulder and across the room to the window. She saw the car approaching.

She lifted her head, and as she did, the loud voices and footsteps eased into earshot. Someone shouted. She released her grip on Todd and turned toward the sounds, confused. Something drew her eyes to the hallway floor. She noticed the trail of footprints. Were they bloodied? Her gaze traced the red path from the hallway to where she stood. Were those Todd's footprints?

She heard a sound outside, and she glanced through the window to the road. The car neared.

"I'm going home, Todd," she said, moving toward her suitcase. "I just want to go—"

Finally, she looked at him, really looked. His face bled profusely. Bloody patches reddened his clothes. She glanced to where his shirt had met her dress. His blood had turned her black dress blacker.

"What did you do? Why are you bleeding?"

She tried to focus. If only she hadn't taken so many pills, snorted so much cocaine.

"I couldn't stand it when they put their hands on you," he said. "Steve, Marcus, and especially John Michael. You know he loves you."

"What are you talking about?"

"First Steve put his arms around you. Then Marcus. You know I hate the way they coddle you."

"Todd, no. It's my grandmother." She closed her eyes. "They were sorry for me."

"But you don't see it, Rachel, how beautiful you are." His hands tightened. "How much they love you. Every one of them. Lenny, too."

"Oh, Todd, not now."

"Rachel," he said, leaning and whispering in her ear. "Both Marcus and John Michael admitted they still love you. After they passed you from arm to arm when you were leaving, I went crazy. Kept hitting them. Lenny stopped me and—"

She freed herself, stepping away. If only she could clear her head.

"Lenny?" She put a hand on her forehead. "What are you saying?"

"I lost my mind." He drew her back into his arms, murmuring words she could not comprehend.

Down the hall, she heard footsteps. Big, loud footsteps coming closer. She tried wiggling loose, but Todd held firm.

"What did you do?"

"I swung a poker at them. Hit Marcus. John Michael, too. He came at me and we fought. I hope he's not dead. Then Lenny—"

"John Michael? You beat John Michael? And Marcus?"

"I get so jealous," he whimpered. "Lenny came and—I stabbed him."

The approaching footsteps halted, and Lenny appeared beside them, the front of his shirt covered in blood.

"Lenny." Rachel turned. "Are you all right?"

"I-I'll be okay," he stammered. "B-but John Michael is hurt bad."

Todd jerked Rachel around. Stood between her and Lenny. "Get out of here, you flunky."

"L-let her go. Sh-she needs to go home."

"Lenny, you need help." Rachel reached a hand toward him, but Todd shoved it back.

"Get away from us, freak." Todd led Rachel out the front door and tried to slam it shut, but Lenny stopped the closing door with one hand.

Lenny skirted around them and shoved them both back inside the building. Then he reached through the doorway, ripped Todd's hand from Rachel's arm, dragged him outside, and slammed the door shut. Immediately, the big wooden door began thumping as Lenny banged Todd against it several times. The sound of knuckle against bone sickened Rachel. She listened helplessly as Lenny's big hands landed fist after fist against Todd's face.

"Don't hurt him, Lenny, please," she wailed.

She fumbled with the doorknob and slapped her hands against the wood. When the door wouldn't budge, she fell against it, forearms and cheek flat. Her face and body felt the vibration of each punch. She begged and pleaded for Lenny to stop, but the wooden tremors continued. When she could take no more, her weary body slid to the floor.

"Please stop," she whimpered.

After a few more strikes, she heard the click of running feet both inside and outside. Someone hollered. The beating stopped. She felt a warmth, then the tepid, wet floor. She gazed down at the blackish-red trickle of fluid and realized the balmy substance was blood, Todd's blood oozing beneath the door. That gore was the last she remembered of the morning.

## Chapter 36  Home

Sitting in her childhood home, where a house full of people bumped shoulders and spooned food onto plastic plates, Rachel watched her mother. How unlike Gee her mom had always seemed. Gee had a strength her mother lacked, yet now, surprisingly, her mother's soft soul unleashed a staggering strength.

For the first time, Rachel realized a woman's reticence might also be her fortitude.

She considered Lisa, Izzy, and other simple women. Strength existed in different manners. She glanced toward her sister, who no longer held the straight, childlike lines of a young girl. Shorter than Rachel, blonde, and as delicate as a china doll, she had inherited their mother's gentle demeanor—and quiet strength.

Rachel sipped her coffee, responding congenially when visitors offered condolences. Despite her despair over losing Gee, comfort surrounded her. The funeral had been a beautiful tribute to a life well lived. Everyone adored Gee. The large attendance at this morning's funeral mass and now at the wake, consoled Rachel. Made her feel lucky to have had such a wonderful grandmother.

And not having drugs in her felt—how did that feel? Wonderful.

The first forty-eight hours at home had ravished her. She faked the flu until a few hours before the funeral-home viewing.

Fortunately, she didn't use every day like Todd and the others. But coming down from the drugs she pumped into her system on the night Gee died had sent her into an agonizing withdrawal. She couldn't hold food down. Choked on water. Threw up dozens of times and then gagged on the bathroom floor long after anything remained in her stomach to throw up.

To date, McDaniel had not permitted a single student to leave Project Dream for anything other than the death of a parent or sibling. But Annie Sherman had gone to bat for her. She told Jerry that Rachel must go home, and Jerry approved Rachel's leave. Kids heralded Annie as a hero.

But Annie had nothing to do with why Jerry McDaniel approved Rachel's trip home.

Rachel dropped her plastic fork into her food, rose, and made her way through the crowded room to the kitchen. She tossed her plate in the garbage and glanced at the cooler of beer. She closed her eyes and massaged her throbbing temples, determined not to extinguish the fire in her head with drugs or alcohol.

"You shouldn't be drinking. You're not even legal." Lisa caught Rachel by surprise. "Do they let you drink at school?"

Rachel turned away from the cooler, grinning.

"Actually, yes, they do. Somewhere at the end of year one, they realized we were teenagers, not objects, so they bent the rules."

"Well, please don't make it a habit."

"I won't." She meant that. At least, she wanted to mean it.

Lisa tossed a stack of paper plates into the trash and began rinsing dirty serving dishes. "How's Todd?"

"He's good." Rachel grabbed a platter and began scraping food remains down the garbage disposal. "I don't know how I would have gotten through the last year without him."

"Is there a chance you two will go to the same college?"

"Maybe. They want me to go to college in California, but they know I want to come home. I'm fighting to, anyway."

Hope suddenly crossed Lisa's face. She set her dish down and curled her soft fingers around Rachel's forearm. "Do you think they'll let you?"

"I don't know. I'll be in some branch of the military during college. After that, we relocate to a military reserve affiliated with Project Dream."

"To do what?'

"Search for terrorist attacks in whatever region we are assigned to."

"Where will you be?"

"They say Torrance, California, for four years, but they aren't completely sure. Everything is still being flushed out. I'm vying to serve my reserve time in Erie after college."

*Vying? Is that what I'm doing?*

"I'm almost afraid to ask, but which college?"

"Pepperdine."

"Wow, that's impressive. I'd love to go there." Lisa thought to herself for a moment. Her eyes widened. "If I apply and get accepted, we could room together."

"You know you can't leave Mom."

Lisa's face blushed. "You're right. I wasn't thinking. I just worry about you, too."

"You don't have to. Todd has been great. He's filled the void in my life since—" Rachel hesitated briefly. At first, she had blamed Lisa for Chase's plane crash. They'd had several arguments, but now she was too tired to fight. "Since Chase left."

"Did you hear any more about him?"

Lisa had never believed his plane crashed. But then she hadn't seen the pictures, the plane's name, Foxtrot, front and center.

"No, just that his plane went down in the Pacific. That's all."

Lisa didn't respond.

"That's why I thank God for Todd. He took my mind off Chase."

"I'm glad you found some comfort."

Rachel fanned her face with a towel. She had grown bored with the conversation. Her gaze swept the room. The dirty pots and casseroles of food, the cupboards, nooks, and crannies so cluttered from years of living jumped at her. The glib chitchat from the living room filtered in around the edges of the kitchen door, pelting her.

She clanked a casserole dish into the sink. "It's so stuffy in this kitchen. Let's get out of here."

"What?"

"Let's sneak away. Run to the park like we did when we were kids."

"We can't go now."

"Sure we can." Rachel tugged her shoes off by the heels and hurried to the back door. She slipped into a pair of sneakers and grabbed a sweater and jacket from hooks on the wall, tossing the jacket to Lisa.

"But—" Lisa glanced toward the dining room. "We should be here for—"

"Oh, c'mon. Let's go for twenty minutes. Mom won't miss us. She has a house full of people." She slipped into the sweater, opened the door, and nudged her head toward the back yard. "I'll race you."

Without much thought, she took off. She sprinted through their yard and headed toward the back yard of the neighbor who lived behind them. Lisa called to her quietly, but Rachel ignored her. She darted down the neighbor's driveway and turned right onto the street behind theirs. She kept running and didn't look back.

Lisa would follow. Lisa always followed.

At the edge of the street, she turned left, passed three houses, entered a path, and felt her sneakers sink into the park's wet, muddy grass. She made her way to the swings. By the time she sat down, straightened her legs, and pushed up into the air three times, Lisa had taken the swing beside her.

Rachel continued pumping, swinging high into the air.

"You're crazy," Lisa laughed.

"Remember sneaking out at night? After mom and dad fell asleep? We met Eddie, Geoff, and Sally here?

"I only went a few times." Lisa leaned back on the swing, stretched her own legs straight up in the air, and smiled.

Rachel loved how happy Lisa appeared in that moment. Content and free, not a bit fragile. "You always worried Mom would get mad at you, but she never found out."

"She must have known something was up when she saw our muddy shoes the next morning. She knew more than she let on."

"Maybe." Rachel stretched her legs and swung higher. "Whatever happened to Geoff Filutze?"

"He came home after he did four years in the army."

"I had a crush on him, but he never gave me a look."

"He did so. You never noticed."

"No, he didn't. I wore my best clothes to the park, trying to get him to notice. In my dreams, he developed this mad crush on me."

"Rachel." Lisa pumped harder. "Every boy in this neighborhood had a crush on you. Geoff was just so much older."

"What's he doing now?"

"He's a cop."

Rachel dragged her feet on the ground and brought her swinging to a halt.

"What happened to Ben Morgan? The cop who turned my name into the FBI?"

Lisa dragged her own feet. "I hear they're going to make him chief."

"I bet they are. He solved the worst crime in Erie history because of you."

"No, because of you. He solved the case because of you. And the man you sent to prison will never hurt another girl as long as he lives. He'll be there until the day he dies."

"Well, how lucky for Officer Morgan. Glad it turned out so great for him."

"He didn't know they would take you away."

"Yes, he did. He should have kept his mouth shut."

"He came by the house one time to talk to Mom and Dad, Rachel. He apologized."

"Well, I don't care." Rachel pumped her feet again. "I'll never forgive him."

"You know you will."

"Won't."

"Rachel, stop swinging." Lisa stood and put her hand out, grabbing the chain of Rachel's swing. Rachel nearly tumbled to the ground. Her swing swerved left and right. "I know you. You always gravitate toward older guys like Geoff Filutze. I know you're in a relationship with this Todd kid, but what's going on with you and the director?"

How did Lisa always know everything? Rachel didn't respond.

"I know more than you think."

"What do you think you know?"

"I know you brought me out here because you think they might be listening to us in our house. I know you can't tell me anything about this project. You can't tell anyone. And I know you're sleeping with the director. That's why you're here. He gives you special privileges."

"You're crazy." Rachael got off the swing and stomped toward the park's entrance.

"I'm not crazy." Lisa caught up. "I know you're never going to get out of this program."

Rachel stopped. A fury in the pit of her stomach rose to the middle of her throat. "I'm going to get out of this program if it kills me."

"It will," Lisa yelled, reaching for her. "They will kill you if you don't listen to them."

Rachel dodged her hand and shot her a vicious stare but could think of nothing to say. She stood speechless in the cool breeze. The wind picked up, and the leaves on the trees fluttered around her. A bird whizzed past, wings flapping.

Finally, Lisa spoke, "I'll never forgive myself. I should be at Project Dream. I saw where the man hid the bodies of those girls, not you. You did this for me. But I swear." She closed her eyes. "I didn't know it would be a lifetime commitment."

Despite her anger with Lisa for tainting their little break with doom, Rachel mellowed. Lisa seemed so pitifully sorry. "I know you didn't."

"No, but I did know you would have to go away."

Rachel cleared her throat. They both had known.

"I talked to Gee about it." Lisa wiped a few falling tears from her cheeks.

"What did she say?"

"She said it had to be this way. That you had to go, and I had to stay. But I would have fought harder to go if I had known you'd never be able to get out. I'm so sorry."

"Gee was right. You had to stay." This project affected so many lives. "You couldn't know the American government would take twelve- and thirteen-year-old kids from their families and handcuff them to a program for life."

"I should have gone," Lisa whispered. She closed her eyes again.

"Do not blame yourself. This isn't your fault."

"Yes, it is."

"Stop saying that."

"I could have done something. Told the police. Told the man who came to the house." Lisa grabbed her stomach, bent in agony.

Rachel recognized the expression on her sister. She had seen it many times. She grabbed Lisa, yanking her upright.

"There was nothing you could have done."

Lisa gasped for air.

"Stop it. Right now."

Rachel shook her, but Lisa couldn't catch her breath.

"This is ridiculous. Stop!"

Lisa wouldn't or couldn't. Rachel glanced around. There was no one else in the park, not a single person in sight. Lisa gasped for air. Her face turned ashen.

When they were little, Lisa's breath would quicken until she passed out.

Upset herself and frantic because they were alone, Rachel did something she never thought she would do. She lifted her hand and slapped Lisa across the face.

Lisa drew a long breath in and held it. She stopped panting. Her expression changed from fright to surprise.

Rachel could see the red sting of her hand on Lisa's face. She froze.

At the exact same moment, they threw their arms around each other. Minutes passed as they stood crying. Their shoes sunk into the muddy earth, and the muck of the gloomy day dirtied them. Finally, when they calmed, moved apart, and wiped away their tears, Lisa spoke, "I'm sorry, Rachel."

"It's okay."

"We should head back. We don't want to worry Mom."

"No, we don't."

A gentle wind fought them as they walked toward home. Halfway there, Lisa broke the silence, again.

"Gee left us letters."

They had reached the neighborhood walkway, and Rachel stomped the mud caked on her shoes onto the cement. "What?"

"Gee wrote letters for us to read. They're for the future. We're supposed to read them at different points in our life." Subconsciously, Lisa picked at her fingers. "Isn't that like Gee? To think of us?"

Rachel reached a hand to stop Lisa's picking, and Lisa slipped her hands inside her coat pockets.

"Yes, it is but—oh my God—that's awesome. Let's go read them."

Lisa smiled. "We aren't going to read them now."

"Well, sure we are."

"No, we're not. We are going to read them when we're supposed to. When we graduate from college. Get married. Have a baby. There are a ton of them."

Rachel flung her arms out, palms upward. "You can't be serious. You don't plan on waiting. Where are they?"

"In a safety deposit box at the bank in my name and, yes, I'm serious. We're not reading them. Gee gave me the key. The safety deposit box is paid in advance for twenty-five years."

"Twenty-five years? Are you kidding me?"

"No. Gee knew you as well as I do. She knew you'd read them right away."

"You need to give me that key."

Lisa, the little sister, resurfaced. The one who infuriated Rachel without using so much as an ounce of energy.

Lisa's eyes sparkled. "No, but you can have this."

Lisa slipped a hand inside her coat and removed an envelope from her dress pocket. Rachel glanced down and saw Gee's sloppy handwriting.

*To Rachel, after my funeral.*

## Chapter 37  Lenny

Lenny tossed a duffel bag over one shoulder and lifted his suitcase off the floor. He headed out of his room, down the hall, and exited the main quarters. Outside, he took the trail alongside the building until he reached a side entrance. He opened its door and stomped into dorm nine, heading toward the first bedroom. Glad to see the room available, he entered and plopped his gear onto the bed. Maybe he could get some peace and quiet here.

The small dormitory with a different entrance was reserved for the worst Project Dream kids. Lenny likened it to a work-release program. They attended classes and programs but were confined to their rooms at night.

His new room didn't have its own bathroom, but Lenny couldn't have cared less. Eight small bedrooms lined one side of a hallway. Each room had a single bed and one small dresser. Four bathroom doors lined the other side of the hall. Only three boys lived in this dorm, so technically, each of them had their own bathroom.

Lenny unpacked his clothes, kicked the duffel bag under the bed, and left the room. Swarthy had instructed him to pack up his gear and report to the administrative building.

But first, Lenny had to deal with his three new roommates.

He crossed the hall to the closest bathroom and opened the door. As he suspected, towels, clothes, and paraphernalia crowded the room.

He stepped to the other side of the hall and walked to the second bedroom. He pounded a fist on the door. He continued walking down the hall. Not sure which boy slept in which bedroom, he stopped and pounded on each door until he had knocked on all seven. Hastily, he made his way back to the first bathroom, leaned against the wall, and waited.

Promptly, three doors opened.

A boy inside a room two bedrooms down from Lenny's opened his door and stepped into the hall. "What the hell? Emling?"

Matt Godfrey stepped toward him. By twelve, Matt had accumulated a mile-long record of breaking and entering homes across Chicago. Within his first month at Project Dream, the kids living in his dorm reported a large number of missing objects. Goods showed up in Godfrey's room. Counselors attempted to rehabilitate him but couldn't wipe his sticky fingers clean.

Further down the hall, two more doors opened. Jerry Drake, a big monstrosity of a thief, stepped out, and Ken Legler, a skinny kid who killed a man at age twelve, inched out of his room. Lenny looked each one of them directly in the eye, gazing for the half a minute he needed to study their destiny. Then he slapped the palm of his hand on the first bathroom door and spoke.

"Whose s-stuff is this?"

Ken Legler began shaking. Lenny would leave him alone. Ken had a brilliant mind but slept only two hours a night. In his first year there, he crept around while the others slept. He stole items from the boys and studied sleeping girls. Instructors counseled him, but he couldn't kick his creeping habit. Girls complained, and Swarthy transferred him to dorm nine.

Lenny actually liked the kid. The rumor was he slit his stepfather's throat after the guy molested his sister.

The other two were a different matter.

Matt Godfrey approached. "It's my s-stuff."

Lenny crossed his arms. "Are y-you m-mimicking me?"

"M-m-maybe I am."

In a flash, Lenny lunged at Godfrey and had him up against the wall. Lenny held an arm against Godfrey's throat. Lenny's other arm stretched around the boy and twisted Godfrey's right arm against the wall. Lenny shoved his knee into Godfrey's groin and leaned weight on him. Godfrey's free hand tugged at Lenny's arm, but his strength was no match for Lenny's. Godfrey choked and coughed. His face turned red.

"Make no m-mistake. If you don't m-move your stuff out of this bathroom, I'll kill you."

With that, Lenny released Godfrey. He slid to the floor.

Lenny glanced at Jerry Drake.

"Am I g-gonna have any trouble with you?"

The Drake kid raised his hands and stepped back into his room. Lenny gazed toward Ken. Kids said Matt Godfrey and Jerry Drake had beat the crap out of Ken throughout his years there.

Lenny eyed him. "What's up, Kenny?"

"Not much." Ken's shoulders sagged with relief.

"G-guess I'll be seein' you around," Lenny told him as he exited the dorm.

"Yeah, see you around."

Lenny trudged back to the main building and headed toward the administrative offices. There he knocked on McDaniel's door. Ken Swarthy hollered for him to come in. McDaniel was still out of town. Lenny entered.

He loved how frightened Ken Swarthy was to be alone with him. For a dime, he would have locked the door and watched Swarthy cower. If he wanted, he could wrap his hands around Ken Swarthy's neck and strangle him to death. No one would be able to pry his hands away in time to save him.

Swarthy squirmed in his seat. "Let's get this straight," he said. "They should have dropped you from this program long ago. I've requested they get rid of you. You're trouble, Emling. But for some reason, once again, McDaniel is going to protect you."

Swarthy flipped through Lenny's file on the desk. Lenny said nothing. He simply enjoyed the thick, tense air in the room. Swarthy's gaze volleyed between the file and Lenny as if he expected Lenny to lunge across the desk at any second.

Intentionally, Lenny leaned down abruptly, and Swarthy jumped.

Lenny lifted a pen off the floor and set it on the desk. He smiled.

"I don't want any more trouble from you. Understand? Not one wrong move. Got it? I will get rid of you the next time. That you can count on."

Lenny did understand. He looked into Swarthy's eyes. Swarthy told the truth.

He had to decide right then. Did he want to kowtow to Ken Swarthy, so he could live and go home? Take care of his mother someday when her arthritis became unbearable? Or give Ken Swarthy one horrendous beating and end up dead?

Lenny wasn't afraid to die. He closed his eyes and considered the possible outcomes of his most tempting option. Who would take care of his mother? What about LeeLee? If he lived, he could protect LeeLee and her children someday.

He thought about Rachel. All she had done for him. As tough as she was, Rachel had taken the world on her shoulders. Lenny owed her, too.

And what about the quiet little girl, Kiera? How, oddly, her eyes matched his exactly? Maybe after their time in the desert, they would meet again someday.

He opened his eyes.

How he hated Ken Swarthy. How he wanted to reach across the desk, grab the guy by the throat, and beat him until he heard his last breath. But for his mother's sake and LeeLee's and Rachel's and possibly Kiera's, he said, "N-no, sir, I guarantee you won't have any trouble with m-me. Not from here on out."

Ken Swarthy studied him.

"I m-mean it, sir. You won't have any m-more problems with me. I'm determined to stick it out."

Swarthy held his breath for a moment, sighed, and said, "Okay, Emling, you have one last chance. You're excused. Move your gear to dorm nine."

Lenny stood and headed for the door.

"I already have, sir."

# Chapter 38  Rachel - The Letter

Designedly, she waited until she boarded the plane to read Gee's letter. Lisa begged to see it, but Rachel refused. If Lisa wouldn't give her all of the letters, then Rachel wasn't going to let Lisa read the one letter she did allow her.

On a plane, amongst people she did not know, she sat in her first-class window seat, declining food and fingering the envelope with her name in Gee's handwriting. She unsealed it and unfolded the letter inside.

When they were high in the air, floating over some small city where cars crawled below like confused ants roaming aimlessly, she opened it.

*Dear Rachel,*

*How I love your spirit. Since the day you were born and cried straight for ten hours no matter how your mother comforted you, you've been so strong-willed we could barely discipline you.*

*You have a magnificent gift of grabbing life and squeezing fun into every second you breathe. You have a strength that far surpasses my own and your mother's. Life will challenge you and change you, but you'll get through everything.*

*There will be times when you think, "this is going to kill me." Here is a secret. It won't. Trust old Gee. Hold your head high and your limbs still and muddle through. Look life in the eye and let him know you'll never give in.*

*You're reading this, so I am gone. But really, you and I and Lisa know that's not true, don't we? Our energy lives on. We embark on a new adventure. And oh, how you and I have always loved adventure. This is our true connection. Our adventure and strength. I will never leave you.*

*Watch out for your Momma and sister. They love you dearly.*

*Stay close to Lisa. You need her as much as she needs you. Come home to her after the desert. After whatever time they require, come home to where you belong.*

*And, Rachel, no matter what transpires in that desert, forgive yourself. You did what you had to do to survive and protect those you loved. Harbor no regret.*

*With so much love I'm unable to describe it,*
*Gee*

There in that plane high above her troubled world, Rachel closed her eyes and allowed Gee's love and understanding to comfort her. All she had done for herself and her sister and her friends—Gee understood. She prayed someday she could forgive herself.

She glanced toward the bottom of the letter, and Gee's final words jumped at her.

*And, Rachel dear, never doubt yourself. You'll get through this. You'll survive and find the man of your dreams someday—just as I found Pops. Oh, how I wish I could be there!*

Tears welled in her eyes.

"You're wrong, Gee," she whispered. "I won't. He's gone."

She set the side of her face against the airplane window and closed her eyes.

*He's with you.*

## Chapter 39  Izzy

Just days after Todd Kennedy sent John Michael and Marcus to the infirmary, and Lenny retaliated and knocked Todd senseless, an uprising began.

Lenny transferred to a special dormitory that housed three other dreamers. Kids living there had to leave the main building and enter a side door. Since the dorm halls inside the main building were numbered one through eight, kids called that separate dormitory the "black nine."

Residing there relayed physical and social ostracism. The black nine housed dangerous kids who had limited privileges. All three, now four, of the black-nine students had come in with the original twenty-five detention-center kids. Mostly, the other kids avoided them.

While there was always unrest in the black nine, now turbulence unraveled everywhere. With the huge fight and Rachel Callahan released for her grandmother's funeral, kids began talking mutiny. "If we go north through the mountains, what can authorities do?" someone had said. "Shoot us all?"

Quickly, Ken Swarthy squashed those rebellious thoughts. He stationed five armed guards in the mountains and forbade kids to climb the first range any longer. Izzy wondered if a mole hid in dreamland. Who had told Swarthy about the potential escape?

Morale plummeted. Kids began saying it was true: those who left Project Dream were dead. But then a rumor surfaced that Marcus, always at the bottom of the class, was going home.

Izzy wanted to find out the truth.

So at eight o'clock in the evening, two Saturdays after the infamous fight, she declined to join the others in the desert. Instead, she snuck into the infirmary to see Marcus.

She entered through the kitchen area and snuck into the hallway. She'd heard Todd had gone through some heavy detoxing, so the handwritten post on his door, "No visitors," didn't surprise her. Lenny had broken Todd's nose, jaw, and four ribs.

She slithered by his room, hugging the wall. She slunk to a second doorway and peeked inside. Marcus, hands behind his head, legs stretched straight, and ankles crossed, watched TV from his bed. She stepped inside and pulled the door closed behind her, careful not to send the click of the close echoing down the hall.

Immediately, she glanced toward the corner of the room. A camera.

"Hey, Izzy." Marcus gazed at the camera, too. "No worries. They disconnected it."

"That's what Sonnie said," she whispered and tiptoed toward him. "I hope she's right."

"I told them I was well enough for company. Nurse Ratched is being overprotective."

"I'm surprised no one's around."

"Annie and Merryman went home for the weekend. McDaniel is still in Washington. The rest are taking a late dinner. You'll need to be out—" He glanced at a wall clock, "in about fifteen."

He raised his eyebrows and winked at her, patting the bed beside him. "Want to jump inside and help make me feel better?"

Hot blood rushed across her cheeks. She took a step away from him and waved a hand. "No."

He laughed and swung his legs over the side of the bed. "Don't go rushing away. I was only kidding. Stick around and keep me company. I'm bored to death. I told them I was fine. I could go back to my dorm until someone comes for me."

"Someone is coming for you?"

"Yeah, I was never meant to be here. Never caught on to the whole remote-viewing thing."

"I thought you were doing better."

"No, not really. I was going to give it one more try, but once my parents found out I'd been stabbed, everyone agreed I should go home."

"How are you?"

He lifted his shirt to expose white tape across his stomach area. "No major organs hit. John Michael took the worst of it."

"How's he doing?"

"I'm not sure. If Lenny hadn't shown up, he'd probably be dead."

"I can't believe Todd turned on you guys."

"It was the drugs. I hear he is still detoxing."

"Yeah, we all heard that."

"Doesn't anyone know I'm going home?"

She lingered in stillness for a moment. "There was a rumor going around, but no one took it seriously."

"Yeah, well, I'm sure they aren't going to make a big deal about it, or kids will be stabbing each other to get out of here."

"True. Maybe that's why they didn't kick Lenny out."

"Man, he is strong. I wouldn't mess with Rachel Callahan if my life depended on it. He hovers over her."

"I know."

"He must be crazy about that sister of hers. I hear she's a lot like you."

"Oh, well." She sniffled, scratched her nose. She was never comfortable talking about herself. "She's beautiful, I've heard."

She hadn't meant to say that.

"I mean, not that I'm insinuating I'm pretty like Lisa. I've seen her picture, and she is drop-dead gorgeous."

This was getting worse.

"No, I mean." She closed her eyes and put a hand to her head. "I don't know what I mean. I stopped to see how you were and, frankly, I'm surprised you're doing so well. Even more surprised they've agreed to let you go home."

He leaned toward her, and for one fleeting moment, she thought he was going to kiss her. She wouldn't have minded.

"Can you keep a secret?"

She waited for the rush of blood across her face to subside, hoping he didn't notice her intensifying ruddiness.

"Yes," she said, despite knowing keeping secrets was not her forte.

"Chase Finley isn't dead."

She took a moment to regroup.

"What?"

"He's alive. His plane never went down."

Izzy glanced over both shoulders and pantomimed, "How do you know that?"

"There's a file cabinet in the room at the end of the hall. Eventually, they're moving central records and all of McDaniel's files to the new buildings, but they're storing them in that cabinet while they redo this building. I see his assistant walk back and forth with files all day long. So yesterday I nosed around. The door was unlocked."

"What did you find?"

"A file about a plane crash."

"Wait. I'm confused. So it crashed?"

"No. The Air Force plane that followed them crashed in the mountains. Chase's father's plane made it out. The CIA is still searching for them."

"Oh my God." She looked around again. "Chase is alive?"

"Yep."

"Well, if they are lying about him getting out, why are they letting you go home?"

He leaned away. "I'm not sure, but they sorted out lots of kids before the seventy-five of us came with the second wave. That's how Rachel got in."

"True." She thought faking the death of Chase but allowing Marcus to leave didn't make sense. But there was no sense worrying him. "I'm just glad you're feeling better. Ken Swarthy made it sound as if you and John Michael were sharing a last breath."

"John Michael might be. He may end up leaving, too."

"Kids want Lenny to leave."

"They won't let him go. I overheard the nurses saying a few kids signed a petition to have him removed, but McDaniel won't get rid of him."

"A petition? No one asked me to sign a petition. Whose idea was that?"

"Dawn's. At least that's what one nurse said."

"Dawn Davis?" She raised her eyebrows. "If I were her, I'd keep my mouth shut. She's not the best dreamer. She gets swapped out with the backups in our remote-viewing class occasionally."

"I think she'd like to get permanently swapped out. What's everyone saying about them allowing Rachel to go home for her grandmother's funeral?"

"Since no one else has ever gotten a leave like that, kids hope McDaniel is softening."

"Sleeping with him helped."

Izzy jerked backward, away from him.

"Oh, no, no, no. That's a rumor."

He smiled. His eyes twinkled. "You never see anything bad in anyone, do you?"

"No...it's just...you're wrong about Rachel." She itched her nose again. "She's in the top viewing group. She has extra privileges."

"They didn't let you go when your father died."

"But he lived in Mexico." She scratched her arm. "Rachel wouldn't do that and, well, now you're going home, so maybe the closer we get to college the more lenient McDaniel will be."

"I don't know, maybe. Honestly, I'm surprised they're letting me go, too."

"What did your parents say? They must be ecstatic."

"I haven't talked to them, yet. Swarthy has been talking to them."

"Swarthy?"

"Yeah, I know he's a complete jerk, but he did a three-sixty during this. He's flying my mother up Wednesday. On a personal plane. I leave Thursday."

"That soon?"

"Yeah, that's why I wanted to go back to my morning classes, so I could say goodbye to everyone. I suppose they don't want the disruption."

"Probably not. Kids are really riled up."

"I bet." Marcus glanced at the clock. "You know, you better—"

A slight clicking sound from down the hall slithered underneath the closed door. Izzy and Marcus held their breath to listen. Heels.

"Oh, shoot, you better get out of here. They might get mad."

"Oh my God, oh my God. Where should I go?"

Nervously, she picked her feet up and ran in place.

"Wait." She stopped. "Sonnie said leave by the window."

Remembering what else Sonnie mentioned, she hurried to turn the light out and the TV off, then she dashed to the window. Marcus beat her there. He jimmied the frame.

"I jarred this open last night but couldn't get it up far enough to sneak out. No problem for you."

"Oh, God, help me" She lifted a knee to the small opening in the window. As she did, particles of sand dropped from her shoe. She realized then she had left a trail of sand from the door to the window.

"Look at the sand," she whispered.

Marcus glanced at the floor.

"I'll get it."

"It's probably in the hall, too."

She turned her head sideways, and Marcus helped push her out. "I'll tell them it was Dawn. Everyone thinks she's a mole anyhow. Go on. Run."

"Dawn? A mole?"

"Go. Get out of here."

"Okay."

"And Izzy? I bet you're every bit as pretty as Rachel Callahan's sister."

"Oh," was all she got out before he closed the window.

She bent down and took off running.

## Chapter 40  Rachel and Jerry

When Rachel stepped off the escalator, bright light streaming through a wall of airport glass blinded her. She squinted. Her eyes scanned the limousine drivers. None held a sign with her name. She sauntered by them, wondering if she could keep on walking. If no one picked her up, if they forgot about her, could she stroll out into the streets of Las Vegas and keep going?

She'd find a place to sleep. She was resourceful. Eighteen now, she could get a job.

"Hello, Rachel."

When she heard the sound of his voice, she stopped and turned. Jerry McDaniel looked young in that setting. His thirty-nine, forty-some years—she wasn't sure of his age—hadn't set on his face. He flashed her a wrinkle-free simper, shoulders slouched, hands in pockets. His thick hair seemed messy. His casual clothes, crinkly. People who passed by might consider him somewhat unkempt.

He stepped toward her. Took her carry-on bag from her and placed a hand on the small of her back.

She glanced around to see where their driver was. His next words surprised her.

"My car is outside."

He led her out the glass doors to the front seat of a snazzy black car with its flashers blinking. He loaded her suitcase in the trunk and took the driver's seat.

"I couldn't let them pick you up. I knew you'd have a hard time."

He drove out of the airport and onto a highway ramp. He merged onto the freeway, his car cruising smoothly, effortlessly.

Tears welled in her eyes. She had never felt so fragile in her life. Coming down off the drugs, attending Gee's funeral, and leaving Lisa had drained her.

"You've lost weight."

True. She had barely choked down any food while at home. For years in the desert, she longed for her mother's cooking.

*Careful what you wish for.*

Then when the savory food sat in front of her, she could eat none.

She set her forehead against the glass of her window, breathed in the leathery smells of the car, and watched Las Vegas's bright buildings fade in the distance.

"We don't have to be back until tomorrow," he said. "I thought you might need extra time. I booked a place northwest of Vegas. It's not a long drive."

She closed her eyes. One more day. She sat up and reached for his hand. A few tears trickled down her face when she opened her eyes. She wiped them away quickly. "Thank you."

"Rachel," he said, removing a hand from the steering wheel. He slipped a long arm around her shoulder and stretched his fingers to the center of her back. He rubbed gently. "I'm so sorry. So sorry for everything."

She knew he was. He had been kind to her even before they slept together.

He had a wife and two toddlers. Both boys suffered severe asthma attacks, which kept their mother busy while Jerry was away. Cold-heartedly, she had refrained from thinking about them. She first slept with him six months after his wife gave birth to their second son, Finn.

Technically, the law would call their interludes statutory rape. In her mind, she had seduced him. She toyed and flirted with him until he caved, although, surely, she wasn't his first affair. Men as powerful as Jerry McDaniel often redefined fidelity.

Originally, she simply wanted favors, but after a few months, she grew fond of him. She didn't love him, but she liked the man who surfaced behind closed doors. There was power in knowing the Jerry no one else knew.

Even the most competent men had weaknesses.

She folded her hands in her lap, and he massaged her shoulders off and on until they arrived at a small, remote resort nestled in Nevada's red foothills. They rode toward a twelve-foot sandstone wall with a gatehouse. Jerry gave his name to the guard in the glass booth. The iron gates opened, and the wheels clicked as Jerry drove onto the brownstone pavers of a circular driveway.

He parked between the gilt-edged glass doors of the entryway and the gilded fountain of Venus, her long golden hair swirling around her glistening body. A porter removed their suitcases, and within minutes Rachel entered a suite with two rooms. A small deck flaunting a red-stone mountain view sat outside a long glass wall in the main room.

If only she could appreciate the ambiance. She sat down on the white couch near the glass doors and gazed outside at the breathtaking sight.

"I have to have you back by morning," he said. "I'm sorry. That was all I could finagle. Can I get you something?"

"No, thanks."

She had never been at a loss for words with him before. Always in control when they were alone, he had easily fallen for her, and she had used his affection to garner a slew of favors.

Did he love her? She didn't know. She only knew she didn't love him. The one thing that could truly make her fall in love with him—taking her away from Project Dream—he couldn't provide.

He sat down beside her. She fell into him.

"I wanted to stay home with Lisa."

"I know." He slid the back of one hand gently down the side of her face and kissed her. "I wish I could have made that happen."

"Me, too. Lisa's not as fragile as she used to be, though. She staved off a panic attack. I don't think she's had any for a long time. She talked about applying to Pepperdine."

"Now that I can do. Get her into Pepperdine," he said earnestly.

"Thanks, but no. She needs to stay with my mother."

"Of course."

"I thank God every day they took me and not her. She couldn't have survived this."

For the first time since she landed in Vegas, she glanced at him and felt her lips curve upward. She placed a hand on his chest. "I, at least, have you to watch over me. You don't know how I appreciate your patience and protection. The way you've kept me out of trouble."

Her hand slipped from his chest to her lap. "Lisa would have been alone in the desert. Alone with her morals like Izzy."

"Oh, speaking of, I did get her into the University of San Diego."

"Really? That's great. Thanks, Jerry. She needs to be by her family. And Sonnie?"

"Stanford. That change was easy."

He picked up a strand of her hair and twirled it gently through his fingers. "I have more good news."

She raised her eyebrows.

"Everything is set for you to transfer to Erie after the first session. Washington was never sure which were the most strategic areas for the Project Dream units, so I pulled some strings. I'm sorry I couldn't arrange for you to go directly home. You'll be in Torrance for the four years after college."

"What about Lenny? Where's he going?"

"Cleveland, a junior college. He'll be assigned to that unit after he finishes school, too. That way he can visit his mother on weekends for all eight years."

"And after?"

"He'll transfer to Erie with you."

"Good. He needs to be by his mother. And Todd?"

"Pepperdine and Torrance like you."

"That's good. He needs me."

"But do you need him? I was torn about sending him there. Are you sure?"

"I am. I care for him, despite his shortcomings. His humor has gotten me through this. I'm sorry he became so jealous. Are Marcus and John Michael okay?"

"They'll be fine."

"Todd has a horrid temper."

"It's the drugs. He has a real problem."

She moaned. "We all have a drug problem."

"You seem to be doing better. A few others never succumbed to the drugs. The Jimenez girl didn't."

"No, not Izzy. I'll miss her when we graduate."

"You'll be two hours apart. Maybe you can visit."

"No. I'm better when it's just Todd and me."

She stared out the window. He fixed his gaze on her.

"You can kick the drugs when this is over, Rachel."

"I can." She hoped she was telling the truth. "I'm going to lighten up when I get back. I'm determined to finish these last months and get on with my life."

He turned away, gazing toward the mountains. His fingers lifted and dropped strands of her hair. He raised his chin slightly, tipping his head backward. He stared pensively.

"Oh, no." She sensed trouble. "What's the matter?"

He stood and ambled toward the sliding doors of the deck. He lingered there, leaning against the glass and shoving one fist into a pocket. He raised his other hand, pointed a finger, and touched the window. He eased a fingertip up and down over the glass, tracing the mountains in the distance. He looked like a kid at an easel.

"I've gotten a promotion."

"You have?" She hadn't expected that. "That's great, Jerry."

"It's a big opportunity. More responsibility." He stopped tracing. "I'm being transferred to Washington."

She let a breath escape.

"When?"

"Next month."

He pushed off the glass with a shoulder, strode to the bar, and poured himself a bourbon. He tipped his head backward and spilled the contents of the glass into the back of his throat.

"Who's taking your place?"

He turned and faced her, leaned his backside to the bar. She could see telling her was painful.

"Ken Swarthy."

She closed her eyes. "Dear Lord, help us all."

## Chapter 41  Izzy

When Rachel Callahan stepped out of Jerry McDaniel's car, all hell broke loose. Five kids approached Izzy and begged her to have Rachel talk to McDaniel for them. Several others approached Swarthy under a united front, insisting college assignments be revisited. Yesterday Merryman had announced placements, and only Rachel Callahan's friends were assigned the colleges they requested.

Izzy couldn't squelch the soaring rumor Rachel was sleeping with McDaniel. She prayed no one mentioned it to Todd.

Two days after Izzy had visited Marcus, Swarthy and Merryman met with dreamers and informed them that Todd, Marcus, and John Michael were quarantined. Anyone caught in the infirmary would face dire straits—whatever that meant.

A crimson flush swept across her face during that announcement. She hadn't told a soul she visited Marcus, but she'd asked around if anyone else had. To her knowledge, she was his only visitor. She hoped Sonnie had been correct about the blind spots in the camera's view.

"We can go in the maintenance door in the early evening. They leave it unlocked for deliveries. The camera on that side of the building only catches the top half."

Sonnie had opened her computer, pressed a few keys, and showed Izzy the camera view and blind spot.

"We can crawl in that door and slither alongside the steel ovens." She pulled up another view inside the kitchen and pointed. "There is a half door along this wall. It's beside the infirmary. They hand food to the nurses through it. You can't see it."

Next Sonnie hit a key, and a screen full of Project Dream views appeared.

"You have access to all the cameras?"

"Yeah. I've been trying to find the safest way into the administrative offices."

Izzy held a hand up. "I don't want to know."

"Don't worry. The plan is dead in the water. They already began moving files around. Mason and I haven't been able to break into the security system on the new buildings yet."

That explained why Izzy hadn't heard more about their break-in plans. It also enlightened her on why Project Dream's other top geek, Mason Howard, had been spending so much time in Sonnie's room lately. For months, Mason had followed Sonnie around like a lost lamb. Finally, Sonnie noticed, and Izzy was happy for her, but she couldn't help but feel a pang of envy, too. So many kids paired up these days, while Izzy rolled along like a shared third wheel.

"But we can definitely go see Marcus and Todd," Sonnie had said.

"What do you do when you get inside the infirmary?"

"They're moving the administrative offices to the new building, so they're converting those offices to a conference room. They knocked out the wall beside the infirmary. The cameras facing the infirmary hall are temporarily out of commission. I'm sure they never expected three people would be recuperating there. They ordered new cameras, but they won't be installed until Thursday."

"How do you know that?"

Sonnie shrugged, then brought up an accounting screen displaying purchase orders.

"You are unbelievable. So you're sure the cameras aren't working?"

"Not in the infirmary wing."

"We could walk down the hall without being seen?"

"Yep, then leave the same way."

"What if Susan Jo checks on them while we're there?"

"Who?"

"You know, Susan Jo, the nurse."

Sonnie laughed. "Nurse Ratched?"

Rachel named her that. The nickname referred to an insane asylum nurse in an old movie.

"Yes; what if she checks on them while we're there? This is a stupid idea."

"We wear dark clothes. If she comes, we go out the window. The cameras outside were removed. A temporary camera faces that side of the building, but it's not night vision."

Sonnie's fingers danced over her keyboard and, magically, an outside view of the infirmary appeared. "If we turn the lights out so they don't shine through the window, they'll never see us. We jump out and run."

"I'm not going and you shouldn't go, either. What would Mason say? You know he's liked you for months."

Sonnie shrugged.

"I'll tell you what he'd say. He'd say you and Marcus have a thing going again."

"That was a short fling over a year ago. Mason knows it's over. Besides, Marcus likes you."

"Me? You're crazy. He's been in love with Rachel since day one."

"Him and everyone else." Sonnie closed the computer windows. "Including McDaniel."

"Don't say that."

"You know she's sleeping with him."

"Well if she is, I bet he forced himself on her."

Reasons why Rachel would sleep with someone as old as McDaniel had been rolling around in Izzy's head for weeks. Finally, because she couldn't fathom any other conclusion, she surmised he must have coerced her into sleeping with him.

Sonnie seemed to consider that possibility, then blurted out, "I don't believe that. She is just so depressed these days that she doesn't care about anything."

"She doesn't care what people say, that's for sure. And she takes too many chances. Just like you're talking about doing now."

By the end of the conversation, Izzy had convinced Sonnie not to visit Marcus and Todd.

But then on Saturday night, lonesomeness bit into Izzy's conviction. All of the kids were out in the desert, including Sonnie and Mason. Izzy found herself alone in her room, wondering if Marcus did like her.

She had a little crush on him. He did party hard. Used drugs too often. Wasn't a great dreamer. Sometimes he landed in the lowest tier of their remote-viewing class, but he was good-looking, sort of.

Sonnie had sparked her curiosity, and without Rachel there to drag her out to the desert, she felt lonely. Even though every ounce of her said she shouldn't go, she went anyway.

Then on Monday, Swarthy forbid anyone to set foot in the infirmary, and she immediately regretted the act. She scratched her arms and legs all day. Did he know she had been there? Her blotches blistered and oozed.

On Tuesday, Swarthy called a morning meeting and said the infirmary ban had been breached. Izzy froze. Did he mean before or after Monday's lecture?

Her arms went numb, and the books in her lap slid to the floor. The bang drew everyone's eyes toward her. Her face reddened. A rumble of laughter filled the room. Swarthy eyed her evilly, then resumed his lecture.

"Stay away from Todd, Marcus, and John Michael," he warned.

Late Tuesday evening, an ambulance, no lights flashing, entered the infirmary and exited quietly. Izzy had no idea who they wheeled away on the gurney.

Now, Wednesday morning, Izzy sat near the window and watched the front road during her morning classes, certain a car would come and Marcus's mother would hurry into the makeshift hospital.

By lunchtime, no car had come. In the cafeteria, Rachel barreled toward her with her tray and sat so close they rubbed shoulders.

"They are packing up Marcus's room," she told her.

Izzy breathed a sigh of relief. It was true. Marcus was headed home.

That thought was short lived. Sonnie sat down. "Marcus is on life support."

"What?"

"They took him to the landing mat, and a helicopter came for him. Probably flew him to Phoenix."

Shocked and momentarily confused, Izzy sat thunderstruck. The unusual quietness of the cafeteria hit her. All around kids leaned elbows on tables, whispering.

"No, you're wrong," she finally managed.

"I watched them take him out on the camera," Sonnie admitted in a low voice. "I saw his face. It was Marcus. He had a tube down his throat, IV, wires everywhere."

Izzy couldn't speak. All through lunch kids stopped by their table to ask if the rumor was true. She ate subconsciously, still staring out the window, expecting a car to come. She refused to believe the story.

Toward the end of their lunch, someone saw Ken Swarthy coming down the hallway. Kids turned in their seats. He entered the cafeteria, marched toward the front of the room, and grabbed the microphone. The speaker buzzed.

"Your attention, please. I have some sad news. Marcus Williams has been flown to a Phoenix hospital."

Izzy felt a tingling in her toes and fingers. The sensation spread through her like fire.

"Is he going to be okay?" One of the girls up front asked.

Ken Swarthy paused, wiped sweat from his forehead. The air conditioner seemed slightly off today. The Nevada heat filtered in stiflingly.

Izzy began to sweat. Her throat tightened. Under the table, she counted on her fingers how many days ago she visited Marcus. Less than four days had passed since he flashed that striking smile at her. Talked about the files at the end of the hall, the airplane crash, Chase being alive. How he looked forward to going home.

She felt her stomach churn.

"I'm sorry to tell you, but Marcus Williams never came to. He's been in a coma since the fight. They don't expect him to live."

An eruption sparked. Conversations raced around the room. Voices rebounded off the walls, making Izzy's head spin. She felt an uncontrollable surge from her stomach. She belched and then emptied her entire meal into her tray.

## Chapter 42  Izzy and Rachel

"I'll tell you once, and then I'm never going to talk about it again." Rachel sat down on the blanket. She was so close to her, Izzy could see the blue in her eyes despite the darkness. "It's true."

"Oh my God, Rachel, did he force you to sleep with him?"

"It's not that simple."

"Simple? Jerry McDaniel rapes you, and you say it's not that simple?"

"It definitely wasn't rape. I've slept with him more than once, and don't give me one of your long, drawn-out Catholic lectures. I liked sleeping with him."

"Wait. What?"

"I slept with him by choice."

"You can't mean that." Izzy scratched the side of her nose, squeezed her eyelids shut, and shook her head. "You wanted to sleep with him? He didn't force you?"

Rachel sighed, leaned back on two arms, and rested the back of her head on her shoulders. She gazed toward the sky. "This is why I never tell you anything."

"When did this all start?"

"Don't ask so many questions."

"I want to know."

"Well, if you must, well over a year ago."

"Over a year ago?"

"Quiet." Rachel glanced around. "I originally slept with him because I wanted a few favors. His good looks were a bonus.'

"You've been sleeping with him for over a year? My God, how many favors did you need?"

"Just a few. I kept sleeping with him because I liked it."

"Don't tell me that. I don't want to hear that." Izzy put her hands over her ears and then quickly dropped them to her sides and continued. "What favors did you get? More drugs?"

"No; how do you think you landed San Diego and Sonnie got Stanford? And did you think they decided themselves to send Todd to Pepperdine? With his drug problem?"

Izzy covered her face. When she slid her hands away, she couldn't look Rachel in the eye.

"You shouldn't have done that for me."

"I didn't. I did it for myself. I couldn't listen to you and Sonnie cry about where you wanted to go. I was already sleeping with him." She folded her legs Indian-style on the blanket and sat up. The full moon lit up her unabashed face. "So I asked him. Shoot me."

"Did you ask for Pepperdine?"

"Only after he told me they wouldn't approve a college in Erie. He tried to get them to send me to Mercyhurst, but they don't have connections there yet, and I don't know."

"You don't know what?"

"I don't know anything anymore."

"Well, you know they will never let us go, don't you? You realize you're sleeping with the man who will never let us out of this program?"

"I realize I'm sleeping with a man who's not a bad guy." Now Rachel covered her own face with her hands. She rolled her palms over her flesh forcefully, as if she could wipe away the truth.

"Rachel!" Izzy stood, paced back and forth on the blanket, and then dropped to her knees. "He's married. Has kids. I hear those boys have health issues."

"Asthma and stop! Don't you think I know that? We do what we have to do to get what we want."

"But you didn't get what you wanted. You're going to Pepperdine, not Mercyhurst."

"Eventually, I'm going home. McDaniel has plans to have the Cleveland unit changed to Erie."

"After college? You're going to Cleveland?'

"No, I'm going to Torrance, near you and then Erie once they make the switch."

"But sleeping with him? My God, Rachel."

"Trust me, Izzy, I didn't mind." She spoke quietly and crossly. "I like Todd. Maybe even love him. But Jerry McDaniel can please me in the bedroom like no drug addict can and don't go spilling that to Sonnie."

"That is so wrong."

"No, it isn't and quiet. You can't tell anyone. I know you. You have a hard time keeping your mouth shut."

"Oh, that's what you think? Believe me, I can keep a secret." Izzy hesitated because Rachel's countenance changed. She looked suspicious. Izzy changed directions. "But you? You go ahead and sleep with the entire army and all of Washington."

She rose to gather her things. "For as long as we live, none of us will ever get out. Not me, not Todd, not Sonnie—" She twirled around and faced her.

"Not even you, Rachel."

# Chapter 43  Izzy

Life changed when Ken Swarthy held the reins. He reinstated a curfew, and the late-night free-for-alls in the desert ended. Annie Sherman transferred out two months after he won the coveted director's seat. Other personnel requested transfers. One by one, the best instructors exited until only an evil shadow of the original administration remained.

Swarthy added daily lessons in national loyalty. Before dinner each evening, he required they stand and recite an oath to their country. He sequestered them to the auditorium several times a week, at will, and subjected them to extravagant lectures.

At those addresses, Swarthy bellowed out rules in a monotone voice. Kids said he looked like Hitler. He warned of secret executions in the military. Said any dreamer who crossed the spikes on the mountain, entered the infirmary or administrative offices without permission, obtained confidential information in any manner, or divulged Project Dream classified information, could be executed.

He talked incessantly of one final test in the mountains that would make or break them. He mentioned this closing "trial" so often in that last hot summer, some kids started the rumor he planned on sacrificing one of them.

Others scoffed.

"He's not going to sacrifice anyone," Todd said when Izzy insinuated murder was not beyond Swarthy.

"Then what's this trial about?" Izzy spoke in a low voice at her dinner table. Since they were no longer permitted to congregate in the evening, meals were the only time they talked.

"He's faking everything. Trying to scare us into not divulging any secrets when we go to college."

"Six kids are scheduled to leave in three days. He said the trial would be before anyone leaves. So we should find out soon," Izzy whispered.

"Who cares." Rachel took a bite of food.

"You don't care because you and Todd are protected. You sold your soul to McDaniel," John Michael said. "The rest of us have to worry."

Rachel stopped chewing.

"What the hell is that supposed to mean?" Todd jumped to his feet. Rachel hastily tugged him down.

"Quiet," she spit through her teeth.

"Say it again." Todd leaned over the table, glaring at John Michael.

Why Swarthy allowed those two to continue sitting at the same table, Izzy wasn't sure. Maybe to kill each other.

"Come on, Todd, he's lashing out because they're not sending him to Boston College. Ignore him." Izzy turned to John Michael. "Stop, will you?"

Rachel widened her eyes and glared at John Michael. "Can't we all get along these last few days?"

She tugged at Todd's arm, but Todd continued inching across the table toward John Michael

"If you are insinuating what I think you are, I'll kill you, Turnbull."

Todd was a ticking bomb. His drug usage had escalated. In the last few weeks, Rachel had stopped chastising him about it. In the past, she had harped on him relentlessly. Now she seemed subdued. Worn might be a better word.

Swarthy had come down hard on her. Clearly, he didn't like Rachel.

She wasn't as popular with the kids, either. A barrage of rumors had surfaced: She had slept with McDaniel. She wouldn't sleep with Swarthy. She did sleep with Swarthy. And the most outlandish of all, she'd had an affair with the commanding officer, Randall Scott, who visited once a month after McDaniel left in order to check on the out-of-control Swarthy.

Izzy only believed the gossip she knew to be true: Rachel had slept with Jerry McDaniel. And she did everything in her power to keep that information secret. "John Michael's saying that to get a rise out of you, Todd."

"So you'll go ballistic, and Swarthy turns on you," Sonnie added. "We all know they're going to make an example out of someone."

Todd seemed somewhat appeased. He sat back and shoveled a forkful of food into his mouth. "Well." He swallowed. "It's not like they're going to kill one of us."

All eyes turned toward him, and not a second later, Ken Swarthy entered the room dressed in boots and full military attire. Several instructors followed behind him. He headed toward the front of the room while the instructors handed out individual envelopes to each of the kids.

"Do not open your envelopes," Swarthy commanded. "Until I say you may."

When everyone held an envelope in their hand, the instructors lined up along the far wall, and Swarthy relaxed into an at-ease stance.

"After dinner you are to retire to your rooms, finish packing, and prepare to meet on the second mountain range."

A tense hush crossed the cafeteria.

*The second mountain range?*

They'd been forbidden from even the first range for months.

"I want everyone in full camouflage with all tactical gear. You are to be standing on the black-peg line by 2100 hours. If you're late? You know the consequences."

Silence rang through the cafeteria. Not a utensil clanged. Even the kitchen help held their breath.

"Come prepared."

Izzy gazed at Rachel and Sonnie. "Come prepared" meant bring two days' worth of supplies. As if Swarthy read her mind, he continued.

"Forty-eight-hours worth of supplies in your backpacks, children. Allow me to offer one last piece of advice. Remember your oath." He hesitated and then added, "You may open your envelopes."

Izzy's hands shook. She glanced across the table just as Lenny unfolded the note inside his envelope. His paper held a simple name. Mary Alice.

Izzy fumbled with hers. She glanced toward Rachel. "What does yours say?"

Rachel held up the paper.

"Lisa. Just Lisa."

Izzy ripped the paper out of hers and unfolded it.

"What does yours say?" Rachel asked.

Izzy could barely get the word out. Her throat felt parched.

"Sammy."

# Chapter 44  Lenny

Someone was going to die.

Lenny had looked each dreamer in the eye. He was fairly certain of today's outcome. There was no altering fate. From the onset, he'd understood the gravity of the program more than the others, but he had held his tongue for everyone's sake.

Now the day had come. A putrid acid rose from the pit of his stomach to the back of his throat.

He would miss them. Rachel, Sonnie, Kenny, Kiera, little Izzy. She did remind him of LeeLee.

He sighed.

Enduring pain had never been problematic. His early, wretched school days had given him the strength to muster through his years at Project Dream. Like Izzy's poverty had done for her. Rachel's loss. Todd's regret. John Michael's evil.

Even the worst of the dreamers had good in them.

Lenny zipped his suitcase closed. Soon he would leave for Cleveland. In the end, Rachel Callahan had seen to that. Slept with Jerry McDaniel for herself and her friends.

In less than eight years, a Project Dream military unit would be developed in Erie, Pennsylvania, and Lenny would move home. Because of Rachel, he would be able to take care of his arthritic-stricken mother, who had lived her entire life thinking only of her son and other less-fortunate souls. He'd gladly protect her until her dying day.

But today? Today he would protect no one.

He had looked directly into Rachel Callahan's eyes and knew the outcome. Only God could overpower fate. He would remain calm and stoic when called to the mountain. He'd remember the debts he owed his mother, LeeLee, and now, Rachel.

He ambled to the mirror, mustering the nerve to glance at himself to be sure. As always, he saw his future.

A gentle breath escaped him.

He would live to repay his debts.

# Chapter 45  Izzy

Izzy stepped out of the shower and tucked a towel around her. She opened her suitcase and removed her camouflage gear. She hadn't thought she would wear those in these final days. She dried herself off and dressed, thinking about the note. About Sammy.

She combed her hair and drew the thick, wet, black strands tightly back into a ponytail. She glanced in the mirror, leaning close to see if her eyebrows were straight, if the hives on her cheeks had surfaced. She wanted to blend in with the sandstone if she could today. She leaned away and gave herself a final straightening, nodding at her reflection.

"Okay, Izzy, you look fine, plain. Don't screw anything up. You leave for San Diego in four days."

She had spent yesterday gathering instructions and packing. Leaving the desert proved to be an ordeal. There were documents to sign, oaths to recite, and secret computer codes to learn.

Secrets.

*Sammy?*

She didn't like secrets. She thought back to past months, to Marcus and the one secret she had kept from Rachel. Tonight, after their final test, she would whisper to Rachel that Chase was alive.

Paranoid at that thought, she glanced around the room. Could someone read a person's thoughts? Before Annie Sherman left Project Dream, she warned Izzy to protect herself.

"Just as you remotely view places, others can remotely view the room around you. If you find yourself feeling closed-in, as if someone is crowding you, be cautious."

Could Annie possibly have meant someone could read her mind? She closed her eyes. What had Jerry McDaniel told Rachel before he left? Two project dreamers could read minds? Swarthy would shoot Rachel if he knew she told Izzy.

He'd shoot Izzy, too. Why had McDaniel told Rachel that, anyway? Was it some sort of test? He knew she couldn't keep a secret. One shot or snort, and Rachel's secrets became public knowledge.

But then, what good was keeping a secret if someone could read your mind?

"Clear," she said out loud as she'd been taught to do.

Yet, try as she may, she couldn't clear her mind. Her thoughts kept coming back to Marcus. How alive and well he was during her visit.

*Clear.*

Swarthy had lied. He said Marcus never came out of his coma.

*Clear.*

Marcus passed away. Sonnie had confirmed his obituary.

*Clear.*

She opened her eyes.

What if they had beaten it out of him? Made Marcus tell who left that trail of sand in his room. Would he say her name? Would he lie and say Dawn Davis's name? That wasn't good, either.

*Clear, darn it, clear.*

She placed the palms of her hands on her temples and squeezed. She couldn't expunge the incident. She wanted to tell someone, needed to tell someone. Hadn't she learned her lesson?

"Don't tell them about the angels," her mama had warned.

But she told the lady not to go to New York City.

"They'll come for you," her belo had cautioned.

And they did come for her.

How she wished she hadn't told the sad woman not to go. How she wished she hadn't visited Marcus that night. How she wished she hadn't received the note with Sammy's name on it. What could it possibly mean?

*Don't think.*

A knock made her jump. Her heart skipped a beat. She rushed to open the door and found Lenny Emling standing on the other side. He wore his camouflage gear, boots, and his backpack was slung over one shoulder.

He glanced directly into her eyes, nearly frightening her to death. Lenny never looked anyone in the eye. He said nothing, at first. Merely stood staring. Then he lifted his big hand and placed one long finger over his mouth. A faint "sh" whirred over his lips.

"For once," he said. "F-for once in your life, Izzy Jimenez, d-don't say a word when we reach the mountain. Your life depends upon it. Stay quiet and you'll live to s-see your niece grow up."

Shocked, she said nothing. Was someone going to die? She couldn't speak. Lenny's gaze fell to the floor.

"Trust me. Say nothing," was the last thing he said before he left her.

## Chapter 46  Project Dream

The sun dipped behind the highest mountains and hovered over the lower hills. The dreamers lingered near the black line of the second mountain range. Some sat, others paced, and most chatted nervously, guessing what the night would hold. None dare cross the line. Though no one could see the militia, surely they were there in the mountains. Their brown suits blending in with the rock.

Project Dream officials now had the authority to stop anyone who crossed that line by any means. Tim Sackett, the youngest dreamer, turned eighteen today. This morning they had all raised their hands and swore an oath to different branches of the United States military. Each dreamer held the government's remote-viewing secret privy. Individually, they represented minuscule yet unique fragments of the country's national security. Transporting those secrets out of Area 51 without permission was treason. The top-secret training they received could not be revealed to another country or another human being. Because of their knowledge, crossing that line on the mountain meant desertion.

It was simple. This was the United States government.

Kids gestured toward Swarthy when he came into view. His Jeep stopped at the last switchback before the black line. He wrapped an arm around a roll bar, swung out onto the ground, and headed up the last hill, still wearing his boots and military gear. The scene mirrored a bleak ending of a gloomy war movie.

Two marksmen flanked him as he climbed. On a nearby hill, the faintest roll of a pebble proved more gunmen watched them. Yes, they were there, lingering in the foothills below and on the mountain tops above.

By the time Swarthy reached them, Izzy could feel her hives bursting out of her skin. He halted on the flat path before the line, his lips tight and his limbs stiff. The two guardsmen behind him spread their feet apart, stilling like statues. They stared straight ahead, machine gun straps crossing their chests.

Swarthy removed his sunglasses and tucked them into a chest pocket. "Tonight, you'll complete your final task of Project Dream. Line up in front of the posts."

Uneasily, kids scrambled toward posts, forming two crowded lines of fifty. Each had been assigned a place in their lineup since the beginning. Occasionally, places changed according to instructors' choices. Swarthy redid the lines a month ago. Virtually all of Izzy's table, and certainly the top ten, stood in the first line. Behind them, the slope of the hill allowed the second line full view.

Lenny, taking his spot six people down from Izzy, turned and set a finger against his lips. She dipped her chin in a nod so faint only he could see.

*I know. Not a word.*

When everyone stood at attention in line, Swarthy gave another command.

"Draw your pistols. Point them downward. Hold them tight against your legs."

Izzy's knees nearly buckled. Would he command them to shoot someone? And if he did, would they? Could they? Could she?

She felt blotches burrowing out of her skin as Swarthy walked in front of the long line, his pace painfully slow. She was sure he would notice her hives and stop, but he walked by. Kept moving down the line, looking each of them in the eye with an evilness she had never witnessed in a man. By the time he stared into the last person's eyes, circled around to the center, and faced them, the sun hid behind even the smallest hills, bathing them in gray mountain shadow.

"Today you will witness a military execution."

A hint of groans flowed across the desert. Kids mumbled.

"You think he means an actual execution?" Izzy's eyes focused straight ahead as she whispered to Sonnie.

"No; we'll execute a military tactic, hopefully."

The grumbles continued.

"Silence," Swarthy hollered, and without so much as taking a single breath in between sentences, he said, "Rachel Callahan, step forward."

Izzy closed her eyes.

*Stay still. Remember what Lenny warned.*

In her peripheral vision, she saw Rachel's figure. Swarthy had moved Rachel toward the center of the line last month. With McDaniel gone, he badgered her relentlessly.

Izzy's last meal rose to the back of her throat.

Without McDaniel's protection, who knew what Swarthy would do to Rachel. Izzy swallowed the nasty taste in her mouth and gazed to the right. Unlike her, Rachel appeared calm. Without hesitation Rachel stepped forward, obeying Swarthy's command. Izzy could only see the side of her face. She prayed Rachel wasn't smiling.

*For once, don't be stupid, Rachel.*

"There has been a breach of confidentiality." Swarthy's voice bounced against hot rock now cooling in mountain shadow. "There can be no breach. Someone must pay."

Izzy's legs wobbled. Swarthy wouldn't shoot someone, would he? Despite her terror, she couldn't let Rachel take the blame for her. Swarthy had asked many times which dreamer broke the infirmary ban order. She turned her head. Considered stepping forward and admitting it was her. But as she twisted her neck, her gaze fell to Lenny. He stared back. Shook his head.

*Trust me.*

Her head snapped forward. Lenny would never allow anything to happen to Rachel.

*Trust Lenny.*

Did Lenny know she had visited Marcus?

Swarthy continued. "Hand me your revolver." He held a palm in front of Rachel.

She handed him her gun.

"Get down on your knees." Swarthy's voice held a wicked hatred.

Izzy's vision swirled, but she didn't move. Somewhere down the line others did. Someone gasped. Someone staggered. She heard a boot scuff rock. But Izzy didn't falter. She stared straight ahead. Motionless as the mountains.

*Trust Lenny.*

*****

Rachel dropped down, lodging two knees into the dirt. She placed her hands behind her back as she had been taught to do, and she smiled up at Ken Swarthy. She hoped kids down the line could see the dimples appear on the sides of her face, so if he killed her, they knew she went out smiling.

She stared directly at him with no fear of death. Life had long lost its value. He appeared perturbed at her smile.

"Today you learn what breaking confidentiality means for a dreamer." His voice carried down the line in both directions. "There will be no leaks in communication."

He stepped toward her. She kept smiling, staring upward, daring him. Even when he raised his gun in the air, not a tremor struck her. She wouldn't let him see her fear.

She heard gasps and sounds. Someone's feet scuffed dirt. Instantaneously, the two guards raised their guns to eye level.

"If I hear so much as one more sound, even a breath by any of you," Swarthy yelled. "You'll take her place."

The mountains seemed to moan around them. Everyone held their breath. The wind whistled over stone and rock. The valley whimpered. And the dark crawl of the mountains' shadows up the hillside seemed to be shrieking.

Ken Swarthy inched his pistol toward Rachel. Placed its muzzle against her forehead.

The cold gun against her head jarred her memory. She heard Gee's words.

*There will be times when you think, "this is going to kill me." Here is a secret. It won't. Trust old Gee. Hold your head high and your limbs still and muddle through. Look life in the eye and let him know you'll never give in.*

She looked Ken Swarthy straight in the eye.

*Let "him" know.*

Years later, she would recall this as the bravest moment of her life. He cocked the gun. She widened her smile. He nudged her forehead, forcing her head back a bit. She could see the anger rise in him when he couldn't break her.

"We will execute any dreamer for so much as a one-word breach of your oath." He spit his words. "And, if you breathe a word to anyone of what happens here tonight, this same retribution will fall to your most-loved family member—the person whose name appeared on the note you received today. So no one move."

Slight gasps sounded.

"None of you are ever to reveal anything about today's military execution. If you do, the person named on your paper will die."

The muscles in Ken Swarthy's face tensed. His stare adjusted faintly toward the right. He appeared to concentrate elsewhere. His scathing glance jumped to someone else. Who? Rachel's smile began to fade. What was he doing?

He swung his arm to the right. Rachel only had time for one thought—Jerry McDaniel had saved her life. She heard the discharge of the gun. The bullet landed squarely on Dawn Davis's forehead. Her body lurched backward across the black-spike barrier on the mountain. Her gun flew from her hand, and blood splattered on the rocks and dreamers around her.

Instantly, the clicking of guns echoed around them. Rachel gazed up to see the men on the mountain tops, guns raised, the sun falling behind them.

She could hear kids dropping to the ground from fright. Some were throwing up. Others screamed. The pungent smell of Ken Swarthy's deed drifted around them. He stepped toward Dawn's body, bent to pick up her gun, and lodged the grip of it into the fingers of her outstretched hand.

His body stiffened to attention.

"Today, at approximately 2100 hours, Dawn Davis attempted to escape the desert with national secrets. When we called to her, she aimed her gun in our direction and, for the protection of all, I shot her."

He paused long and cynically. A smile formed on his lips, and Rachel realized why he took her gun. She would have shot him.

"Her intent was to sell those national secrets on the black market. Tell a soul different and the person you love most in this world will find the same fate as Ms. Davis."

*LeeLee.* Rachel thought.

*****

*Sammy.* Izzy thought.

Sheer terror swept across her. If she fell backward, across the line, would he shoot her, too?

Kids began inching forward, some fell to the side, bent and retching. Was someone else going to die? Izzy noticed the horizon. The mountain peaks. The valley. The militia. How long had they been there? How many gunmen stood on the mountain tops as the sun set behind them, their black shadows lurking like executioners in a horror film?

Would they shoot more dreamers?

Izzy's knees buckled. The formation of their line no longer discernable, Lenny darted toward her. Lifted her to her feet, and then hurried down the line to help another small girl, Kiera.

Sonnie threw her arms around Izzy. Mason stepped toward Sonnie and hugged them both. John Michael collapsed to his knees. Rachel stood and turned in time to see Todd stagger backward. She lurched toward him, grabbed his arm, and yanked him forward, away from the black-peg line.

"Drop your guns," Swarthy cried. "Drop them or we shoot you."

Those who hadn't dropped them already set them at their feet. Ken Swarthy laughed. Izzy would hear that evil laugh in her dreams for years afterward.

"Leave her body as it is. Move away."

Kids scrambled farther away from Dawn Davis. Some leaped over the line of blood trickling from her head as they searched for friends. Those who still could, watched Ken Swarthy turn and descend the mountain, his two dog-like guards backing away after him. More kids collapsed. Cries heightened.

In the frantic hysteria of the darkness, as the sun set in the night, the truth hit Izzy: none of them would breathe a word to anyone of what happened that evening. They would not tell a soul about the secret execution of Dawn Davis.

Her gaze found Rachel. Todd slouched, and Rachel helped steady him with her strong arms. Izzy stepped away from Sonnie and Mason. She glanced across the hillside and all around. She took in the expressions on the faces, breathed the smell of the gun powder, and listened to the wails of the weak. She absorbed the scene, so she would never forget the insidiousness of the incident. She wanted to remember that she had seen raw evil and lived.

When her eyes circled back to Rachel, her heart sank.

*Sammy. I must protect Sammy.*

She wouldn't tell Rachel that Chase's plane hadn't crashed. That he was alive. So many secrets of their time in the desert would remain with them forever. No one would know she had snuck in and talked to Marcus on that evening. That Dawn Davis had taken a bullet to the head for her.

Suddenly darkness seemed upon them.

She stepped to the front, located her gear, and hoisted her bag over one shoulder. She reached into her pack and pulled out a headlamp. A calmness fell over her. Perhaps the peace was shock or God or the realization that despite all odds she had held onto her dignity. She had not succumbed to alcohol and drugs and promiscuity as many of the others had. She had been stronger than that.

She glanced toward Lenny. Her only remorse fell in not stepping forward to confess her breach into the infirmary. Why had he told her to remain quiet?

Lenny seemed to read her mind. He stepped toward her.

"It had to be this way," he said. "No matter what you did here today, they were going to kill Dawn. You'll understand someday. Trust me."

In him, too, there was tranquility.

*Trust Lenny.*

She would trust him because she had to. She couldn't bear life otherwise. She would live in this Project, protect America, but she would never compromise her morals. She had gained an insurmountable strength from the desert's wickedness.

She nodded at Lenny. They were stronger than the others.

Lenny nodded back, and then she, Izzy Jimenez, started down the mountain. She walked alone, turning her back on Sonnie and Rachel and the others. She wanted no more of them. She wanted to forget. Forget everything and everyone from Project Dream.

She thought of little Sammy in Mexico. How she could visit her at Friendship Park, spend time with her mama, see Enrique.

Determined to block this day and her years at Project Dream, she marched down the hill, her head held high, her resolve to protect Sammy and to live herself, unmatched.

All of the other dreamers noticed her small, straight frame—once judged weak and clumsy—walking bravely away. They watched her, and eventually, they followed.

Izzy Jimenez left for the University of San Diego four days later and like the others, she would not mention a word about Project Dream or that final execution.

She understood her destiny.

There was no way out but by death.

# A Note About the Author

CJ Zahner is a digital-book hoarder, lover of can't-put-down books, and the author of *The Suicide Gene, Dream Wide Awake,* and *Project Dream.* She has two novels pending: *Within the Setting Sun,* and the sequel to *Dream Wide Awake, The Dream Snatchers.*

CJ grew up in Erie, Pennsylvania, the second child of hard-working parents, Pasquale and Donna Mae Filutze. Her brother Mike, eleven years her senior, married when she was nine years old. Often alone, CJ created characters and wrote stories to while the time away.

She fell in love and married her soul mate, Jeff Zahner, and is the proud mother of Jessie, Zak, and Jillian, and the blessed grandmother of Layla Grace.

In 2015, she began looking at life differently when her brother and his wife were diagnosed with dementia and early-onset Alzheimer's. Then, her husband pulled her aside and said, "Quit your job. You're a writer." After twenty years of service, CJ picked up her purse one day at work and quietly walked away. She never returned. She began her career as a novelist.

Now, she reads, writes, runs, and dreams up her next novel in her lovely little hometown of Erie. On Saturday mornings, you'll find her running with friends at Presque Isle State Park. If she's not there, she's visiting her children, granddaughter, or hiking in one of America's great National Parks with Jeff.

Read her personal blog or find book club questions for her novels on her website at www.cyndiezahner.com.

Read sample chapters of other CJ Zahner novels on the following pages.

# The Dream Snatchers

## Chapter 1  Sammy

Sammy Jimenez's long legs kicked up tiny rocks as she ran toward town, her long, black hair whipping around behind her. Here and there along the path, boys hollered disgusting comments to her as she sailed by. A few tried to catch her.

Sometimes she would slow her pace to get within spitting range of the boys. Then she'd hawk in their faces and speed away, laughing.

One boy, Jerald, she allowed to run alongside her.

"In a hurry to see your scumbag father?"

"You should talk, Harry Jerry. When's the last time you saw your old man?"

"Heck, I'm not even sure that is my old man." The boy labored to breath. "You coming with us next week?"

"You're crazy." She slowed a bit. Jerald never could keep up with her, but then which of them could? "You'll smother in the back of that van."

"Didn't you hear?"

"Hear what?"

"Old man Sanchez dug a tunnel. He's going to let some kids go through to try it out. He said we have to be fast."

"Then he won't let you go." She laughed while she ran.

"You could go." He struggled to breathe.

"I told you. My aunt Izzy is getting me out of here. Taking me to North Carolina. Just signing the final papers."

The boy tripped but then regained himself as they passed the City's welcome sign. Sammy picked up the pace, darting down one street, turning on another, and then racing toward an old, broken-down white van.

"She's been trying to get you out for years," he called, several steps behind her now.

"She's going to get me out this time. She promised. My aunt Izzy never breaks a promise."

"Well, if you change your mind."

Right then a man stepped in front of her with his hands out, and she crashed into him so hard that she knocked him off balance. She tumbled to the ground on top of him. Jerald couldn't slow his feet in time to help her. He passed them, fell to the ground himself, and rolled in dirt.

Sammy kicked so violently that a cloud of dirt arose around her. She hollered, cussed. Several people stopped walking to watch, but no one approached.

The man stood up with her in his grasp, his thick arms secured around her waist. She flailed her arms and kicked her feet, shimming down him so that the top of her pants broke free from beneath his grip. In a flash, one second, she whipped the knife out and slashed the side of his face so deep he released her. With hardly a hesitation, she ran toward the van.

"You bitch," the man yelled.

Sammy ignored him. She picked up her pace. She could see the wheels of the white van beginning to move. No matter what, her father never waited if she was late. He'd been driving people to Friendship Park every Sunday since some woman named Betty opened the border for families to visit each other. Papa waited for no one.

She ran faster. Hollered.

"Mani, the door! Please?"

One door on the back of the beat-up van opened. A young boy on his knees beckoned to her with one hand while holding the side of the van with his other.

"C'mon," he yelled, and then all around her people began hollering. Cheering.

This wasn't the first time she had run for the van, but she hoped it would be the last. As she neared, she saw her father's face in the side mirror, a cigarette hanging from his lips, his eyes jockeying from the mirror to the road, an exuberant smile curving his lips.

The van sped up.

"Slow down, Papa," she screamed.

People came out of storefronts and shacks to watch her run. They yelled.

"Correr, Sammy!"

"A trapa ese tonto, Sammy."

"Don't let that scoundrel leave you, Sammy."

And as the van slowed just a tad to turn the corner, Sammy surged forward, came up to the bumper, and threw herself inside. The beckoning boy grabbed her pant loop and pulled her in.

Up and down Mantelli Street, cheers rose and people clapped. Inside the van, Sammy scrambled toward the center as hands patted her shoulders. "Buen trabajo, Sammy." "Mi Dios, esa chica es rapida."

She stood, brushed herself off, and moved toward the front of the van, her steps bouncing from side to side.

"Papa!" She hollered, her eyes wide. "Belo got a computer!"

The driver, Enrique Jimenez, turned toward her, a cigarette dangling from his lips. His black eyes twinkled, his smile widened, and he spoke out the side of his mouth.

"A tower or a laptop?"

"A laptop."

Five hours later, Sammy and twelve others exited the van and lined up to get into Friendship Park. Sammy waved goodbye enthusiastically as her Papa drove off. He would pass the time in a bar three miles down the road and pick them up when the gates closed for the day.

Papa had long been banned from Friendship Park.

# Dream Wide Awake

## Chapter 1  Jack

He felt her eyes on him before she spoke.

"Daddy?"

Her breath warmed his cheek. She stood so close that the remnants of last night's snack—her mom's favorite, watermelon gumdrops—mingled with mint toothpaste and reminded him she was a little Lisa, only fearless.

He kept still. Held the sweet smell for a moment and waited for the familiar poke. The prod came. One miniature finger pecking three times, knocking at his shoulder.

"Daddy? Are you in there?"

He loved that she pictured him inside his own head. Yet, he hated it, too.

"Yes, Mikala." He stretched his legs, being careful not to wake Lisa. "I'm in here."

"Marky is close now."

His eyes snapped open.

"How close, sweet pea?"

"In my room."

Jack Daly sat up and swung his legs over the bed, feeling for his shorts on the floor with his toes. He placed his feet in the leg holes, stood, and pulled them over his boxers.

"I can see the movie better," she said softly, shuffling her pink puppy slippers backward to give him room.

"Quiet, darling, let's not wake Mommy," he whispered, but the request was in vain. The covers rustled as Lisa rolled over. She tugged a pillow over her head to muffle their words. She didn't approve of their morning chats.

"Okay," Mikala whispered softly from the doorway. A ray of moonlight cheated its way through the corner of a window blind and fell faintly on her eager form. She stood, hands raised, fingers wiggling.

He whisked her up in his arms, her one-size-too-big flannelled pajamas bunching over wiry arms and legs, and her long blond locks cascading over tiny shoulders. He turned and backed out of the room, closing the door behind him. When he released his hand, the doorknob clunked to the floor, and the door drifted ajar.

"Damn it," he whispered, tucking Mikala close as he leaned over to look for the handle. "Oops, sorry, sweetie."

"It's okay, Daddy."

Normally, he refrained from swearing around the kids, but his procrastination had thrust him into a parental slip of the tongue. Shirking home-upkeep chores naturally accompanied tough work cases. Plus, he hated odd jobs. Twirling a screwdriver and dipping a paint brush had never been his forte. He hoped the knob-less door didn't remind Lisa he hadn't patched the wall in the boys' bedroom or touched up the kitchen backsplash. Their homey little tri-level needed a makeover.

For lack of vision, he swirled one foot over the hall carpeting until he felt the knob against his foot, and then he kicked the nuisance to the side and glanced down the hall toward the fluorescent yellow lights of the cartoon clock in Mikala's bedroom. 4:44. The time was always about the same when the dreams called her from the night. His fingers found the hall light switch, and their world lit up.

"Let's go downstairs, so we don't wake your brothers."

"Daddy?"

"Yes?"

"We don't have time for coffee."

He smiled. She knew the routine: milk and coffee in their favorite mugs at the kitchen counter. He shouldn't be amused. He knew what was coming, but despite all, her youthful wisdom still grabbed him.

"Okay, sweetie." He sat down at the top of the staircase, and her little frame collapsed into his lap. One of her arms landed squarely around his shoulder. "You said Marky is in your room?"

"Yes, he played the movie, bigger."

Her voice tickled his eardrums. He loved its young, high-pitched tone that hadn't kept time with her six years. He savored the youthful shrill, knowing that when she grew older, like Lisa, the years would age her sweet voice, and life would cloud her innocent interpretation of the dreams.

He yawned and threaded the thick, caramel-colored hair garnishing his forehead with his fingers, smoothing an annoying clump to the side. The tuft bounced back defiantly. He frowned. "Can you see the other little boy yet?"

"Yes, but I didn't look at his face. I wanted to wait, so I am safe with you."

"You're safe, sweet pea."

"I'm scared." Her fingernails pressed into the skin on his shoulder.

"Scared?"

Her dreams seldom frightened her. He could lead her away from the bad parts, talk her around the actual crime, so she didn't experience the horror. He wasn't completely sure about all this. Her psychologist said she didn't seem damaged in the least from her nightmares, but then they hadn't been completely truthful about everything. These weren't really nightmares. "Why? You aren't normally afraid."

"Because I recognize the room in the movie."

He turned to face her. "It's familiar?" He scratched an itch at the back of his neck with his free hand and yawned again.

She nodded.

"What do you recognize about it?"

"It's Danny's room."

He stopped breathing.

Doubting his daughter's words had long escaped him. Since she first explained about the movies—dreaming wide awake, she called the phenomena—their accuracy had dissolved any disbelief. But this couldn't be. She must be wrong this time. Marky, the boy in her dreams, relayed movies of strangers. Visions that remarkably resembled abductions in their hometown.

Years before, he merely suspected she had inherited her mother's gift. Now, he knew. She was Lisa's replica. The one difference? Mikala was strong willed like her aunt Rachel, grounded at age six. Lisa couldn't handle the dreams. Mikala could more than handle them. Like a miniature newscaster, she announced each scene to him until she came too close to the scary parts, and he nudged her by them.

As an investigator promoted within the police force three years ago, the fact that his own daughter had a sixth sense was anything but coincidental. After all, his occupation and this curse of a trait so alive in his in-law's family is what had led him to Lisa in the first place.

But this was different. Now the gift—curse—befell his daughter.

"Danny? As in your cousin Danny?"

"Yes. Can I close my eyes now?" She poked her chin out and shut her eyes before he responded.

"Sure, sweetie, but I think you're confused."

"No, I'm not confused." She scrunched her eyelids tighter. "I can see Danny's Superman bed."

"There are lots of Superman beds." He kept his arms around her still while she concentrated. As if absence of movement could clarify her vision, erase his nephew from her mind's eye.

"No, it's Danny's. I can see the three Batman stickers. The ones Aunt Janice yelled at him for putting on his bed."

This wasn't normal. Typically, she described streets, houses, faces of strangers, never people or places she knew. A week ago, two months after Marky Blakley turned up missing, she'd described the boy's lisp to perfection. Said he appeared to her. Showed her the scar on his finger where the spokes of a neighbor boy's tricycle had cut a piece off—a bit of information never released by the department. Then Marky began showing her movies of two other little boys. In her head. Scenes of an abductor targeting children of single mothers flooded her mind.

But this couldn't be. This was Danny, his sister's son.

"The bad man broke the glass of Danny's window and then held up the white washcloth—the sleepy cloth."

Chloroform.

"Mikala, look at the boy in the bed, his face. You're confused."

She was quiet, still, her expression soft. Lip relaxed against lip. Then her eyes opened.

"He can see me."

At first, because of her casualness, he thought he'd surely heard her wrong.

"Who can see you?"

"The bad man."

His calmness faded to confusion. He tightened his eyebrows. Premonitions, they called these episodes. His wife experienced them, now his daughter. But they were never interactive.

"What do you mean he can see you?"

"He said my name. He has a guide."

"A guide?"

"You know, Daddy, someone who shows him movies. He knows who I am."

"No, Mikala, the bad man does not know who you are."

"Yes, he does, Daddy." For the first time, he heard panic in her voice. "That's the reason he is at Danny's house."

A creak in the floor behind him grabbed his attention, and he turned his head. Lisa darted from the bedroom, ripped Mikala from his arms, and handed him something in her place.

"I told you not to allow this. I said you were playing with fire."

"Lisa, she's wrong. He can't see her."

"Yes, he can, Daddy."

"No, he can't, Mikala." He lowered his voice to sound stern.

"Yes—yes he can. He's with Danny right now. Run, Daddy. Get Danny!"

"Go." Lisa screamed so loud one of the boys in the next room woke crying.

Jack glanced at his lap—at the ratty sneakers Lisa had placed there. For the moment it took him to put them on, he wondered if he should run or drive the block and a half to his sister's house. He decided, descended the stairs, and bounded out the front door bare-chested, leaving Lisa behind switching on lights and talking into the scanner. She would call for a cruiser to go to Janice's house, to her own house. But Mikala was wrong about Danny. She had to be. He was going to be in a heap of trouble with the chief later.

He ran down the driveway and disappeared into the black night within seconds. His legs turned over like an Olympic sprinter's, his breath labored, and sweat beaded on his upper lip. He rounded Third Street and nearly slipped in the wet grass on Nevada Drive but caught himself. He saw her house in the distance. Janice, four months separated from her husband, was alone there with her son. Alone like the others. Three single mothers of three abducted little boys.

His mind raced. The police would be at his house in two minutes. At Janice's in three. They protected each other's families.

When he was four houses away, he began screaming his sister's name. Trying to scare anyone off. Make the bad man drop the child? Leave without the child? He didn't know why he screamed. By the time his feet hit her driveway her light had turned on. The front bedroom window opened.

"Jack?" Janice's voice slithered through the screen.

He passed her window and ran toward the back of the house, toward Danny's room. He could see broken glass on the ground shimmering with the reflection of a street light.

*Dear God, no.*

This couldn't be. These abductions could not have hit his family.

"Danny!" he yelled.

When he reached his nephew's window, the whites of Danny's two little eyes glowed in the dark room. He was there. Standing and looking out the bare, open window back at him. Waiting.

"Hi, Uncle Jack," Danny said, his little face peeking over the window ledge, his stuffed bear, Tony, nudged under his chin.

Jack leaned his hands on the house and huffed, trying to catch his breath. Trying to digest that Danny was okay. Alive. Mikala was wrong.

"Thank God, thank God," he uttered out loud. When he caught his breath, he gazed up at his nephew.

That's when horror seized him. Above Danny's little face, secured on the broken glass, a scribbling on Christian stationery paralyzed him. It was the abductor's fourth message, but the first to make Jack's blood circulate like an electric current. The words he read flowed over his lips in a whisper, expelled with terrifying breath.

"One mulligan for Mikala."

# The Suicide Gene

*Wednesday, May 13, 2015*

## Chapter 1 The Funeral Parlor.

The face in the casket was her own. It nearly freaked her out.

She stood between her brother and sister, knees wobbling. Her high-necked dress clung to her skin, choking her throat, squeezing her long, slender body tighter and tighter until she felt her lungs might explode. *Damn panic attacks.*

Her siblings moved closer, tightening their grip on her when they heard her struggling to breathe. Together their tall frames—movie-star handsome—melded into a dark mass at the foot of the casket. It took all the energy the three of them could muster to keep her upright.

"Are you okay?" Melanie asked her.

She nodded.

"Try not to embarrass yourself," Matt whispered.

Again, a nod.

She wasn't sure she could get through the day without fainting. There were no breaks at a funeral, and she just wanted to get away from the grim whispery-whirrs of the bereaved and the sickeningly-sweet waft of the flowers. But she couldn't leave. Matt would kill her and, besides, she had no cigarettes. Her sister was her supplier. *Now she's dead.*

The parade of mourners stretched out of the room and down the hall and it was only 2:05. Some faces in line she didn't recognize, which infuriated her. Her sister had no real friends. *Nosy bastards. They just want to know what happened.*

She tried to ignore surrounding conversations and remain composed. But like Medusa's venomous mane, muffled words of hand-covered comments serpentined toward her from all directions. She couldn't block them. They echoed in her head like garbled phrases over a worn intercom. "Why did she do it?" "Like her mother." "Was it suicide?"

That last question nearly sent her to her knees. Her body sagged. Melanie caught her and Matt pulled her close, so she could lean on him until it passed.

"Don't look if looking makes you queasy," Melanie told her, but her glance drifted back to her sister's pasty face. *That's what I would look like if I were dead.*

She, herself, had considered suicide for so long it was hard to believe she still feared death. She hated funerals, could barely walk through the front door of a funeral home without hyperventilating. Yet, she had to go to this one. Her own identical twin sister lie in that ugly copper box, her head sunk low in billowing white silk.

"I'm sorry for the three of you." Her aunt Carol's hoarse voice coaxed her attention from the coffin. Notably thinner—grief now topping her midmorning chemotherapy cocktail—her aunt dabbed a tissue at tear-stained cheeks. She was in the third round with breast cancer and getting her butt kicked. "I can't believe this is happening to our family again. Did you know she was that bad?"

"Well." Melanie paused. "She's always had those tendencies, but we thought—with the counseling—she was doing better."

"Counseling?" Aunt Carol's cheeks pinked.

"Yes," Matt said. "Six months ago we started seeing a psychiatrist—all four of us."

"We thought a counselor might help," sweet Melanie continued. "We decided maybe we did have some baggage about Mom's—" She took a deep breath. Her gaze moved to her sister.

*Don't say it, Mel, don't say suicide.*

"Death." Melanie looked away.

"How horrible." Aunt Carol straightened. She appeared

appalled. "You should sue him—that counselor."

"Her." Matt shook his head, eyes glaring. "She's a psychiatrist."

"We will sue her." The twin's voice rose, but she stopped, glanced at Matt, and tightened her jaw. "She didn't give a damn about us. Now my sister is dead. She'll pay."

It happened then—at 2:10 p.m. She felt Matt's piercing gaze and watched as he released his grip on her arm. Her aunt Carol became so emotional that Matt had to help her to the back of the room. Family members congregated there amidst her wild sobs while Matt held her, and a rush of people came toward her and Melanie at the casket. One after another. Melanie let go of her, too, and she had to stand on her own.

For the first time in her life, she was alone. Her eyes rested on the lifeless body of her twin. Her comrade. Her best friend. There was never a time in her life she didn't have her sister to talk to, fight with, or cry on. They knew each other's inner being, finished each other's sentences, felt each other's pain. What would she do without her?

Her eyes zigzagged over the casket. *Oh no, I'm not feeling well.* She couldn't see her sister's dimples, her smile, the rose tattoo on her ankle that perfectly matched her own. What shoes did she have on? Was she wearing any? She'd never be jealous of those expensive, black stilettos on her feet again, or the designer purses cascading over her shoulder when they shopped. They'd never pack a picnic lunch and take Mel's kids to the park, ride bikes at the peninsula, or complain to each other about their ex-husbands. *Here comes the blackness. I'm falling now.*

She went down hard on the floor but didn't feel a thing. Her last thoughts were her beautiful sister really was gone, and oh, sweet Jesus, what had she done? *I'll kill that bitch. Emma Kerr will pay.*

\*\*\*\*

The funeral director stood with his back against the glass of one front door, and guests sauntered in languidly. Emma stepped past him and slipped into line, scrunching her heather-gray infinity scarf upward so the airy fabric hugged her chin.

Everyone warned her to stay away—Giff, Ally, Sharon, her insurance attorney. She peeked around the gray hat of the woman in front of her, tugged her own beret down her forehead, adjusted the readers she purchased, and prayed no one recognized her.

She glanced ahead. Was Father Mike there? She hoped not. Mourners queued up crookedly along the lavish funeral parlor hall that stretched past the two large viewing rooms on its left side. Today, only one person was laid out, and the motorized curtains between the two rooms were open, so family members and guests of the McKinney family had additional space. Several roamed in the first room's open floor, and a few relaxed on the velvet couches that hugged the walls.

Emma cowered by the door of that room, waiting in the long snaky, viewing line, her tall but small frame well hid behind two large women she chose to follow in. From where she stood, she could see through the first room and into the viewing room where the McKinneys hovered beside their sister's casket.

She watched an elderly woman approach them, knowing the thin, frail woman must be their aunt Carol. She stretched her neck to see Matt, but could only catch a glimpse of his arm around his sister. She waited, watched from behind the gray hat. Suddenly, his broad shoulders came into view when the woman, Carol, sagged to the floor. A muffled moan from the crowd in the viewing room arose and echoed through the parlor. People's heads snapped to attention all around her and Emma, along with the others at the end of the line, watched Matt escort his aunt out of sight.

She tilted her head and attempted to listen for the voices of the sisters, but they were too far from her, and all she could hear were the annoying whispers of the two women in front of her.

"Carol has been sick for a long time," the woman with the

floppy gray hat said. "Melanie has taken care of her for years."

"That Melanie is a saint," the second woman said, then lowered her voice. "Not like those other two."

Emma glanced at her watch and tried to block their voices. The people in front of her weren't moving. Several more had arrived behind her now, and the line stretched out the funeral parlor's front doors. There was no way she could give her condolences and be back to counsel Charles Brown by 2:30. But then, did she really believe she would actually make her way through the viewing line? And say what to them? She was sorry?

"I hear she overdosed and slit her wrists just like her mother," the second lady leaned under the gray hat of her friend. "They're both crazy. I bet the other one kills herself, too."

"Mary Jane told me they were seeing a counselor."

"I heard that, too, and God help the counselor."

The muscles in Emma's neck tightened. She held her breath.

"No one wants to be in the McKinney's sour graces."

"That's for sure. Carol has sued just about every doctor in town. That's how she's lived all these years. She's settled with every insurance company in Pennsylvania." The woman with the hat leaned toward the friend. Emma had a clear view of the sisters but her thoughts had now turned to the women in line, her face exposed to all. "And Mathew's no better. He scares the daylights out of me."

"I hear he's dating that newscaster. I can't remember her name."

"Yes, that pretty little thing, Heather something. I heard that, too. I don't know what she sees in him. He's good looking but scary. I hear he didn't get along with the twins."

"Oh, that's true. Mary Jane said he hated them, absolutely hated those two."

A second muffled sound rose, and Emma's gaze shot toward the sisters. People scuttled toward the viewing room.

She stepped closer to see past the scrambling black suitcoats and dresses. One sister was lying on the floor. Matt McKinney came back into view. He stooped down and put his hand beneath her head.

"Get some water," someone yelled.

"Oh my God, she fainted," the woman in the gray hat shouted.

Emma watched as Matt began lifting his sister off the ground and as he did, his eyes stretched through the crowd, landed on Emma's, drifted away, and then snapped back to her. Their eyes locked and he stopped. Emma felt a paralyzing fear.

She realized then, she shouldn't be anywhere near them. What was she thinking? But she couldn't tear her eyes from him. She stared straight back...and it appeared as if...had he shook his head? At her? Just a small movement that warned her to get out?

She took a step back, dropped her eyes to the ground, turned, and left the funeral home. When her feet hit the tarmac of the back alley, she began running.

61123177R00177

Made in the USA
Middletown, DE
17 August 2019